All My Tears

Five Novellas

Kathy McKinsey

Scrivenings
PRESS
Quench your thirst for story.
www.ScriveningsPress.com

Published by Scrivenings Press LLC
15 Lucky Lane
Morrilton, Arkansas 72110
https://ScriveningsPress.com

Printed in the United States of America

Second Edition
Paperback ISBN 978-1-64917-117-7
eBook ISBN 978-1-64917-118-4

Cover by Diane Turpin, dianeturpindesigns.com

(Note: This book was previously published in 2019 by Mantle Rock Publishing LLC and was re-published as is when Scrivenings Press acquired the publishing rights in 2021.)

To my mother, Lila Mae Brinkmann, who has shared this dream with me for almost 50 years.

To my husband, Murray McKinsey, who has encouraged me like no one else in my life.

To my daughter Rebecca, who is my personal editor.

To my daughter Sarah, who listened to all my ups and downs as this book was written.

To my sons Ping-Hwei, Caleb, and Benjamin, who are the smile of my heart.

GIFTS FROM MY BROTHER

*W*hen I opened my eyes, my brother Jeff sat beside me, his head in his hands, asleep.

Where was I? I didn't know this room. What . . . "Jeff?" My voice croaked.

He jerked awake, then looked straight at me. "Cassie. Hey."

"Why are you here?" My eyes were heavy and my mouth dry. Turning my head, I saw the IV attached to my arm. "Is this a hospital? Why, what, why are you here?"

Jeff leaned over and put his face right beside mine. "Because there's nowhere else I'd rather be right now."

"What—what happened?" I lay in a bed, and my head was confused and groggy. "Jeff?"

"You're hurt." He laid his hand on my shoulder. "But yes, this is a hospital, and you're going to be okay. Just sleep now. I promise I'll stay with you."

Relaxing, I closed my eyes. He wasn't going anywhere.

THE NEXT TIME I woke and found my brother sitting beside my bed, I was more alert. "Jeff?"

He closed the magazine in his hands and turned toward me. "Hey, little bird, how are you?"

I couldn't meet his eyes. "I think I heard . . . one of the nurses said . . . I tried to kill myself. Is that true?"

He knelt on the floor beside my bed and laid his head close to me. "Yes, honey."

"I don't remember anything about it. That's, that's scary." It was a struggle to sit up. My hands, covered with bandages, hurt when I put weight on them.

Jeff pushed some pillows to prop me in a more comfortable position. "It is scary." He put his hands on my shoulders and gazed straight in my eyes. "But we're going to help you."

"I don't understand. Why would I?" restless, I twisted, trying to sit up more.

He rested his hand on my cheek. "Shh, try to relax. The doctor said you can leave the hospital on Tuesday. Today's Saturday." He looked worried, and his smile didn't reach his eyes. "Sharon and I want you to come stay with us and the kids for a while, as long as you need. We'll help you. We'll find doctors and counselors there. You're not going to be alone with this."

My head pulsed. In the hall outside, a page came over the loudspeaker. "What about my apartment? My job?"

He squeezed my fingers. "Those things can wait a while, so you can get well. There's nothing you need to be in a hurry about. I'm going to keep telling you not to be in a hurry."

My eyes closed, and I took a deep breath. That was not how I handled life. I always kept myself under pressure, trying to stay one or two steps ahead of things at work. Biting my lip, I shook my head. After all, how well had I handled my life?

"One day at a time, remember?" Jeff still held my hand. "Jesus said to take things one day at a time."

I swallowed. "I'll try,"

4

~

AFTER SLEEPING for most of the flight home with Jeff, I was barely awake enough to notice Sharon and the kids when we got to their house. Everything was quiet when I found myself lying in bed, Jeff sitting in a chair beside me.

"We haven't had enough time together." Jeff shook his head. "Nine years between us, such a big difference. By the time you started school, I was already in high school." He reached to straighten my pillows.

"I tried to tag along after you, but you were so much quicker than me." My voice slurred with weariness. "And then you got a car."

He grinned. "Ah, my escape. And when you were a teenager, I was finishing college and starting to work."

I sucked in a breath. "Yes. You were gone."

"I know." He laid his hand on my shoulder. "I wish I'd figured out how to spend more time with you." He rubbed his face. "Once you were in college, I'd moved farther away and started a family and career. You were always my baby sister. I never knew how to deal with you, except to play with you like a baby or treat you like a kid." He chuckled. "Then you graduated from college a couple years ago, and it seemed like all of a sudden, you were this grown up, professional lady."

"You were always my big brother, the Superman. I was pretty sure you hung the sun and moon and stars in the sky."

Jeff held my hands in both of his. "Well, now maybe we can get to know each other better, and hopefully, you won't be totally disappointed in me."

*T*he next day, I sat up wide awake and looked around the room. This was my first time in Jeff's new house. Except for the dresser sitting at the end of the bed, the space around me looked like a basement rec-room, with a couch, three or four chairs, a small table, and several laundry baskets filled with toys.

"I wonder if they added the bed and dresser just for me. Wait. What's this?" Pushing to my feet, I moved to a half-closed door and found a small bathroom with a shower. "Pretty nice."

As I sat back on the bed, Jeff came down the stairs.

"Hey." He bent down and gave me a hug. "Looks like you're ready for breakfast."

I tapped the clock on the table beside my bed. "I'm thinking I missed breakfast by several hours."

Jeff sat on the bed beside me. "That's okay. You need the rest."

"I need to know what happened. I feel awake this morning, not fuzzy headed. I know . . ." My throat tightened. "I know things have been rough for me, but . . ." My fists clenched. "Please, tell me."

He hesitated a minute, then reached over and took my hand, smoothing it open. "What do you remember?"

6

"The last thing I remember is coming home from work that Friday. Nothing all that weekend. It happened on Monday, right?"

"Tuesday." He swallowed. "You didn't show up to work on Monday, and you didn't call. They said that was not at all like you, and they tried to call you, but no answer. When you didn't show up or call on Tuesday, your friend Linda decided to come to your place." He paused and took a breath. "There was no answer when she knocked, but the lights and TV were on."

His jaw tightened, and his hand convulsed around mine. "She was able to find a maintenance guy to let her into the apartment. They called 911 when they found you."

He stopped again.

"Go on." My lips trembled. My stomach clenched.

"Linda said there was an empty bottle of sleeping pills on the table beside your bed. Maybe you took them first. But there must only have been enough to make you throw up. Then it looks like you decided to take everything that was in your medicine cabinet." He shifted his position but held onto my hand. "There were a lot of empty bottles on the floor in the bathroom. Prescription pain killers, left over prescription pills from bronchitis or something, older sleeping pills, aspirin, over the counter allergy medicine. But again, it didn't have much effect except to make you sick."

He closed his eyes for a minute. "So you cut your wrists. The doctor said if Linda hadn't gotten there when she did, you would have died."

A wave of cold rushed over me, and I gasped.

Jeff wrapped his arms around me. "God has some pretty special plans for you. He wanted you to stay alive."

"Oh." My body shook, and tears trickled down my cheeks.

"I'm so sorry, little bird." Jeff was crying too. "I failed you. You needed someone after Dad died, and I wasn't there for you."

∾

Jeff's wife Sharon had always been sweet, but shy. I didn't know her well. Would she resent having to take care of me?

But she was smiling when she came downstairs that afternoon. "I've been shopping. We can go together when you feel better, but I thought I'd get you a few things to start with."

She sat down on the bed beside me and handed me a shopping bag. "I was thinking you might like some long, loose-sleeve shirts while your wrists are healing." Her voice was soft. "There are so many pretty things, including for warm weather."

My breath caught. "You guys think of everything."

"Maybe. But for sure Jeff already thought of making a doctor's appointment for you tomorrow, and I thought you'd like something nice to wear."

Grasping the shopping bag, I looked at her. "I . . . I'm sorry I have to be such a, such a burden to you guys right now."

She leaned to give me a hug. "Please don't say that again. We want to help you however we can." She smiled. "I've never had a sister, and we haven't spent much time together. I'm looking forward to us becoming friends."

Wiping at a tear, I steadied my chin. "I guess I should try these on."

CHAPTER 3

*J*eff had an appointment set up for me the next morning with their family physician, Dr. Edwards. She was young, informal, and worked to set me at ease.

She gave me a basic examination and asked Jeff and me a long list of questions.

"Jeff had your records from the hospital sent over. I have a good idea of what's going on. You lost a lot of blood, and the pills you took have made you pretty sick. But you're gaining strength, and with a little time, you'll recover well."

She sat down on a stool, putting herself at my level. "There are some things that I'm going to recommend, though, and I hope you'll follow through with them. I'm going to give you two names of people I want you to call. One is a psychiatrist, who can help with your medication. The other is a counselor. I know them both well and have had good reports about them from other people I've referred."

I nodded. She had a kind face, and I had a hard time holding her gaze. My whole being was filled with shame.

"She'll call them," Jeff said, his voice quiet but firm.

As we drove home, Jeff asked, "You've been here a couple of days now, had a lot of time to yourself. Are you bored yet?"

"Bored? What do you mean?" Where was he going with this?

"Are you ready to have dinner with the family? Spend time with the kids?"

"Oh." I gulped. Never having spent much time with small children, including Jeff's kids, I didn't know how well I would handle this new relationship. "Uh, sure. Of course."

Jeff patted my hand. "You'll have fun. They're cute kids. And they'll love you."

Meetings with supervisors and potential buyers had come easy to me over the last couple of years, but now my stomach flipped with nervousness about having dinner with a six-year-old and a four-year-old. The last time I'd seen Tommy and Naomi was at my Dad's funeral about a year ago. We had little interaction. Before then I'd rarely spent time with them, and they'd only been babies or toddlers.

There was no need to worry, though, as I found out that evening. They weren't shy.

Tommy, the six-year-old, brought a huge pile of papers from the counter and set them beside me. "Do you want to see what we've been working on in school?"

Naomi sat on my lap with a book, which had a very pretty princess on the cover, and asked if I'd like to read it to her.

"I do want to. Would you like to look at Tommy's school papers first?"

"I saw them before," she told me, her face serious.

"Yes." How was I going to handle this? "But I'd like to look at them, and I want to hold you on my lap. Then, Tommy, will you listen to the story about the pretty princess with us?"

"Yeah, I guess it would be okay."

Naomi had a few suggestions about things Tommy could have done better on his schoolwork, and he pointed out a couple of dumb things the princess did in the book. But since I had many questions about almost everything, we were all still laughing when Sharon said it was time to eat.

"Can Aunt Cassie sit by me?" Tommy asked.

"No." Naomi shoved him. "I want Aunt Cassie to sit by me."

"Oh, Sharon, can't they just call me Cassie?"

"Or call her little bird." Jeff grinned.

"Yeah! Yeah!" both kids yelled.

"No. Jeff." Sharon sighed. "Where did little bird come from anyway?"

Jeff put his arm around my shoulders. "Because when she was little, she used to flit around the house from room to room to room, singing and giggling and whistling and just making a lot of noise."

"I don't remember back that far." My mouth twitched. "Sounds like that must have been a lot of fun."

"It was a joy." He gave me a toothy smile. "Now, everybody, sit down. She's going to sit by me because she's my sister. And after supper, she gets to help me do the dishes."

CHAPTER 4

*T*he next day, Jeff went back to work.

It rubbed against my grain, not going to work myself. And this was another woman's home. How could I stay out of the way here without being a hermit in the basement?

Naomi came down while I was still in bed. "Come have breakfast with us, and then we'll push Tommy on the bus."

Tommy didn't need convincing when the bus came, but Naomi still ran to the door with him and giggled while she pushed him out.

Smiling as I looked at her happy face, I took her hand. "Naomi, do you want to make our beds?"

We completed this important task and even found a small amount of trash to pick up.

"Sharon, is there anything else I can help you do around the house?"

"I'm pretty caught up." She looked over the living room. "I have some work I need to do for an online class I'm taking, so if you would play with Naomi for a while, it would help me a lot."

Naomi had a beautiful dollhouse she told me had been her Mommy's when she was a little girl.

"This box is full of furniture." She set the box on the floor between us. "We need to set it all up in the dollhouse."

We did, and then we rearranged it all five times. Both of us did a good bit of giggling, but when I put the bed in the bathroom, Naomi decided it was time to pick up.

"We need to put all the furniture back in its special box."

When the furniture was put away, Naomi took out her dishes. "Now I'll make us lunch. I hope you're hungry."

"Yes, thank you. I'm very hungry."

Naomi handed me a separate plate for each item. "Here you go. Spaghetti. Meatloaf. Here's a hot dog. Potato salad. Raisins. Angel food cake. Chocolate pudding. And brownies."

"Mmm, yummy, thank you. I'm not sure I'll need to eat again for two days."

Naomi giggled and tapped my knee with one of the plates. "That's silly, Aunt Cassie. This is just play food. We'll have a real lunch later."

After our second lunch, Naomi planted herself in my lap. "Will you come sit by me while I take a nap?"

"Sure."

Naomi held my hand and led me up to her room. "Here we are." She crawled in bed and scrunched into a ball with her head on the pillow. "Tuck me in." She yawned.

Watching her face as she fell asleep, I was sure I'd never seen anything so beautiful, and peaceful. A feeling I couldn't recognize squeezed my chest.

NAOMI MADE sure I was around to help "Pull Tommy off" the school bus. She wiggled beside me. "We get to have an after-school snack with him."

Tommy told us about what had happened during every hour of

the day. "I brought some math papers." He drew them out of his backpack and placed them on my lap.

"We started a new book today. About a dog." He took a bite of his banana. "I didn't bring it home tonight, but I will tomorrow."

When it was almost time for Jeff to get home, I told the kids, "Okay now listen, this is important. As soon as your Dad comes in the door, yell at him 'It's Daddy the superman!'"

I loved them. They were very cooperative.

"Already you're teaching my children bad habits." Jeff tried not to smile.

It was Jeff's job to do the dishes every night while Sharon got the kids ready for bed. Now it was my job to clear the table and dry the dishes.

Jeff splashed water at me. "I can see you had fun with the kids."

I nodded. "I had a very relaxing time with Naomi. Is she always so calm?"

"No, she's not." His voice was dry. "Don't worry. When they get used to you, they'll be more natural around you."

When I headed for the basement, Jeff stopped me and pointed to the couch. "Did you call to make appointments with the doctor and counselor?"

Sitting on the couch, I turned away from him. My mouth trembled. "Yes. I have appointments with both of them in the next two or three weeks."

He put his hands on my shoulders and turned me to face him. "Hey, what's this all about?"

With my eyes squeezed tight, I tried not to cry. "Jeff, I'm so ashamed."

He sat quiet for a minute, holding my hand, looking down. "I wish you wouldn't be," he said finally. "You've been hurting a lot. That's not anything to be ashamed of. It's just something that needs to be addressed." He looked up. "Please let me be a part of this. Let me help you."

"I'm scared." My voice was a whisper. "What if I try to—to hurt myself again?"

He pulled me close to him and didn't speak for a while. After a minute I heard him whispering. When I turned my face up to look at him, I realized he was praying. When he was done, he wiped at a couple of tears on my cheek. "I'm going to be with you, honey. So is Jesus. You're not going to be alone."

CHAPTER 5

"*A*unt Cassie? Little Bird? It's time to wake up."

When I opened my eyes, Tommy stood beside my bed. "Tommy?" I rubbed my eyes. "What's going on?"

"It's time to get up." He danced from one foot to the other. "It's time to get ready for church, and Daddy's making pancakes."

Church. That's right. I knew that. Jeff had told me the night before. I hadn't been making it to church very often the last few years, but, of course, they went at Jeff's house. The thought made me a little nervous.

"Pancakes, huh?"

"Mmm hmmm. Daddy makes good pancakes. He puts M&M's in them."

"Does he now?" Yawning, I pushed myself up. "Then I guess I'd better get up."

Why was I nervous? We had grown up going to church. It had been important to my parents. It had been important to me at one time.

~

STANDING outside the door to the sanctuary, I hesitated.

"You okay?" Jeff stopped beside me, his hand on my shoulder.

"There sure are a lot of people in there."

He put his arm through mine. "Stick with me. Everybody loves me here."

The church held two services, and we went to the one with contemporary music. Eric Richmann, the pastor, was young and upbeat. It was not hard to listen to him.

"Don't be surprised when I start yelling if I notice any of you drifting off." Eric smiled. "We have a lot of important things to cover this morning."

Jeff and Sharon appeared to have quite a few friends. They were kind to me, but nobody peppered me with questions. My body relaxed.

After the service, a man came up to us, carrying Naomi on his shoulders. "This is my best friend Mark," she told me, laughing and clapping the sides of his head.

I smiled. "Are you?"

"I am." He nodded. "And you must be Naomi's new favorite Aunt Cassie."

Jeff came up and slapped Mark hard on the back. "The rest of us don't really like Mark much, but to keep Naomi happy, we let him go out for lunch with us on Sundays."

IT WAS easy to slip into Jeff's family routines. Pushing Tommy on the bus, dinner with the family, dishes with Jeff, church. Jeff and Sharon were wonderful parents and made time to share with their kids. They read to them, played with them, and told them stories.

"Daddy, tell us the story about how you and Mommy first met." Naomi bounced, her face all smiles. It was bedtime, and everybody sat on the floor in the living room.

"No." Tommy scooted up closer to Jeff. "I want you to tell the story of Daniel in the lion's den."

Jeff wrapped his arms around both kids. "Quiet now, and I think we'll have time for both stories."

Jeff and Sharon gave the kids lots of hugs and, to my surprise, they gave me almost as many. All four of them were forever showering me with hugs and attention. I saw myself leaning toward this, like a dry plant toward water.

*M*y first appointment was with the psychiatrist. Dr. Carver was business-like and straightforward. "I'll monitor your medication, Cassie. We're starting with a fairly general course for treating depression. But along with Dr. Edwards, I strongly encourage you to set up a regular schedule with the counselor." He reached for some papers on his desk. "What questions do you have for me?"

Twisting my fingers together, I bit my lip. "Questions. I'm not sure . . . I don't think I have any questions right now."

He nodded. "All right then. Here is my card. Please call me if you do." He stood. "You can make your next appointment with the receptionist." He handed me the papers and walked out the door.

Pressing my hands to my cheeks, I stared after him. "That was quick. Thank you, Dr. Carver. It was nice to meet you too."

JULIA, my counselor, was a comfortable lady. She was a little overweight, hair turning gray with no apology, probably in her fifties.

She sat in a chair close to mine, but not too close, relaxed and listening.

"Cassie, I know Dr. Edwards suggested that you come to see me, but I'd like you to tell me why you're here."

Not speaking for a minute, I looked at my hands folded in my lap. "Yes, Dr. Edwards referred me to you. Dr. Carver recommended it too. Jeff, my brother, insisted I come. I don't think I had a choice."

"Would you rather not have come?"

"No." I laughed and shook my head. "I'm sorry. I'm not laughing at you. I'm laughing at myself. I mean, I don't mind coming. Of course, they're right. I tried to kill myself." Looking down again, I worked to moisten my mouth. "I need help."

"Okay. Let's start with something easy. Just tell me a little about yourself. You're not from around here, are you?"

"No. I came here to stay with Jeff and his family for a while after —when I got out of the hospital."

Julia was easy to talk to. I told her about growing up and my time at college. "I've always loved to draw, so I managed to take a couple of drawing classes in college. My major was in business, with a focus on public relations. I convinced myself that drawing would help with my advertising skills."

"That sounds reasonable to me."

I shook my head. "With all the computer art programs now, nobody in business needs to do their own drawing. But they liked me at my job. They did let me include some of my own drawings in my proposals."

"What was your job?"

"I worked in the PR department for a large manufacturer of dress clothes for teens." Getting up, I walked to the window behind Julia's desk and watched cars go by on the street below. "I made an important spot for myself in the business. I got along well with everybody, my coworkers, supervisors, customers. Senior staff contacted me when they had urgent deadline projects."

My chest tightened, and I stopped, then turned back to face Julia. "I'm not sure why I told you that. That's not how things ended up."

"Then I think we can stop for now. We've made a good start today."

CHAPTER 7

*B*ang, bang, bang.
        What?
Bang, bang, bang.

Catching myself before I rolled out of bed, I pushed up and looked around the room.

The noise came again.

The window?

I crossed the room and bent to look outside. Jeff was kneeling on the ground, grinning at me. The window screeched as I unlocked and pushed it open. "What are you doing, waking me up?"

"Man, little bird, you have lived alone too long. You've forgotten the joy of waking up early on Saturday mornings."

"I don't think I ever knew that joy."

"Come on." He snapped his fingers. "Get dressed and come out and help me check the pepper plants and tomato vines to see if there's anything left worth salvaging." He stood up. "Then you and the kids are gonna help me stuff the plants into trash bags."

"Oh, we are, are we?" Grumbling, I got dressed and went outside.

"I don't remember you helping Mom with the garden much when

I was little." Walking to stand beside Jeff, I kicked my foot at some tomato vines.

"That's probably because you weren't helping." He tossed a small green tomato at me. "You were inside playing with doll clothes or Lincoln Logs or otherwise being lazy."

"Hmmm."

"Hey listen." He moved along and ripped more tomato vines. "We wanted to ask you a favor."

"Yeah?" Kneeling, I searched through the vines to find a rotten tomato I could toss at him. "What might that be?"

"I want to take Sharon on a date tonight, dinner and a movie. I was wondering if you would babysit."

My hands stilled. "Babysit? Me?"

"Yeah. What do you think? I wasn't around when you were in high school, so I don't know if you did any babysitting back then."

He made it sound so natural. "I . . . did some." I chewed my lip. "Jeff, are you sure?"

"Sure about what?" He pulled pepper plants out of the ground.

My eyes stayed focused on the bucket with the few vegetables he'd found. "Are you sure you feel comfortable leaving me alone with the kids?"

"I am."

"And you're sure Sharon is comfortable?"

"Yeah." He came back to squat in front of me. "What are you worried about?"

"I don't know." My hands tightened around the handle of the bucket. "I, I'm not sure."

Jeff reached into the fallen vines. "Here, I found you something." He handed me another green tomato, then leaned back on his heels. "Are you afraid you'll hurt the kids?"

"I don't think so. No." I pressed the tomato against my cheek.

"Are you afraid you might hurt yourself?"

"Maybe." I swallowed. "I don't understand why I tried to kill myself. I don't remember it."

Jeff leaned forward and took my hands in his. "You've got to let yourself get well, honey. You've got to trust God that you can. Sharon and I see you with the kids. We are not afraid."

Sitting still for a minute, I let my hands rest in Jeff's. "I'll babysit the kids," I whispered. "I want to be able to do that."

~

IT WAS HARD NOT to have fun and relax with the kids.

"Hey, since Mommy and Daddy got to go out for dinner, we should have junk food," Tommy suggested.

"Yes." Naomi danced around the room. "Hot dogs, potato chips, and cookies."

"Sounds good to me." I took out paper plates and juice boxes. "Let's have a picnic in the living room. On the floor."

They had plans for after dinner too.

"Let's make a house out of Legos." Tommy rubbed his hands together.

I smiled at him. "Tommy, all you need to do is snap your fingers, and you'll look exactly like your dad."

Tommy attempted to snap his fingers. "I'm learning how."

The three of us lay on our stomachs, placing each Lego piece with care so we wouldn't knock anything down. When they finally said they were finished, I was impressed at the complex house they constructed.

"It's a masterpiece." I hugged them both close then reached for my phone. "Let me take a picture."

"Text it to Mommy and Daddy." Naomi bounced and clapped her hands.

"Excellent idea." She made me smile.

We read a few books, not wanting to do anything else in the living room to disturb the house we'd built until Jeff and Sharon got home and could see the real thing. The kids probably talked me into more books than their parents would have read before they finally were willing to go to bed.

Sitting on the floor between the doors to Naomi and Tommy's rooms, I could hear them breathing as they slept. It was such a sweet sound . . .

A small body crashed into mine and jolted me awake. "Tommy?" I wrapped my arms around him. "What . . . Are you okay?"

"Help." He sobbed. "Aunt Cassie. Help me." His whole body shook, and tears streamed down his cheeks as he clutched at my shirt with both hands.

I held him tight and pressed my face against his. "I'm right here, sweetie. You're okay. I'm right here. It was just a dream. You are okay, sweetie."

Sharon told me Tommy sometimes had nightmares where scary men chased and grabbed him. I held him until he quieted, then carried him back to bed and covered him. Kneeling beside his bed, I put my head down next to his and rubbed his back. Long minutes passed before his breathing became normal again. In his sleep, Tommy worked his hand out from under the quilt and laid it on my cheek.

CHAPTER 8

*T*wo days later, we were waiting for the "It's Daddy the superman" welcome home. "Here he comes," Tommy said. "Whoa, he's got pizza."

Naomi and I joined Tommy at the living room window. Sure enough, Jeff was walking up the drive with pizza boxes in his arms.

"Sharon?" I called. "Did you cook?"

"I did not." Sharon walked into the living room wearing a dress. "You and I are going out to dinner. A thank you for staying with the kids the other night."

"But you don't have to —"

"Cassie," Sharon said out of the side of her mouth. "I need a girls' night out."

"Oh. Um, going out to eat sounds like fun."

"Not to me." Jeff came in and set the pizzas down on the dining room table. "I'm pooped." He sprawled onto the couch and flopped his arm over his eyes. "You kids have some pizza and keep it quiet, okay?"

Naomi giggled and jumped on his stomach. "Oh, Daddy, get up. You have to help us."

"Come on, Daddy, get out some plates." Tommy pulled on Jeff's feet. "Did you buy soda?"

Sharon winked at me. "You ready to go?"

I looked down at my sweats. "It'll only take me three minutes to change. Promise."

∽

"YOU GUYS HAVE BEEN AWFULLY good to me." Looking up from my salad, I managed a smile for Sharon.

"We love you, you know." She put her fork down. "I've told you what it means to me for you to stay with us." Her eyes crinkled with a smile. "And I think you know how Jeff feels."

"Yeah, I guess he's a pretty good guy."

She picked up her glass of water and turned it in her hands. "He really wants to help you. He wishes he could have been there for you more when, when both of your parents died."

"He had his own life to live." I shrugged and picked up a slice of bread, tearing pieces off of it. "When Mom died, Jeff had already started a job, and you two were engaged, weren't you?"

Sharon nodded. "How old were you then?"

"Fourteen. It was Dad and me who weren't any good for each other." Biting my lip, I looked down. My salad was covered with scraps of bread, so I pushed the plate away. "Mom and Dad were really close, especially during the last months . . . when Mom was so sick . . ." I swallowed. "And Dad spent every minute he could with her, took care of her, everything she needed."

I stopped and pressed my eyes closed. "Afterward, he was overwhelmed with grief. I guess to deal with it, he buried himself in work. I needed him to comfort me, but he couldn't."

The server set a plate down in front of me. Pasta, I think. I couldn't remember what I'd ordered. Now that I'd started talking, I wasn't able to stop.

"I guess I decided to do the same thing Dad did. I worked hard at

KATHY MCKINSEY

school. I figured if I got good grades and got into a good college, maybe I could make Dad proud." I took a breath. "And if not, at least I could learn to take care of myself." Tears streamed down my face.

Sharon reached her hand across and covered mine. "How was college? Did you make friends?"

"I was too busy studying. Until I met Curt." My jaw tightened. "He was like me. Another business student, hard-working, intent on getting good grades."

"When did you guys meet?"

"When we were seniors. Neither of us cared about a big social life. We studied together and went out when it was convenient."

"Then he asked you to marry him."

"Yeah, on the night we graduated." Picking up my fork, I poked at the food on my plate. "But we couldn't find jobs in the same city. We ended up several hours apart."

I took a drink of water and cleared my throat. "We were okay with that, though. We visited each other whenever we could. We thought, we thought it would work out. We'd focus on getting our careers started. The right time for us to be together, it would work out."

Sharon squeezed my hand. I didn't look at her.

"Then he called one night. He said he was so sorry but . . ." My throat tightened. "He'd met somebody else, and they were going to get married immediately." My fork fell on the plate. "I'm sorry. I'm not going to be able to eat this."

Sharon got up and came around to slide into my side of the booth. She wrapped her arms around me. "I'm so sorry. I guess I didn't handle this girls' night out dinner very well."

CHAPTER 9

One Sunday at lunch, Naomi's best friend Mark sat down next to me in the restaurant we'd gone to after church. "You know, Cassie, it's way sad you've let yourself get stuck in that old people's Sunday school class that Jeff and Sharon go to."

"Really?"

"Oh, yeah. Almost everybody over thirty, most of them married. Stuck in their ways. Boooring."

"Yeah, boring," Tommy said.

"I'll show you boring." Sharon laughed as she spread a napkin in Tommy's lap then tickled his neck.

"I hadn't thought about that." I slid a straw in Naomi's drink.

"You're a young person," Mark went on. "You need to be with other young people, in a more vibrant, exciting group."

"I'm young." Naomi popped her head around me to look at Mark.

"Yes, you are." I kissed her head. "If I don't want to be in Naomi's class, how could I find such a group, I wonder."

"Funny you should ask." Mark bent down to pick up a fork Naomi dropped on the floor. "I happen to be in just such a class at our church."

"No." My eyes widened.

"Can you believe it? A lot of singles, only a few married couples, almost nobody over thirty. People who are excited about the Bible. About life."

"Young, vibrant people," I suggested, catching Naomi's drink before it also went on the floor.

"Exactly. You've got it." Mark slapped his hands down on the table.

"And what Mark isn't even bragging about"—across the table, Jeff reached to steal one of Tommy's fries— "is that he is the teacher of the class."

"I don't like to think of myself as a teacher." Mark shook his head. "Too old school, buddy. I like to think we can all learn from each other. I'm just like a ... a discussion starter."

"Hmmm, discussion starter," Jeff said, reaching his hand toward Tommy's plate again. "Sounds like a good excuse for not having to prepare what you're studying beforehand."

Tommy clapped his hand down on top of Jeff's. "Hey."

I nodded at Mark. "You're right. It does look like Jeff is getting pretty old."

WATER SPLASHED AGAINST MY HAIR.

"What?" Looking up I found Jeff grinning at me as he handed me a plate to dry.

"I'm just trying to get off all the water I can for you."

"Right."

"Are you going to Mark's Bible class?"

Placing the plate in the cabinet, I came back and stood a little farther away as I waited for the next one. "I don't know ... Sure. Why not?"

"It probably would be fun. More people your age. And I've been in Bible studies with Mark. He's a pretty good teacher, uh, I mean discussion starter."

Jeff stood quiet for a minute, looking down at a plate in his hands. "Maybe I'm being nosy, but . . ." He hesitated. "It seems to me that you're not as excited." He shook his head. "No, excited isn't even what I mean. You don't seem as comforted by your faith as I remember when you were younger."

"You're probably being nosy." I handed back the plate he'd given me. "This plate is still dirty. But maybe . . . Maybe I'm not as comforted. About faith."

"How come, honey?"

Twisting the dish towel in my hands, I stared at it then looked up at him. "I don't want to hurt your feelings. I know how important your faith is to you. But I guess . . ." I shook my head. "I guess it doesn't work for me anymore."

Jeff washed a few dishes without saying anything then dried his hands. "I have something for you." He left the room. When he came back, he handed me a Bible, a worn-looking Bible.

I looked down at it then back up at Jeff. "I have a Bible."

"It was Mom's. I have Dad's. I just wanted to give it to you."

When I looked down at the Bible again, I remembered it, lying on the table beside my parents' bed. The cover was bright red, Mom's favorite color. I wrapped my arms tight around it and squeezed my eyes against tears.

Jeff put his hands on my shoulders. "Look, I'm not trying to pressure you or be pushy or anything." He took his hands off my shoulders and slapped his legs. "Listen, let's stop trying to be nice to each other." He took a deep breath. "This is what I truly want to say. I want you to find some peace. And I believe that Jesus and the Bible are the best ways for you to do that. I'd like for you to try reading the Bible again. Please."

Looking down at Mom's Bible, I opened and flipped through it. Page after page had underlines and notes written in the margins.

I swallowed and tried to speak, then cleared my throat and tried again. "It looks like Mom made it easy to know what to read."

Jeff moved beside me and looked down at the Bible, then smiled. "She had a lot of favorites." He reached over and turned a few pages. More and more underlines. "That seems like a good place to start, those underlines. Listen to what God has to say to you. That's all I want for you."

Setting the Bible on the counter, I wrapped my arms around him. "Okay." My face pressed against his chest. "I guess that's not so hard."

MY MOTHER'S Bible lay open on the bed in front of me. The cover was worn smooth from years of handling, and many of the pages were wrinkled. My eyes blurred as I saw Mom's hard-to-read handwriting in the margins.

At one time I'd read the Bible every day.

I turned the pages, reading some of the verses my mother had underlined.

Psalm 103:2-3: "Praise the LORD, my soul, and forget not all his benefits - who forgives all your sins and heals all your diseases."

In the margin, Mom had written, "Thank you, Father, for your unbelievable grace."

We were challenged in our church youth group to memorize Scripture and to remember the location of verses we discussed in Bible studies. I was charged, one of the students who did all the Bible work I could.

My hands flipped more pages.

Philippians 4:8: "Finally, brothers and sisters, whatever is true, whatever is noble, whatever is right, whatever is pure, whatever is lovely, whatever is admirable—if anything is excellent or praise-worthy—think about such things."

Here Mom had written, "Help me teach this to my children."

My parents were serious about their faith and taught this to me and Jeff as babies. It was an easy decision for me to ask Jesus to be my Savior when I was twelve.

The youth group I belonged to was filled with teachers and other kids who were excited. The Bible was exciting.

2 Corinthians 1:3-4: "Praise be to the God and Father of our Lord Jesus Christ, the Father of compassion and the God of all comfort, who comforts us in all our troubles, so that we can comfort those in any trouble with the comfort we ourselves received from God."

Here Mom said, "Thank You, Father, for your sweet love for me."

In my mind I saw Mom, sitting by a lamp in the living room late at night, her head bent over the Bible, her lips moving, a pencil twisting in her hand. I wiped at a tear so I wouldn't smudge any of her notes, then cradled my face in my hands and cried harder.

My mother died, and my father pulled away from me. And more and more it didn't seem so real that God had that much interest in me.

I went to college, then started a fast-paced job. The Bible and church didn't find a place in my life anymore.

But after a while, working hard didn't help me like it had before. The weekend came when I tried to kill myself, and I didn't remember that at all.

Julia asked me a few days earlier, "Do you have to remember it, Cassie? To move on, do you really have to remember?"

Did I have to remember? What did I need to do?

Sitting up, I clasped my mother's Bible between my hands. Jeff thought reading the Bible could help me find peace. Mom used the Bible to guide her through every day.

What about the verses I'd read? It had been a long time since I'd prayed.

"God?" Would He listen to me? "What am I supposed to get from these? I'm supposed to think about good things. You will comfort me? And forgive me? And be compassionate to me?" I rubbed my hands at the tears in my eyes. "I don't know, God. I think it's going to be hard for me to believe all this again."

"Hey, whose car is that?" Tommy stood at the window, watching for Jeff, while Naomi and I played with plastic jungle animals on the floor.

Naomi ran to look out, so I followed. "That's my car," I said, surprised. "And that's my friend Linda."

Sure enough, my car was parked in the driveway, and Linda stood next to it, talking to Jeff. As they walked toward the front door, a familiar sense of shame came over me. My chest lurched, and my shoulders hunched. Linda found me when I tried to kill myself. How could I face her?

Shaking myself, I moved to give her a hug. I had to do this.

"What in the world are you doing here?"

"I've come to take you out for dinner." She squeezed me, then stepped back and laughed. "And, by the way, I brought your car."

"That is so great. When do you have to fly back?"

"Tonight, right after dinner, unfortunately. I tried to get tomorrow off, so I could spend some time with you, but a rush job came up." She shrugged. "You know how that is."

"Yeah, I do know."

Linda looked down at her feet, and I chewed my lip, neither of us sure what to say next. Jeff finally stepped in. "You'd better get moving if you want time for anything but fast food while you drive Linda to the airport."

～

"THANKS so much for bringing my car." We were settled at a table in a steak house, Linda's favorite. The salads had been served, and country music played loud.

"I won't pretend." Linda grinned. "It was Jeff's idea."

"Hmph. He probably just didn't want me to start asking to borrow his car."

She laughed then stretched her hand to touch mine. "How are you?"

"I'm okay." I hesitated. "I guess . . . I know I have a lot to thank you for."

My breath caught when tears sprang to her eyes.

"I was so scared." She took a drink of water and cleared her throat.

Swallowing, I squeezed her hand.

"None of us knew you were feeling that bad. I mean, we knew you weren't yourself, but . . ." She shook her head.

I stared down at my salad. "There's a lot I don't remember." Raising my eyes then, I met her gaze. "I was hoping you could fill me in more about what happened."

Linda rested her chin on her fist. "It's not like you didn't have enough to deal with. I mean, your Dad dying, and then Curt treating you like he did. We could tell you were having trouble with work."

I sucked in a breath. "Why didn't I know?"

Linda blinked.

With my fork, I smashed a crouton. "I guess I knew I didn't feel right, but I thought, at least . . ."

"Cassie, just take it easy for a while." She laid her hand over mine. "Let yourself heal a little. You have a great brother, and it looks like he's got a sweet family."

I managed a smile. "Yeah, they're pretty terrific."

For the rest of the meal, Linda caught me up on what was going on with people at work, her family, and her dog. No time at all passed before I'd dropped her off at the airport.

"MY FRIEND LINDA from work was in town a couple days ago." Standing at the window in Julia's office, I ran my fingers over the plant sitting there and watched the rain.

"How did that go?" Julia spoke behind me.

I didn't turn to face her. "Good. She brought my car. Then she flew home."

"What did you talk about?" Her voice was soft, kind.

"About work, mostly."

"Tell me about it."

"She said everybody at work knew that I was having a rough time."

"Why does that surprise you?"

I pinched a leaf on the plant. "I guess I thought I concealed things better." My voice sounded bitter. "They seemed to know what was going on more than I did. She said they knew I wasn't doing well with my job. I thought I was fine, that my work was good anyway."

"Why does that upset you so?"

My jaw clenched.

"People have trouble with work, Cassie. It's not a character flaw." Julia's chair creaked as she shifted. "You have a lot of guilt, a lot of shame. Maybe not for any good reason."

"They were paying me." I took a breath. "And I like to control myself better than that."

"So your pride is hurt."

"I'm not sure that's fair." When I realized I'd broken a leaf off the plant, I snatched back my hands and fisted them against my stomach. "Maybe. But I had a job to do. I was committed to that."

"I'm guessing your work was still productive enough to make money, or they probably would have fired you." Her voice was still kind, but firm. Insistent.

"I don't know." As I turned to face Julia, tears streamed down my cheeks. "I was clueless. About what was going on. I still am."

As I lay awake that night, listening to water drip in the bathroom sink, my eyes refused to close. Sitting up, I clicked on the lamp beside my bed then picked up my mother's Bible.

Psalm 34:18: "The LORD is close to the brokenhearted and saves those who are crushed in spirit."

I pressed my hands against my face. "God, I guess I've been pretty broken hearted. Crushed in spirit?" I gulped. "Yeah. Can You comfort me? Do I . . . do I even have the right to ask You?"

What would it be like to have God's comfort again?

*J*eff and Sharon invited guests over for Thanksgiving, an elderly couple from church who didn't have family in the area, and Mark.

Naomi and Mark were huddled together in a corner of the living room, so I sat down next to them. "What's up?"

"Mark's helping me fix my horse," Naomi said. "She broke her neck."

The plastic toy Mark held in his hands certainly was broken. "Oh, that looks pretty bad. Do you have medical training?"

"Absolutely." Mark's face and voice were serious as he applied glue and lined up the broken pieces with caution. "From the best school."

Naomi giggled. "Mark, that's silly. She's only a toy, not a real horse."

"Oh sure, now you tell me." Mark tapped a dab of glue onto Naomi's nose.

She giggled again and jumped up. "I'm gonna go see." She ran to the bathroom.

With my lips pursed, I stood. "I think I'll help her get that glue off before Sharon sees it."

"Do you need any medical assistance?" Mark examined the toy in his hands.

He made me smile. "I'll be sure to give you a call."

As Mark was getting ready to go home, he stopped in front of me. "Want to go to dinner with me tomorrow night?"

I blinked. "What?"

He lifted an eyebrow. "Dinner? Tomorrow night? You and me?"

"Oh. Um, sure. I mean—sure." Could I sound any more stupid?

He smiled and patted my arm. "I'll pick you up at seven."

After all the guests left and we'd finally finished washing dishes and cleaning up, Jeff lay sprawled out on the couch, looking stuffed and exhausted.

Gazing down at him, I shook my head. "I'd take a picture of you right now, if I could think of anybody to send it to."

"Don't bother," he mumbled, his eyes closed. "I hear Mark asked you out."

"He did, yes."

"He told me he was going to. He didn't ask me if he could. He just told me he was going to."

"Should he have asked you if he could?"

"Well … yeah."

"I see." I sat on the arm of the couch next to his head. "Why is that?"

"It's just . . ." He opened one eye. "It's proper."

"Proper, huh?"

Should I remind him I was already engaged to be married once? No. That probably wouldn't be a very good argument.

"Are you still going to allow it?"

"Yep." He yawned. "I checked with Naomi."

"Naomi?" I laughed. "Good idea. And it's okay with her?"

"She said you can give it a try. She wasn't really expecting him to wait for her."

"That's good. I certainly would have hated to break Naomi's

heart. But she does understand we're not getting married or anything, doesn't she?"

"I'm not sure if she does understand that. You may have some trouble convincing her."

"Great."

Sharon came in the room. "I think they're both finally asleep. Whoa." She stood still and stared at Jeff. "Could anybody look lazier than this?"

"Hey, be nice to me." Jeff waved her away. "There were a lot of dirty dishes."

"And I think he's feeling a little left out as a big brother too." I patted his shoulder. "He might need a little TLC."

"TLC, is it?" Sharon perched on the edge of the couch next to Jeff. "Doesn't that mean tickling's the lucky one's choice'?"

"It certainly does." Jeff jerked up and grabbed her hands.

Laughing, I went into the basement and closed my door against the shrieks and growls coming from upstairs. My mother's Bible lay on the table beside my bed. Picking it up, I hesitated then opened it.

Hebrews 11:1: "Now faith is confidence in what we hope for and assurance about what we do not see."

"I guess that's fair. I haven't had confidence in You for a long time, God. I'm sorry, but I'm going to have to ask You to help me have faith again."

The book opened again, but this time to Psalm 103:8-9: "The LORD is compassionate and gracious, Slow to anger, abounding in love. He will not always accuse, nor will he harbor his anger forever."

"Can You really love me, God?" My face ached. "Can You forgive me? I've been angry with You for so long."

CHAPTER 12

"Icopped out when it came to choosing a restaurant." Mark rested his hand on my arm as the hostess led us to a table. "I figured since we come here so much on Sundays, you'd probably like it."

"What if I don't? What if we just come here because Jeff and Sharon like it, and I can't stand it?"

He reached over and tapped my knuckles with a menu. "Tough luck for you. Because I love the place."

He did most of the talking. I asked questions, to put off talking about myself. Mark had a big family, two sisters, three brothers, and "a passel" of nieces and nephews.

"You must have a lot of experience gluing broken toys back together."

"I do." He nodded and made a serious face.

Mark was an occupational therapist. "I do home health, mostly in the homes of elderly people."

He took a bite of his sandwich. "It's an honor, really, being allowed into their homes." He quirked an eyebrow. "And very natural. So funny when they are still wearing their pajamas when I get there. Not just the patients either."

"I've noticed you get along well with the older people at church."

"They are a lot of fun. And fascinating. I could spend hours listening to the stories they tell. And you wouldn't believe the kind of stuff people have in their houses." He held out the bottle of hot sauce to me.

I shook my head. "Um, no. Thanks."

"Your loss." He shook hot sauce into his potato soup. "Anyway, what people have in their houses. Some of it's really interesting, beautiful antique furniture. Wooden toys from over a hundred years ago. Some of it's just collected and crammed-up junk.

"I love looking at the old family pictures." He rested his spoon on his plate. "They're interesting to see, you know? The clothes and hairstyles and everything look so old. But I especially like when they tell me about what was happening."

He took a drink. "There are pictures from when the men went into war, weddings, family pictures. Most are really formal. I like to ask them to tell me who everybody is."

We were quiet for a minute.

"What do you want to tell me about you, Cassie?"

Looking down at my plate, I hesitated. What to say? I told him a little about college and my job. "I guess what I liked most about both was when I was able to draw."

"What do you draw?"

"Anything. Everything. Food, animals, landscape, people." I laughed. "Nothing's safe I guess."

"Are you good?"

"I want to be. Not bad." I shrugged. "Not so good I'll make a living at it."

It was a relief when Mark didn't ask me when I was going back to work. Jeff told me once that if anybody asked him about me, he just explained that I was on medical leave. He suggested that I do the same thing and to open up more to whomever, and whenever, I felt comfortable.

I looked across the table at Mark. He had a kind face and a smile that made you want to smile right back. It probably wouldn't be long before I could tell him a little more about what was going on with me.

Mark leaned back in his chair. "Want to take a drive and get a start on Christmas?"

"Do what?"

"This town loves Christmas. There are already a ton of houses around here with lights up. And believe me, our people know how to decorate for Christmas."

That sounded pretty safe. "I'd like to do that."

We didn't talk for a few minutes as we drove by houses decorated with lovely strings of lights and live Christmas trees in the yards.

"There's something you might want to draw."

In one yard sat a large turtle covered with colored lights. On top of it perched a smaller turtle, a baby atop its mama.

I laughed. "I would like to draw that."

We passed a shop with a large ice cream cone out front, topped with two dips of colored lights.

"Now that's what I call a Christmas treat." Mark smacked his lips.

"Mmm hmmm." I relaxed in the seat.

Mark laughed. "Look at Rudolph."

A large plastic Rudolph had a big rubber ball clenched in his mouth. "Excellent. I think this would be a nice town to live in."

Mark closed his hand around mine. "I'm glad you think so."

As we drove up to our house, he chuckled. "Look at that, the living room light's on. Big brother must be waiting up for you."

"Big brother the superman."

"Is that what you call him? I'll have to tuck that away for future use."

As I opened the car door, Mark got out and hurried around to my side. "Let me walk you in. We don't want Superman to think I'm not doing my job."

He took hold of my hand as we walked.

"I do like that restaurant," I told him when we were standing on the porch.

"I know." His smile flashed in the front door light. "I asked Naomi. She told me it was your favorite."

CHAPTER 13

"Whoa, that's good." Sondra, a girl from church, rested her hand on my shoulder as she gazed down at the drawing in front of me. "Can I show it to my dad?"

I sat in the classroom before Mark's Bible study, finishing a drawing for Tommy and Naomi.

When I heard Sondra speak, I looked up. She went to the same Bible class I'd joined, was about my age, and had made a special effort to talk to me.

"I'm serious." She tapped her finger on the pad of paper in front of me. "Could I show that to my dad?"

I looked back to the picture. Naomi and Tommy both sat on galloping horses. She chased him downhill toward flowering bushes.

"Why would your dad want to see this?"

"He owns one of the papers in town, *The Observer*. He's been looking for someone to do some drawing. Some kid stuff. Maybe some cartoons. Would you be interested in something like that?"

"I, I'm not sure."

"Please. Mom and Dad come to the later service. Just let me show this to him, and I promise I'll bring it back to you this afternoon."

With more than a little hesitation, and fear, I handed her the pad.

~

"WHAT'S UP?" Jeff found me standing at the living room window, staring at the traffic. He tugged at my sleeve. "Cassie?"

I opened my mouth then closed it.

Jeff took hold of my hand and led me to the couch. "What is it?"

"Sondra took a picture I drew to show to her dad."

"Okay."

"She said he's been looking for someone to help at the newspaper, doing some, some drawing."

He leaned back and nodded.

Trying to make myself more comfortable on the couch, I squirmed to face him. "I mean, it's not like they've offered me a job or anything."

"Would you like to do something like that?" He picked up my hand again.

"I'd like to. But what if I can't . . . What if . . ." I swallowed and dug my nails into my palms. "What if I get sick again?"

Jeff pulled me to sit closer beside him. "Remember, you're on medical leave. You can agree to do as little or as much as you want. If it makes you feel less pressured, you can even offer to volunteer."

I looked up at him. "Volunteer?"

He put his arm around me. "Come on, little bird. Do something you enjoy. Live a little."

"I don't know. We'll see. Sondra's coming over later this afternoon." I looked down again.

"Now what?" Jeff tugged my hair.

Finding a button on the couch seat, I wiggled it. "We started reading the Gospel of John this morning in Mark's class."

"Okay."

The button twisted in my fingers. "Mark said John talks a lot about God's grace."

Jeff stayed quiet.

"Jeff?"

He laid his hand over mine. "Don't tear my couch."

"Oh, I—" I snatched my hand back.

Jeff grinned.

My hands clenched in my lap. "I haven't paid much attention to God in a long time. I was mad at Him. Because of Mom and Dad, then Curt." I swallowed then bit my lip. "Will God—will He let me come back?" I shook my head. "I feel so messed up."

Jeff laughed and wrapped both arms around me. "You have so many worries, honey. And I have so few answers. But one thing I know for sure. God will definitely take you back. He's been waiting on the edge of His seat for you to ask Him."

Pushing back from him, I grasped his hands. "Are you sure?"

"I am sure." He loosed his hands to rest them on the sides of my head. "Cassie, take a deep breath. Work for the paper if you want. Ask God to help you believe He will take you back. Your mind is whirling." His hands were gentle as he squeezed my head. "Try to relax a little."

"Relax. Right."

CHAPTER 14

When Sondra brought the drawing over later that afternoon, we went out to get coffee.

"Dad would like you to come in to the paper tomorrow and talk. He was excited about your work." She spooned sugar into her coffee. "He thought maybe you could look at some of the ideas he has for a children's section and maybe do a couple drawings. Talk to people around the office. See what you think."

Holding my cup in both hands, I took a deep breath. "Sondra, I've been . . . I haven't been well. I had to quit work for a while. I don't know how much time I could promise or how much work."

She didn't hesitate or look at all curious or pitying. "Totally up to you. It's a family-owned paper. I'm a reporter there. A lot of people are family."

She took a sip of coffee and set her cup down. "Dad's not interested in being in a big competition with the other paper in town. Don't get me wrong. We're not shoddy. He does expect quality work. But our paper's just got a different kind of purpose. And I'm sure Dad would be willing to work out with you whatever hours you're comfortable with."

"What if I feel like being a volunteer right now?"

She blinked. "That's new." She took another drink of coffee. "Look, Cassie, he liked your drawing. If it works out for you to help us some at the paper, Dad's not going to cram money down your throat." She smiled at me. "Come in and check us out. Talk to Dad."

I DIDN'T SEE Sondra's dad right away the next morning, but I did meet other interesting people.

Rex, the sports writer, who wore his sweatshirt backwards and told me he would have played professional baseball, but he couldn't bear the idea of leaving his hometown.

Jason, the advertising director, who was always in a hurry, but every time he dashed by me he'd say, "I have so much to do. Do you think you'd like to help with advertising?"

Rob, the photographer. He sat on the desk in front of me and leaned back on his hands, gazing at me. "You know who you remind me of, Cassie? Last year's Miss America. I'm being serious here."

Sondra's mother came through the office, her arms stacked with newspapers. "Hi, Cassie," she called as she passed by. "Listen, don't believe anything these guys say."

Sondra and Lorie, another reporter, both sat near me. They burst out laughing.

"Hmph!" Rob slid off the desk and walked over to Rex. "Do you have any idea what she's talking about?"

"Not me." Rex shook his head, and the two men walked out together.

Finally Sondra's dad, Joe Bradley, came into the newsroom and pulled up a chair beside me. He held a drawing I'd brought in that morning, a family of pineapples painting a house.

"Sondra tells me that if you work for us, you don't want any pay."

I nodded.

"I can deal with that, for now anyway. Part-time too, that's fine.

We're busy around here, but we won't pressure you. We like your work. We want you to like us, to be comfortable here."

"Okay." I took a breath. "Thank you, Mr. Bradley."

He turned his head from side to side, looking around the room. "I'm sorry, who are you speaking to?"

My lips twitched. "I mean, thank you, Joe."

"Oh me." He shrugged. "I haven't done anything yet. I want you to know, I'm a little uncomfortable not paying you. I'll have to at least give you gifts. Even my dog gives us gifts. I'll share one with you that he gave me this morning."

He laid the family newspaper on the desk in front of me. It'd been so torn and chewed, when I tried to unfold it, the front page was unrecognizable.

I laughed. "This is perfect."

WORKING at the paper was wonderful.

To keep myself from wearing out, I didn't come in more than three days a week, and I never stayed for the entire day. The newsroom was loud and busy. These were funny people, creative, full of energy, eager to help each other.

My energy was nowhere near their level, but I listened to Joe's ideas about cartoons and jokes he had in mind for kids. I was surprised at how many ideas I came up with on my own. Almost on my own.

"That kid has a puppy sticking out of her backpack." Joe stopped by my desk and looked at the drawing I was working on.

I nodded. "It was Tommy and Naomi's idea."

"Maybe I should give them a job here."

I picked up my pencil. "They could probably use a job. They're trying to talk Sharon and Jeff into getting a dog."

"I've got a dog they can have. Cheap." Joe tapped my drawing. "At the bottom write, 'Can't I take him to school, Mom? Please?'"

I sat at my desk while a whirl of noise and activity surged around me. Looking down at the drawing in front of me, I swallowed, and blinked. Drawing had always been my fun, my relaxation, my joy. I pressed my hands against my cheeks. "Can this really become my work?"

CHAPTER 15

I stared at myself in the mirror. "God, things are going well. Is it safe to be happy?" The girl in the mirror blinked, surprised. "Am I praying? Is it safe for me to talk to You?"

Someone hammered on my bathroom door. "Hurry up." Jeff, of course. "It's only Mark. You don't have to make yourself look that special."

I smiled at Mark when I came into the living room. "I'm sorry for keeping you waiting. I meant to be ready and just come out to the car when you got here."

"Oh no." Mark shook his head and tucked my hand into the crook of his arm. "I came to the front door and knocked. I don't want to do anything to upset Superman."

"Right, the perfect gentleman you are." Jeff punched Mark on the arm. "Have a nice evening, buddy. I hear this is a chick flick you've got yourself into."

As we drove, we passed more houses decorated with lights and yard objects.

"Did I not tell you that this town knows how to do Christmas?" Mark tapped my hand. "I think that's the tenth Frosty I've seen today. Wait." He slowed the car. "Is that a live cat on his head?"

After the movie, we stopped by a café to grab a burger. "Tell me the truth, Mark. You didn't really like that show much, did you?"

"What are you talking about?" He reached across the table and dribbled ketchup on my hand. "It was great."

"Good. Then we can see it again."

He pushed his foot down on top of mine under the table. "Don't press your luck, lady."

WORK at the paper made me smile too. I was making friends.

"Jason." I stopped him one day as he hurried past my desk. "You know, maybe, maybe I could help you some with advertising."

He almost dropped the stack of folders he carried. "What?"

I clasped my hands together on the desk in front of me. "It's something I have experience with. I could get information for you sometimes from people wanting to buy ads, look for art on the internet for you to choose from." Was I talking nonsense? "Anything we could think of where I might be useful."

Jason set his folders on my desk. "I think I'm going to kiss you."

I EVEN READ from my mother's Bible most days.

Romans 15:13: "May the God of hope fill you with all joy and peace as you trust in him, so that you may overflow with hope by the power of the Holy Spirit."

My mother had written in the margin, "Thank You, Father, for peace."

"God, can I really have peace?"

ON NEW YEAR'S EVE, Mark and I went to a party at the house of a lady he worked with.

"Hi, Cassie. I'm Barb." She shook my hand then took my coat. "I hope Mark didn't promise you an exciting party. We're a small group, and we're not very rowdy."

"That sounds just like my kind of party."

As midnight drew near, we watched the ceremony in Times Square on television. "Are you having a nice time?" Mark sat on the arm of my chair.

"Yes." I smiled up at him.

"Good. Are you ready to go?"

"Huh? The ball hasn't dropped."

His eyes crinkled. "I want to be somewhere else at midnight."

I shrugged. "Let's go."

We parked in front of the ice cream shop with the lighted cone outside. "Watch the clock on the dash," Mark told me. As soon as it showed midnight, he leaned across and kissed me. "Happy New Year. I think . . ." He grinned. "I know I am excited about this year."

CHAPTER 16

The weather grew colder as we moved deeper into January. Bleak. Exhausting. One afternoon I sat home with Naomi while Sharon went to the grocery store.

"Cassie. What are you doing?" Sharon's voice woke me.

"Huh?" I sat up and rubbed my face. I'd fallen asleep on the couch.

Sharon stood in front of me, frowning, her eyes wide. "Naomi opened the front door and came out on the porch when I got home." Sharon waved her arms. "She didn't have a coat, or socks . . ." She stopped and took a breath. "I thought you were watching her."

"I was. We were playing with her dishes . . ." I looked around the room. "Where is she?"

"In her room getting some socks on." Sharon shook her head. "She's just four. Come on. You can't take a nap and let her run around the house and do whatever she wants, go outside . . ." Sharon sighed and waved her arms again.

"I'm sorry. I didn't mean to fall asleep." Taking a breath, I stood up. "She's okay, isn't she?"

"Yes, she's okay but . . ." She jerked her shoulders and turned away. "I've got to put away groceries."

"Sharon, I'm sorry. But, Naomi's okay, right? So . . ."

She walked on to the kitchen. "I've got to put away groceries."

~

A PROJECT I was working on at the paper flopped. Sitting at my desk, I stared at the drawing. I couldn't think of what to do with it. Nothing I tried looked right. I drew a couple lines, then stopped and dropped the pencil.

"Did you finish the cartoon with the elephants yet?" Joe stopped by my desk.

"No. It didn't work." I crumpled the piece of paper in front of me.

"That happens. No big deal. You okay?" He laid his hand on my shoulder. "Cassie?"

"What?" I couldn't look up at him. "Yeah, I'm fine." My mouth was dry.

~

ONE NIGHT as I put away laundry, I saw an envelope sticking out of a favorite pair of old jeans. A card from Curt. "Hey, Sweetheart. I'm looking forward to seeing you this weekend. Love you."

"I bet he didn't come that weekend." I tore the card in tiny pieces. "He always had a reason why he couldn't come."

I scrubbed at a tear sneaking down my cheek. "Why do I think I can have a relationship with Mark? I never have been good at it."

~

ONE MORNING when it was time to get up, I sat on the side of the bed, not moving any farther. A knot of fear curled inside my stomach, and I felt the blood drain from my face. The idea of standing up was overwhelming. I couldn't do it.

I told the family I was sick and needed to sleep. This worked on the second day too.

CHAPTER 17

On the third day, Jeff showed up at ten o'clock in my room. "Come on, come on, get up. I need your help."

Rubbing my eyes, I turned my head away from him. "What are you doing home from work?"

"I decided I needed a three-day weekend. Get up. We've got work to do."

"Sharon called you." I managed to sit up on the side of the bed.

"Sharon called me." He sat beside me. "What's up?"

"I don't feel well."

"I'm sorry, what's wrong? Do you have a fever? Let me check."

He reached over to lay his hand on my forehead, but I shook my head. "No."

"Are you sick at your stomach?"

"No." I wrapped my arms around my middle.

"What is it then? You've been asleep the last couple nights when I looked in on you, or you looked asleep anyway."

"I just feel cruddy."

"You want some cold medicine? We've got some pretty good stuff upstairs."

"I don't have a cold."

He stood up. "Get your shoes on and come with me then. Without any symptoms, you're helping me take down the Christmas tree. It is way past time."

I called after him as he started out of the room. "Sometimes you treat me like one of your kids."

He turned back to face me. "Sometimes you act like one of my kids."

When I got to the room on the other side of the basement, Jeff had his arms filled with three empty boxes. "Get those other two boxes and come on upstairs."

By the time I made it to the living room, he already stood on a chair taking down the star from the top of the tree. "Take this and put it carefully in that green box."

It was crazy how fast he moved. He told me to be careful, but he jerked things off the tree and handed them to me to stuff in boxes. In no time, we had taken apart the tree itself and packed it away.

"What are you in such a rush for?" I finally mumbled. "Are you mad at me?"

Jeff slid to a stop as he came downstairs with an armload of decorations from the kids' rooms. He laid down what he was carrying and sat on the floor beside me where I knelt, pushing the last few fallen ornaments into a box.

"I'm not mad at you." He stopped and ran his hands through his hair. "I guess I just don't know what to do to help you." He took a deep breath and slapped his legs. "Let's take these boxes downstairs."

Down in the storage room, Jeff stood on a step stool, and I handed him a box. He lifted it to a top shelf and turned for another. "Can you tell me at all what's wrong?"

I wrinkled my face and shrugged. "I had a fight with Sharon the other day."

"Yes." He waited. "Are you still mad at Sharon?"

"No."

"Do you think she's still mad at you?"

I didn't say anything.

"You know she's not. You know how things happen in families." He waited again. "Is there anything else?"

"I found an old card from Curt." I shoved another box at him. "None of it sounds like a big deal. I don't know. Just a bunch of little stuff. I don't know." I shook my head.

"Okay. That's okay." He thought for a minute. "You know, a lot of people feel down in winter time. And especially people with depression. Whoa. Take that look off your face."

He jumped off the stool and took the box out of my hands. "Come in here." He grasped my arm and walked into my room. Sitting on my bed, he patted the blanket next to him. "Sit."

I sat.

"Why did you scowl like that? Depression is an illness that some people get. A medical illness like heart disease or diabetes." He sighed. "Sometimes I think you see it as a fault or something to be ashamed of."

Keeping my head down, I picked at a loose thread on my shirt.

"I know you've had a lot of bad things happen in your life. But, but a lot of people do." He stopped and rubbed his hands over his face. "Look, I don't know very much about this. But I do know that depression is an illness. Period. Not anything to be ashamed of. And medicine is a miracle given by God to help people."

He put his hand under my chin and raised my face to look at him. "You know you're different now than you were when I brought you home from the hospital, don't you?"

"What about the last three days?" My voice cracked.

"Oh, honey." He leaned back on his elbows. "People who have arthritis have days when they're in a lot of pain. Some people who have heart disease have to carry special medication around with them in case they need it suddenly. You're gonna have bad days sometimes."

Tears trickled down my face. "Dr. Carver said, he said I might never remember the time when I tried to kill myself. Or, I might remember. Just out of the blue. That's really scary."

Jeff sat up and wrapped his arms around me. "I know it's scary. It scares me too."

I tried to push back from him. "What if I try to kill myself again?" My voice rose. "What if—"

Jeff pushed my head against his shoulder and squeezed me tighter. He took deep breaths, and neither of us spoke for a minute.

He lifted my chin and pushed hair out of my face. "Honey." His voice grated. "If you have an illness, you've just got to . . . I know this is terrible, but you've got to figure out how to live with it. Medicine helps. That may be something you use long term. Counseling helps. That may not be long term. But if in a couple years it seems like you might need it again and you go back to counseling, that's okay. It's a tool, another gift from God."

He set me back a little from him. "You've got to trust God to help you with this. As much as I want to, I can't be the superman big brother. I can't fix it. I'm not always going to be there. Although . . ." He made a face. "No matter how far away you go, I'm going to keep in better touch next time. Probably a whole lot more than you want me to."

I managed a wobbly smile, and he rested his hand against my cheek.

"You need to learn how to work with this. Your counselor will help you, and your doctor. I'll help you. You have to learn the different ways you feel bad. You've got to pay attention to when something happens. And when you wake up on a day like today or yesterday, no matter how bad you feel, you have to teach yourself that you can't stay in bed."

We were quiet for a minute. Finally, I nodded.

He studied me, then grinned. "I promise you won't be staying in bed late tomorrow. We've got some early Saturday morning chores to do."

Laughing a little, I wiped tears from my face. "You're precious to me," I whispered.

He wrapped his arms behind my shoulders. "You're precious to me, too."

∽

AFTER JEFF LEFT, I sat on the side of the bed for a while, looking down at my hands in my lap. I picked up my mother's Bible and flipped through the pages.

"Is this how it is, God?" I wiped my cheeks. "I have to accept that I have an illness that I pretty much have to live with. Forever. And I have to trust that You're going to help me with it." My shoulders bunched. "We're just barely getting to know each other again."

I kept turning pages.

James 1:16-17: "don't be deceived, my dear brothers and sisters. Every good and perfect gift is from above, coming down from the Father of the heavenly lights, who does not change like shifting shadows."

"God, Jeff said medicine is a gift from You that can help me live with this illness."

Psalm 34:18: "The LORD is close to the brokenhearted and saves those who are crushed in spirit."

I set my mother's Bible on the table beside the bed. Lying down with my face buried in the pillow, I shook with sobs.

CHAPTER 18

I was able to get an appointment with Julia on Monday.
"I've had a rough few days."

Julia always left her desk and sat in the chair near mine. But I couldn't stay seated. I paced the few steps between her desk and the window.

"Tell me about it." Julia's voice was calm.

"I don't know. It was a lot of little things." Her nameplate lay flopped onto its back, so I set it upright. "I couldn't make myself get out of bed."

She stayed quiet.

"Jeff left work and made me get up." I looked out the window at the drab snow. "I asked him what I should do if . . . What if I tried to kill myself again?" The wall clock behind me ticked. "He didn't have an answer."

"Did you think about trying to kill yourself?"

"I don't think so. No. I just didn't want to get up."

I walked back to her desk, reached for her family picture, then clasped my hands against my stomach. "Jeff thinks I have depression as a long term illness."

"What do you think?"

Turning back to the window, I yanked at my hair. "I don't know. Maybe. I guess that makes sense, but . . ."

"But?" Julia persisted.

Outside, a couple walked by on the sidewalk, leaving more muddy footprints in the snow. "But it seems so hopeless." I turned to face Julia.

She held a cup of tea in both hands. "What does Dr. Carver say?"

Shrugging, I flapped my hands. "He makes it sound so, so, common. Every day." I paced to the desk, then to the window and back. "Maybe not common, but, but . . ."

"Acceptable? Like something that can be handled?" Julia smiled at me.

I let out a breath. "Now you sound like Jeff."

ON WEDNESDAY, I went back to work. Relief washed over me when I saw papers piled on my desk, ad requests from Jason and notes for children's drawings from Joe. Last week I'd made a mess of a cartoon Joe wanted for the kids' section, and I'd been afraid he'd be upset with me. I hadn't been there for days to help Jason. Would he think I wasn't dependable?

People came into the news room and stopped to talk to me, and my shoulders relaxed a little. This was a good place.

Rob ran in. "Cassie. Good. You're here." He sat on the desk in front of me. "Tell me, have you ever thought about being a model?"

"No, I haven't."

"I'm serious. You could do it." He did look serious. "Here's what I've been thinking. You and I can start working on photo shoots. No hurry. And when we've got some proofs we're both happy with, I'll submit them to modeling groups."

He smiled and clapped his hands on his knees. "You and me, baby, we could be a great team."

I couldn't help laughing. "Yes, you're right. That's definitely something we should think about. Carefully. For a long, long time."

"Oh, see? You're making fun of me. And that's definitely not something one friend should do to another."

Mrs. Bradley came by then. "Cassie, I told you, don't pay any attention to anything he says."

"Now, don't start that again." Rob sounded hurt. "Already Cassie doesn't believe me."

I was busy searching for some of the advertisement work when Joe came in, holding something in a paper bag. He'd continued to bring me gifts from his dog as my payment—a collapsed rubber ball, a chewed-up tennis shoe, part of a tree branch, an empty candy wrapper. It was a good joke between us, but it had never been in a bag before.

I narrowed my eyes at him. "Good morning."

"Good morning. I see you're hard at work." He sat on a chair near me and laid the bag on my desk.

"Uh huh."

"Good. That's good." He scooted his chair a little closer. "Now. You know how I feel about the fact you won't let us pay you for your work."

"Yes."

"Well, I guess we'll have to keep talking about it. But for now . . ." He picked up the paper bag. "My dog did bring in an especially nice gift this morning." He stuck in his hand and pulled out a dead squirrel.

"Whoa!" I scooted my chair back and threw out my hands in front of me. "Okay. Okay. It's a deal. You can pay me. I give."

"Why, Cassie." Joe dropped the squirrel back in the bag and laid it on the desk again. "I'm so glad to hear you say that. What changed your mind?"

"And please take that bag off my desk."

"Hmmm? This bag? Oh, you don't want the gift? Funny, my wife didn't either."

He picked up the bag and held out his other hand to me. "Welcome again, for real this time."

"Thanks." I hesitated. "Umm, I think I'll wait to shake your hand until you've had a chance to wash it. And still part-time for now, if that's okay."

"Oh sure, however you're comfortable." He looked around the room. "Where is everybody? I'll see if I can't find somebody else who wants this fine gift."

He walked out the door calling for Sondra and Lorie. Smiling, I went looking for something to wipe my desk where the paper bag had been. "Lord, You've given this to me as a gift, this job." My eyes teared, and I hugged my chest. "You do love me?"

"Hey, Little Bird. What's wrong?" Jeff came down most mornings before he left for work to make sure I got up. This morning when he came down, he found me sitting on the side of the bed crying. He handed me tissues from the table next to my bed, then sat down beside me.

I groaned and scrubbed at my face with my hands. "Nothing. Just a bad dream. Sometimes they're hard to shake."

"I'm sorry. Was it scary?"

"No. Yes . . . I don't know." I blew my nose. "It was dumb. I was carrying Naomi up a tall flight of stairs. Every time we almost reached the top, I dropped her. Again and again." Shrugging, I worked to calm my breathing. "It was just a stupid dream. I don't know why it upset me so much. I'm sorry."

He rubbed my hair. "You don't have to be sorry. Dreams are weird."

My breath caught. "Sometimes I feel like I'm crazy."

He wrapped my hand in his. "You're not crazy."

We didn't speak for a minute. Looking up at him, I opened my mouth then closed it.

"What?"

"You know," I said, then paused. "I've been reading the Bible a lot lately, and praying. I think I'm not so mad at God anymore."

"I know." He hugged my shoulders. "I'm proud of you."

I looked down again.

"Yes?" Jeff lifted my chin and searched my eyes.

I shifted on the bed. "I guess you've been praying for me, about learning to handle this whole depression thing."

"And a few other things." He grinned. "For a bunch of years."

Jeff reached for Mom's Bible. "Let me show you something." He turned pages until he found what he wanted. "Look at this."

John 10:10: "The thief comes only to steal and kill and destroy; I have come that they may have life, and have it to the full."

After reading the verse a couple of times, I looked back up. "Okay."

"Look at that, a full life." He leaned back against the wall. "I don't mean to be telling you that you have to settle for a hum-drum life. Or more than that even. A life of sickness." He reached over and tugged my hair. "Jesus promises us a full life, honey. That's a good life, happy, exciting. Even with an illness."

"Hmmm."

He knocked on my head. "I mean it."

"Okay. We'll see." With a laugh, I grasped his hand between both of mine. "You're good for me."

"Hey, aren't you going to eat any popcorn?" Mark shook the bowl at me.

We sat on Mark's couch, a bowl of popcorn between us. He'd invited me over to his place to watch a movie after Sunday lunch.

I couldn't pay any attention to the movie, though. "Mark?"

"Hmmm?" He grabbed another handful of popcorn.

"I need to tell you something."

"Sounds serious." He picked up the remote and turned the movie off. "I'm all ears, ma'am."

"I haven't told you yet about why I moved here to live with Jeff and Sharon." I looked down at my hands and swallowed. "Why I left my job."

He set the popcorn bowl on the table in front of the couch and moved closer to me. "No. You haven't."

My fingers twisted together. "I . . . I was in the hospital."

"Okay."

I still couldn't look at him. "I, I guess I have depression. Probably chronic depression. I mean . . ." I pushed my face into my hands. "I mean, I'll probably always have it."

"I know what chronic means." Was he smiling?

Taking a deep breath, I ground my teeth together. "I tried to kill myself, Mark. I cut my wrists."

He was silent for a minute. Then he moved even closer and took my hands from my face. "Look at me."

I gulped. And looked.

He touched my face. "Are you afraid I won't want to be with you anymore?"

I couldn't answer.

"Don't worry." He rested his forehead against mine. "I'm already caught. I'm not going anywhere."

With my head resting against his shoulder, I shuddered. Reassuring? Scary? Yeah.

CHAPTER 20

"Where you headed?" Jeff walked to stand next to me as I stood on the sidewalk in front of the house.

"Oh." I jumped. I'd been caught up by the lovely sight of the neighborhood. "You startled me. I just wanted to take a walk. It looks like spring is trying to come."

"Spring, huh?" Jeff shaded his eyes and looked around. "Don't let those couple of robins and a few buds on the trees fool you. We'll have snow again before the end of the week."

I poked him in the ribs. "Spoil sport. I think it's spring."

Jeff clapped my ear muffs then squeezed my mittened hands. "Whatever you say." He turned back to the house, then stopped. "You okay?"

"I think so." I took a breath. "Check back with me in a couple hours."

Jeff nodded and gave me a thumbs-up. "You got it."

I walked as far as the neighborhood park and settled down on a bench. Opening my backpack, I pulled out a thermos of coffee and my mother's Bible.

"All right, God, let's have this out."

Matthew 11: 28: "Come to me, all you who are weary and

burdened, and I will give you rest." In the margin Mom had written, "I have rest."

I wrapped my arms around my middle. "This depression thing, it's not just going away." I took a deep breath. "Jeff says You can give me a good life, even with it."

Standing, I paced in front of the bench. "Everybody seems to think this is something that can be handled." I shook my head. "Even Mark wasn't scared away."

My foot kicked at some old leaves. "I guess there's no way I can be absolutely sure I won't try to kill myself again." Shuddering, I squeezed my arms tighter around me. "That scares me."

A bird called above me, but it didn't sound like the robin singing spring.

I sat down and looked at the verse in Matthew again. "This is way more of a burden than I can take care of on my own." My nose ached with tears. "You'll help me?"

I blew warm air into my cold, mittened hands, then turned more pages in the Bible.

Isaiah 41:10: "So do not fear, for I am with you; do not be dismayed, for I am your God. I will strengthen you and help you; I will uphold you with my righteous right hand."

Lifting my face, I looked for the loud bird.

"Twee-tip, twee-tip."

No, it wasn't the jolly robin. It was one of the same, dull birds who waited through the long winter with us.

I barked a laugh. "Okay, God. So You have a sense of humor."

That bird was still willing to sing.

I took a drink of coffee then held the warm cup close to my face. "Father?" I stopped. It was still a struggle for me to call him "Father."

Taking a deep breath, I started over. "Father . . . Let's give this a try."

72

CHAPTER 21

On an early May Saturday morning, I didn't wait for Jeff to wake me up. I went outside and found him setting out tomato plants.

"Weren't you going to ask me to come out and help?" I sat on the ground near him.

"I was going to wait until there was some more important work to do, like pulling weeds and stuff."

"I see." I watched him for a minute. "Jeff?"

"Mmm?" He kept working with the plants, not looking at me.

"Sondra's roommate just moved out. She's getting married."

"Sondra?"

"No, her roommate." I hesitated. "Sondra was wondering if I might move in with her."

Quiet.

"I'm working enough hours at the paper now, I think I could afford it."

"We should have started charging you rent."

A water hose lay on the ground nearby. I picked it up and aimed it at him. "How do I turn this on?"

"Yeah, yeah. Put it down."

I laid the hose down. "So what do you think?"

"What do you think?"

"I think I'd like to move in today."

He snapped his head to face me. "And why didn't you mention this sooner?"

"I didn't want you to get too nervous." I gulped. "I didn't want to get too nervous."

He rubbed his hands on his jeans. "I don't get nervous." He fell back onto the ground and pulled me down with him, tickling me.

"Stop, stop," I squeaked. "I'll kick the tomato plants."

He rolled me farther away on the grass, tickling harder. "Ah, a challenge."

"Jeff, Jeff, stop . . ." Reaching for his hair, I yanked.

He pulled my hands out of his hair, grasping them and putting his face close to mine. "You want to know what happened to the last person who did that?" he asked, his voice low.

"No, no, please, Jeff—" I gasped.

He pulled us both up to a sitting position and wrapped his arms around me. We sat for a minute, catching our breath.

The back door opened. "Everybody okay out here?" Sharon called.

"I guess so." Jeff cleared his throat. "Cassie wants to move out today."

"I know." She walked over to sit beside us.

"You know, do you?" Jeff looked from one of us to the other. "When was I going to know?"

"When I asked you to come over this morning to help us move some furniture around." I smiled at him.

AFTER I FINISHED LOADING the trunk of my car, I turned back to the house. Tommy and Naomi stood on the front porch steps, both with long faces.

A tear coursed down Naomi's left cheek. "Why are you leaving?"

I sat on the step below them. "So you can have my room in the basement for a play-room again."

Tommy stuffed his hands in his pockets. "That's not funny."

"Sorry." I pulled both of them onto my lap and kissed their heads. "I'll see you tomorrow."

"At church?" Naomi wiped her nose on her sleeve.

"That's right. And if you talk real nice to your dad, he might let me go to lunch with you afterward."

"Doubt it." Jeff walked out of the front door and sat down beside us.

"See?" I tickled Naomi under her chin. "You've got a lot of work ahead of you."

Tommy squirmed off of my lap and onto Jeff's. "Don't let her go, Daddy."

Naomi turned her face against my shoulder and cried harder.

"Would you guys like to come over to my house for dinner soon?" I pulled Naomi's head back and kissed her nose.

"Could I get off the bus at your house?" Tommy asked.

I reached over and untied his shoe. "I'll probably be at the paper most days."

Jeff lowered his head and whispered loud in Tommy's ear. "If I was you, I'd ask her what she'll have for dinner."

"I don't want any dinner." Naomi rubbed her eyes with her fists.

"Smart girl." Jeff tugged on her ear, then bent down to kiss her head.

Tommy sniffed. "Smells like Mommy's baking cookies."

"Maybe a good time to go on back in the house," I said, squeezing Naomi.

Her mouth still quivered. Tommy stood up and grabbed her hand. "Come on. I'll race you to the kitchen."

I buried my face in my hands until I heard the front door close.

"Sure you don't want to go back in the house?" Jeff pulled my hands away from my face. "It smells like oatmeal raisin."

"I'll race you to the apartment." I took a deep breath and stood. "I'll take your car. You take mine."

Jeff passed his keys over to me. "You got it. I'll give you a five minute head start."

~

AFTER THE FURNITURE WAS REARRANGED, I took Jeff for a walk in the neighborhood. Neither of us had much to say. We ended up back by Jeff's car.

"Where's Mark when there's work?" Jeff opened his door and got in.

"He's coming over tonight for dinner. He had some patients he needed to see today."

"Likely excuse."

I looked down at my feet. "Are you really upset that I'm moving out?"

"Certainly I'm upset. What do you think I'm made out of, rock?"

I chewed on my lip. "Well, I'm an adult. You knew I wasn't going to live with you forever."

"Yeah. Of course I knew that. What does that have to do with anything?"

Leaning into the car, I hugged him. "I love you. I'll come visit you a lot. And I hope you'll visit me too."

"Oh, I'll be here. You can count on that." He hugged me back. His eyes were sad.

I stood up. "Will you call me in the mornings for a while, to be sure I make it out of bed?"

"For as long as you like." He reached out and touched my hand. "If you're already up and out of the house when I call, can I search for you all over town?"

"Uh, no."

We were both quiet for a minute, then he finally smiled. "I'll see you later, little bird."

Watching as he drove away, I blinked my eyes against tears. "I'll see you soon, Superman."

After a moment, I turned back to my new house. "Father, Jeff and I will be okay." I took a long breath. "Thank You so much for the gift of my brother."

The front door banged open. "Get in here," Sondra called. "Let's get you unpacked and settled in."

I wiped at my face and ran up the steps to the front door, ready to start the gift of my new life.

THE END

ALL MY TEARS

CHAPTER 1

$\mathcal{T}$he elevator closed behind me, and I started down the hall. Someone sat on a chair outside my apartment door.

It was late, and the light in the hall dim. I turned to go back to the elevator.

"Beth. It's me. Sam."

Still moving away, I looked back. I couldn't see much of him, but the voice?

The man stood. "It really is me."

"Sam?" Hesitantly, I moved a couple of steps closer. "What are you doing here? Where'd you get a chair?"

"From your neighbor across the hall." He pushed the chair out of the way and moved toward me. It surely was my brother. "Can we go inside?"

"Huh?" I shook my head, confused. "Go inside?"

"Please. I need to talk to you."

"It's a mess." Shrugging, I moved to the door and unlocked it. "Come on then."

After shoving a bunch of newspapers and food containers off the couch, I switched on a lamp. "Sit down." Pushing trash off another chair, I sat and hugged my middle.

Sam sat on the couch. He glanced at the mess around him then looked to me. "Did you know Dad's been in the hospital?"

"Nice to see you too. What's it been, two years?"

"Probably. Did you know?"

"Joyce called me. I've been in the hospital too. Had you heard?"

Sam sighed. He was trying to be patient. "Alcohol rehab, I think Joyce said."

"Yep. I got out two days ago."

"Have you had a drink since?"

"Nice of you to be concerned. No, I haven't, actually."

He rubbed his hands over his face. "Look. We need your help."

"You must be desperate."

"Could you, for one minute, think of someone besides yourself, and just listen?"

"All ears."

He took a deep breath. "Did Joyce tell you that Dad has dementia?"

I jerked forward. "Alzheimer's?"

"She didn't tell you." Sam's feet twitched, but he stayed seated. "Not Alzheimer's. I mean, they don't know what it is. It's just dementia. For older people."

"Dad's only sixty-eight."

"That's old enough, I guess." Sam pressed his hands against his knees. "Anyway, he's been having trouble remembering things. To pay bills. To get the mail. To take out the trash. To eat sometimes. He's confused, doesn't always know people." He shook his head. "And he's clumsy. He doesn't always pay attention to where he's going. He fell down the front steps and broke his ankle. Fortunately one of the neighbors saw him right away and called an ambulance."

"Was he hurt any other way?"

"No, thankfully. And it was a simple break. But we went ahead and put him into rehab for a while, to make sure he could take care of himself before he came home."

I closed my eyes. Joyce only called me a few days ago. If she'd tried earlier, I wasn't able to listen.

Sam stood and paced around my small living room. "The bottom line is, he can't live alone anymore."

"Uh huh."

"And he's still healthy you know? Really healthy."

"Except for dementia and a broken ankle."

"A healing ankle." He stopped in front of me. "Like you said, he's still fairly young. He really doesn't need to go into a nursing home yet."

Not speaking, I looked straight back at him.

"You know how far away I live. And with my job, I'm in enough trouble for being gone right now. And Joyce lives a three-hour drive from Dad—"

"And she's got an important job." I stood up and pushed past him a few steps, then turned to face him. "And both of you have families, right? But then there's little sis, divorced, no family, unemployed, what could be better?"

"All right, listen."

"Am I not saying it right? Remember though, I'm a drunk. You sure you can trust me?"

"No, I'm not." He ground his teeth. "But Joyce thinks she can. And remember, I'm desperate."

We stood and stared at each other for a minute, my heartbeat pounding in my ears.

Sam sighed, then turned and went into the kitchen. Cabinet doors banged, then dishes clattered in the sink and water ran. He walked back into the living room with a glass in his hand.

"Do you always wash your dishes before you use them rather than after?"

"It works for me."

He took a drink. "Let's sit down and try this again."

"I'm comfortable standing."

Sam sat back on the couch, holding the glass in both hands. Feeling silly, I finally sat down too.

"Beth, Dad has retirement, plus social security, plus savings. He has enough money to take care of himself and you right now. He needs you." He took another drink and rubbed at his face. He looked tired. "Look, I know he was never a real warm and fuzzy kind of Dad, but he wasn't abusive either. He worked all the time. He was busy working, and that's all. He wasn't bad to us."

"I never said he was."

"He's still our father. We're not such a great family, maybe, but at least we can do better for him than stuff him in a nursing home when he's just sixty-eight and not really that bad off."

Squeezing my hands together, I looked down, then up at him again. "What do I know about taking care of a man who has dementia? I mean, he fell and broke his ankle. How do I prevent something like that from happening again? What if he wanders off?"

Sam got up and paced. "I'm not saying it'll be an easy job. You'll have to keep an eye on him." He shook his head. "I don't know anything about this either. Joyce will have more information for you."

He stopped in front of me. "He's not very active. He just sits in his room or on the couch mostly." He walked away, then turned to face me again. "Maybe this would be a good thing for you for a while. Go back home, away from where you've had a hard time. Change of scene." He took a drink. "Dad can take care of his own personal needs. He may need to be reminded. To bathe himself, take his medicine, things like that. You'll have to shop and cook, keep the house somewhat decent." He stopped, looked around the room, looked back to me, and pressed his lips together.

Meeting his gaze, I pressed my lips together too.

We stared at each other for a minute then Sam smiled. "What do you say?"

My mind spun, and I held my head in my hands. Could I do this?

I set my jaw. As much as I'd thrown blame at Sam, I knew I was the one who'd distanced myself from my family.

And Dad needed me now.

I raised my chin. "I'll come."

CHAPTER 2

"*I* have to leave now, Beth. Let's go over this list one more time."

We'd gone over it a dozen times, but my sister was about to leave me alone with my father, so I didn't argue with her.

Joyce stood at the kitchen counter, looking at the notepad by the phone. "Dad's main doctor's phone number is on the top of the list. He's got an appointment to see the foot doctor on Tuesday afternoon. He'll probably take off that bubble walking shoe thing. The ankle's pretty much healed."

"Got it."

"I have it all written on here." She looked so worried.

"I've got your number first on my cell phone. Not that I'll be calling much," I hurried to add.

Joyce sighed and turned the page on the pad. "Uncle Joe said he'll come over twice a week and spend a few hours with Dad, so you can go shopping and have a break."

"I didn't think Uncle Joe and Dad got along very well." Uncle Joe was Mom's brother.

"Don't complain about happy surprises, as long as they last anyway." She tapped the pad with a pencil. "I've got the name and number here for the pastor at the church Dad attends sometimes. He visited Dad several times at the hospital and rehab, and he said they would be willing to have someone come by and sit with Dad to give us, whoever was staying with him, a break, too. So I suggest that you be willing to give him a call."

Oh, I'd be willing all right.

Joyce closed the pad. "I'll try to come down every two or three weeks for at least a day on the weekends to spell you some."

I wished I could reassure Joyce that everything was going to be fine. She seemed so anxious. But I was terrified.

I'd been at the house with Joyce and Dad for two days. She'd talked with me about foods he might possibly eat, ways to encourage him to shower and dress himself, taking care of his bills, keeping an eye on him in the house, walking with him to the car. Many other details. How much of it would I really need? Dad spent most of his time sitting on the couch, looking at old newspapers.

Joyce checked the time on her cell phone. "I have to go."

"Go." I forced my face to make a smile. "We'll be fine."

Joyce was only two years older than me, but she'd always behaved as the much more mature sister. She gazed straight at me. "Will you be fine? How are you feeling?"

Okay, between Dad and me, she had some reason for anxiety right now.

"I'm feeling fine. I didn't bring any booze with me. I'm going to do a good job with Dad. Honest I am."

Poor Joyce. She looked scared, and probably wished she could change her mind about leaving me alone with Dad. But she had a husband, three kids, and a job she had to get back to.

She came over and gave me a hug, not a normal thing with us. "Do call me if you need to. Seriously. We appreciate this a lot."

"Hey, he's my Dad too. Now get out of here."

S<small>AM CALLED LATER THAT NIGHT</small>. "How are you feeling?"

"I'm just fine, thanks. And you?"

He sighed. "Are you always going to be sarcastic with me?"

"I'm not sure how to talk with you. It's been so long since we've been in touch."

"And that's all my fault somehow."

Ooooh, stab. He had me there. "What can I do for you, Sam?"

"How's Dad?"

"Fine. He had a good-sized sandwich for dinner, and he's nodding over a magazine on the couch right now."

"Is there anything you need?"

"Nothing that you can do from four states away."

"Thanks a lot. That's helpful. Please don't be too stubborn to call if there's something you need from me." He hung up.

That went pretty well.

I turned toward my father on the couch. "Looks like it's just you and me, Dad."

CHAPTER 3

"*L*et's go." Dad squirmed in the chair. I hadn't even attempted to help him onto the exam table.

"Dad, wait a minute. I'm sure the doctor will be here soon." Putting down the magazine I'd been glancing at, I walked over to stand beside him.

"Where is he?" Dad braced his hands on the arms of the chair.

"Dad, wait."

The door behind me opened. "Hello, Mr. Drake."

I rested my hand on Dad's arm and turned as a nurse stepped inside.

"Beth, hello. I didn't know you were in town."

Blinking, I bit my lip. Who . . .?

She walked over and laid her hand on Dad's other arm. "Mr. Drake, can I help you up on the table?"

Jenny. Jenny Bartlett, or whatever her name was now. It had probably been more than a dozen years since I'd seen her and almost twenty since we'd been friends in middle school.

Jenny concentrated on Dad as she helped him onto the exam table. I walked to the other side. When he was seated, I met her eyes. "Hello, Jenny."

"Hey. Mr. Drake, the doctor will be here in just a minute." She stepped back to the door then stopped to smile at me. "I'll try to catch you on your way out."

~

THE DOCTOR TOOK the bubble shoe off. "You're doing fine, Mr. Drake. You can use your cane if it makes you feel more comfortable, but your ankle is doing very well. You need to keep stepping on that foot to get the strength back." He walked out with us into the waiting room. "Make an appointment for about two weeks, just so I can check to make sure you're continuing to heal properly."

Jenny was beside my father in a moment and laid her hand on his arm. "Oh, I'm glad to hear you're doing well. I'll walk out to the car with you. I wanted to chat with Beth a second anyway."

Jenny helped me get Dad settled in the car then walked with me to the driver's side. "It's really great to see you." She looked a little shy when she gave me a hug. "How long are you here for?"

I shrugged. "The long haul I guess. As long as Dad can stand me. As long as I can be helpful to him."

"That's great. I mean, I didn't know if he'd have to go into a nursing home or something."

"None of us are sure how well it's going to work out." I opened the car door. "But Joyce and Sam decided to try letting me stay with Dad for a while."

"I really do think that's good." She caught her lip between her teeth and looked down.

As I remembered, Jenny wasn't usually bashful like this. She hadn't been when we were in the office and she was in her nursing role.

She looked up again. "Can we get together sometime? Catch up with each other?"

"Sure, if you want to come over to the house and have coffee. I don't think I'll be getting out a whole lot."

Jenny took out her phone. "That would be fine with me. Give me your number, and I'll call you, if that's okay."

"Sure. Please. I'll enjoy having company."

As we drove home, I thought about Jenny. We'd been close friends in grade school, middle school too. Then in high school, when she'd started hanging out more with the church youth group crowd and I'd mingled more with the party gang, we'd drifted apart. It would be fun to get together with her. Why had she turned timid? She was probably still a strong churchgoer. Maybe she'd heard rumors about me and was nervous about what I'd be like.

Relax, sweetie. Everybody doesn't have their mind focused on you.

"She probably won't really call," I told Dad.

But she did. The next morning. "How about Saturday? My husband doesn't have to work, so he can stay with the kids."

"I'd like that. What time?"

"How about noon? I can pick up some sandwiches on the way."

"I'll have coffee ready."

"Okay, that's not just sandwiches I smell in those bags."

Jenny grinned as she came inside the front door. "I'll confess. I stopped by the bakery too. I seem to remember you liked the apple fritters."

I grabbed the bakery bag. "I think I'll kiss you. Mrs. Yancey's apple fritters? Yum."

"Well, they're Mrs. Yancey's daughter Julie's apple fritters now, but they're almost as good." She looked around. "Where's your dad?"

"He's asleep. He doesn't have much of a regular schedule really. He was awake until about four this morning, then slept a couple hours, then was up till about an hour ago. He may sleep all afternoon, or he may wake up in fifteen minutes."

"That probably means you don't sleep very well either." Jenny set the food on the dining room table.

"I always have my door open when I'm in bed. Sometimes I fall asleep sitting at the table while Dad's on the couch." I shrugged. "We're figuring it out."

"I brought him a meatloaf sandwich. I've noticed he likes those at church potlucks."

"Dad goes to your church?"

"Sometimes." Her eyes twinkled. "Always, when there's a potluck."

"These sandwiches smell good, but you'll forgive me if I start with the apple fritter."

As I munched, Jenny showed me pictures of her kids, Amy six, and Robby eight.

"Cute kids." I scrolled through the pictures on her phone. "Who's this funny-looking goon?"

She laughed. "Chris, my husband. You never met him, huh?"

"I guess we haven't seen much of each other for . . . a long time."

She reached and laid her hand on mine. "I feel bad about that. We were such good friends in grade school."

I stood and found some napkins on the counter. "Well, it's not like I've been around much for the last few, for a bunch of years."

"It's not just that." Jenny looked down. "When we got to high school, I pulled away from you."

"You did the right thing. I wouldn't have been good for you."

She looked up, tears in her eyes. "We were friends. That was important. And now we've lost years of that."

I got up and carried dishes to the sink, looked for a rag to wipe the table. Anything to keep from looking into her eyes.

"We were just kids. And besides, it's not like we've lost the chance for a lifetime. We're only thirty-three after all."

My back was turned, but I heard her sniff as she laughed a little. "Maybe it has been too long. You seem to forget, I'm only thirty-two."

Circling the table, I bent to hug her. "You're right. I did forget. You were always the young whipper snapper I had to try to keep under control."

She hugged me back. "Yep. You were my old and feeble lady." She picked up a couple of napkins, handed me one, and we both wiped our faces.

"That's enough of that now." I went to get more coffee.

When we were a little calmer, Jenny picked up her cup and held it in both hands. "So, I showed you my pictures. Are you going to tell me what's been going on with you?"

"Oh, and just when we'd stopped crying."

She stuck out her lip. "Come on."

"Joyce, where's my shoes?" Dad shuffled into the room, carrying his winter coat.

I jumped up. "Joyce isn't here, Dad. I'm Beth." I stopped and took a breath. "You don't need your coat. It's August. Here, sit down. Jenny brought you a meatloaf sandwich."

When it was just Dad and me, I didn't usually get so flustered. Would Jenny think I was able to take care of him?

"Here's your sandwich, Dad. Can I have your coat?"

He grabbed the sandwich. "Sure."

Draping the coat over an empty chair, I slowed my breathing and glanced at Jenny. "Looks like you're right. He lost interest in the coat pretty quick when he saw that sandwich."

When I was seated again, Jenny looked across at me. "I don't think you've met Mark Russell yet. He's our pastor."

"No. But I think his name is on the list of phone numbers Joyce left."

Jenny nodded. "He was talking with some of us at church. We were thinking it would be good if people could come by and visit with your dad sometimes for a little while, to give you a chance to get out of the house. I would be happy to do that."

Resting my chin on my hand, I gazed across at her. "I'd rather someone else did, while you and I go out together."

She smiled. "I bet that could be arranged."

"Mmm, that was good." Dad smacked his lips. "Got another one of those sandwiches?"

"I'm sorry, we don't." I laughed. "But you'll never guess what I'm good at cooking. One of the few things."

CHAPTER 4

"Good morning."

Standing from picking up the newspaper from the front steps, I looked around. Who had spoken?

Someone gave a creaky laugh. "Don't you know who it is?"

Finally I saw him, a tiny man, scrunched in a rocking chair on the porch across the street and up one house.

"Mr. Blackstone?" I walked down the stairs and crossed the street, stopping in front of his porch steps.

"So you do remember me. I used to always make you say hi to me when you were walking to school."

This man must be ninety years old. Surely he wasn't living alone. "You didn't have to make me say hi."

"Come and sit down, why don't you?"

"I can't stay long. Dad might need me. But how are you doing? It's good to see you."

"I'm doing. Let's see, you're Beth, right?"

"Very good. Yes, Beth."

He chuckled again. "You see, not all old people lose their memory. I remember a lot of things about you."

"Oh. That may not be so good."

"Ah, you were okay. There were worse kids. You were willing to stop by and talk to an old man once in a while. That made you a pretty good kid, I think."

My cheeks warmed. "I'll come by again, but I need to get home right now. Do you live by yourself? Would you like my phone number in case you need anything?"

"That's nice of you. My grandson lives with me. And I have home health aides who come in to help me. But you stop by when you can. I'd enjoy the company."

I looked down at the newspaper in my hand then up again. "Can I ask how old you are? I'm thirty-three, by the way."

He laughed. "You are a funny one. I was ninety-one on the Fourth of July."

Ninety-one. And a good memory, sitting on his front porch talking and laughing with people who went by. Thinking about my Dad at sixty-eight, my heart squeezed with sadness.

JENNY CAME over on a Wednesday night, after her kids were in bed. This time she brought ice cream.

"You're going to make me fat."

She licked her spoon. "You look like you could stand to gain a few pounds."

"Yum. You even remembered my favorite flavor is peanut butter chocolate."

"Some things are important to remember." She took another bite. "So. You were going to tell me what you've been up to."

My gaze fell to the bowl of ice cream. I'd hoped we could skip that. "I guess I should tell you and get it over with, but it's not pretty like your pictures."

She reached over and clasped my hand. "Beth."

"I'm serious. I'm not looking for pity."

"Okay. I'm not offering any."

Dad's ice cream bowl clattered to the floor. Getting up, I hurried to the couch. "It's okay. No mess. He ate it all before he fell asleep."

Jenny came and helped me shift Dad to a more comfortable position on the couch. I put a pillow under his head and picked up the empty bowl.

"College didn't really work out for me." We were seated back at the table. "I was still into partying more than studying. I pretty much flunked out the first semester."

"What'd you do then?"

"I did a lot of different jobs. Whatever I could find, so I didn't have to come home. I finally was able to get work as a secretary. My last job lasted seven years." Staring at my cup of coffee, I swallowed. "I thought they really liked me there, but it was my boss who checked me into the alcohol rehab program. They fired me anyway."

We were quiet for a minute. Dad's snore came from the couch.

"Joyce told me you were divorced."

"Yep."

"And you didn't have any kids."

I stood and went for more coffee. "It wouldn't have been a good idea. Steve and I wouldn't have made a good family for kids." I sat again but didn't look at Jenny. "I had a miscarriage. After that, Steve said there was no way we should have kids. He said I cried too much. How would I be able to handle kids who were sick and had any number of other problems? We weren't together much longer after that."

Jenny took the cup out of my shaking hands. "Good. Now that's done. We can talk about other things."

"You're a goof." I managed a smile then scooped up another spoon of ice cream. "You see, I haven't been a really good friend for a Christian like you."

"Mmm, I don't know. I think you're a pretty good friend for a

Christian like me. Besides, I'm praying that you become a Christian too."

"That might take a lot of prayer, girl."

She nodded. "I'm up for it."

I laughed. "Good. Please don't stop. I've got a feeling I can use as much prayer as you can pound out."

CHAPTER 5

"*J*oyce is coming to visit today, did you remember?"

Sighing, I sat next to Dad on the couch. When would I stop asking him if he remembered everything? So far he knew who I was. Sometimes he called me Sam or Joyce, but he'd done that when we were children and when nothing was wrong with his memory.

"Dad?"

"I know it." He turned the page in the newspaper. "Is she bringing the kids?"

"Not this time, I don't think." We were quiet for a minute. "When was the last time you saw her kids?"

"I don't know."

Oh good one, Beth. I bit my lip. What could I safely talk about with my dad? "There's still meatloaf left. You guys can have sandwiches for lunch."

"We have meatloaf?"

"Yes. I made it yesterday. We had it for dinner." I managed to stop myself before asking if he remembered.

"Oh. Good. I like meatloaf sandwiches."

We were quiet again. Joyce was coming this weekend so I could have some free time, and she planned to stay overnight. Resting my head on the back of the couch, I closed my eyes.

What should I do while she was here?

The front door opened and Joyce stepped in. "You two look comfortable." She shut the door behind her.

"We are." I yawned. "I guess we didn't sleep too well last night."

"Take a nap before you go out if you want." She set her overnight bag on the floor. "I plan to stay until about noon tomorrow, so you should be able to get some rest."

"Thanks. Dad will probably lie down soon too. He has trouble sleeping." I stopped and lifted my shoulders. "I guess you know that."

"I do know." She sat on the arm of the couch next to Dad and laid her hand on his. "Hey, Dad. How are you?"

"All right. Where are the kids?"

"They're home with Ron. We're all planning to come up for Thanksgiving. Would that be fun?"

Oh, but too much fun. Just imagine Dad trying to handle the house filled with Joyce, her three kids, and her handsome husband.

"Yeah." Dad turned the page in the paper.

I stood. "I do think I'll take a nap."

"Oh hi, Mrs. Jeffers." Nodding to the lady who'd waved at me, I moved my shopping cart down the aisle and stopped to grab a can of coffee.

Even though my Dad lived in a small town, it still surprised me so many people remembered me. I'd been away fifteen years and home to visit very little.

"Beth? Hey, Beth, hold up a minute."

That was a familiar voice.

I stopped and turned as another cart came up behind me. "Dave?"

My, that crooked smile had made my heart skip when I was a teenager.

He bumped his cart into me. "I heard you were back in town."

"I was sure I'd paid off enough people so you wouldn't find out."

He shook his head. "You know better than that around here."

I glanced down, not sure what to say next.

"Do you have to hurry home?"

"No, actually. Joyce is here to give me a little break. Why?"

"I wondered if you'd like to grab some coffee over at Tommy's Diner."

"WHAT'S SO FUNNY?" Dave asked a few minutes later when we were settled across from each other in a booth.

"I was just thinking, this isn't the kind of place we hung out in when we were in high school."

Dave and I had dated off and on for a couple of years, and we'd done quite a bit of drinking.

"We're not in high school anymore."

"No. We're not." Looking down at my coffee, I took a breath then looked up again. "What are you up to these days?"

"Now, I'm a science teacher at the high school."

I shook my head. "No, you're not."

"Okay. I'm not." He stirred sugar into his coffee.

"Are you serious? A science teacher?"

"Truly. I make the kids dissect frogs and pigs and everything."

"I never would've thunk." I stirred my coffee, even though I didn't use sugar or cream. "I did think you'd be married though."

"I was." He took out his phone and turned it to show me a picture of a little boy, probably six years old. "And I have a son. Toby."

"Cute kid."

"He is. I only get to see him every other weekend. That, plus the

fact I'm no longer married. Two big reasons I don't drink anymore."
He paused a minute. "And A.A."

A.A. He'd been pretty honest with me.

My hands clenched together. "They said I should go to A.A., too.
I just got out of alcohol rehab."

CHAPTER 6

I sat on the bed next to Dad. "Where did that photo album come from?"

"Joyce found it somewhere."

The page he had open showed pictures of when we were pretty young. I had to be at least five. A top middle tooth was missing.

"This is fun, Dad."

"Yeah." He turned the page. "Look at that dog." He pointed. "Dumb stray just stopped at the house one day, and you kids insisted on keeping him. See that? A piece of his ear is missing."

"Yeah, Zipper. We loved that dog."

He turned the page and sat, quiet.

I swallowed. "Mom sure was pretty in that dress, wasn't she?"

"She was a sight."

My mother died five years ago. Her funeral was the last time I'd been home to visit. Reaching for the album, I turned the page.

Dad laughed. "There's Sammy. Trapped on top of the shed because the ladder fell over."

"I remember. You took a picture before you would help him down."

Those were the days when Sam and I were still friends, before he'd discovered more interesting companions. Before I'd made myself scarce.

We turned a few more pages.

"Joyce is almost as pretty as Mom in that dress."

"Mmm hmmm." Dad nodded. "You were pretty cute too." He pointed to a picture of me on the opposite page.

Here I was missing a tooth on the top and bottom. Two braids, one coming loose, a hole in my pants and . . . I leaned down to look closer. It looked like my hand was bleeding. "Yeah, in my own peculiar way."

I'd read somewhere that people with dementia often remembered things from the past better than the present. I'd have to ask Joyce if there were more photo albums.

A Bible lay on the table beside Dad's bed.

"Did Joyce find that Bible too? Whose is it?"

"No, I keep it there." He laid his hand on the Bible. "It's mine."

I scrunched my brows. Why hadn't I noticed it before?

SAM CALLED THAT NIGHT. He talked to Dad several times a week, but he and I usually didn't have much to say to each other.

"Is Dad awake?"

"No." We were both quiet for a minute. I cleared my throat. "How are you?"

"All right. How'd he do today?"

"Good. Joyce found an old photo album, and I think he had a nice time looking through it."

"That's good."

On Sam's end, a couple of voices called greetings, then a car door slammed.

"So ... how's Julie? And the girls?"

"They're fine. Why do you ask?"

I opened my mouth to snap back with something rude but bit my tongue. "Just to be polite, I guess."

"Sorry." He sighed. "I need to work on that too."

More quiet.

"Sam?" I took a breath then moved ahead. "Do you remember Dad ever going to church?"

"Church?" He paused. "Yeah. When I was pretty young, he would go sometimes. But Mom never really wanted to go, so I think he just quit. Why?"

"He's got a Bible on the table by his bed. I don't know. I've never seen him reading it." I pushed the salt and pepper shakers around in front of me on the counter. "Some people from a church have come by to visit him, and my friend Jenny said he used to go to services sometimes. Not too long ago, I mean."

"Yeah. I do remember Joyce mentioning something about that."

"I was thinking." Setting the pepper shaker on top of the salt, I balanced it there with my index finger. "I wonder if he'd like me to take him to church. Or, or do you think that might upset him? A lot of people around?"

"Hmmm." Sam tapped the phone. "I don't know that it would bother him. He might enjoy it. He probably gets bored sitting around in the house all the time, just the two of you."

"Thanks."

"You're welcome." Was he smiling? "That might be a good idea. You could always sit in the back and leave if you needed to."

"That would look good."

"I wouldn't think you'd care."

"You're right. I wouldn't." I set the pepper back down on the counter. "I'll ask him. See what he says."

CHAPTER 7

"I didn't tell you I was coming, so you wouldn't have a chance to say no." Jenny carried in an armload of bulging grocery bags and set them on the counter. "I have to get more out of the car." She smiled at Dad, seated on the couch with his head nodding over a newspaper. "Good morning, Mr. Drake."

I followed her out the front door. "What do I not have a chance to say no about?"

"Baking apple pies." She took out a bag with a mixing bowl and utensils and handed it to me. "I didn't know how equipped your kitchen was right now, so I tried to bring everything."

"You want me to help you make apple pies?"

"Please." She groaned. "My mother has three apple trees, and she keeps bringing me bagfuls. My kids have eaten so many apples, they start to cry when I try to hand them one for their school lunches."

We walked back into the house. "Who are we making pies for?"

She cleared her throat. "You can keep as many as you like. I'm taking one to work and a couple to church. Chris will take two or three to his office. We'll hand some out on the street corner."

"I get it, I get it." I laughed. "Maybe I could give one to our neighbor. You know, of course, that I ruin anything I try to bake."

"Excellent. We'll keep practicing. That should get rid of all the apples."

Several hours later I threw myself into a kitchen chair as Jenny cut a piece of pie for Dad. "I need a break!"

"Take a break." She filled the sink with water and started with the dirty dishes.

"Don't you ever get tired?" Standing, I found a dish towel and joined her at the sink.

"Sure, about two hours after I got up this morning. The kids were awake late last night. Did you set the timer for the last pies?"

"Yes, ma'am. That's one kitchen skill I do have."

Jenny grinned. "You didn't do too bad. Let me see your thumb. Is your Band-Aid still on?"

I made a face at her.

"So listen." She hesitated. "Can I ask you a question?"

"Okay."

"Why have you come home to visit so little since high school?"

I dried the cup I held, taking a minute before I looked up. "You like tough questions, don't you? I felt like such a loser compared to Joyce and Sam."

"Beth—"

"Don't, okay? You asked."

Jenny closed her lips, and I went on.

"Sam was promoted three times in his company in less than three years. And Joyce is an elementary school teacher, which made Mom so happy. Mom taught second grade before she had kids, and she always hoped one of us would be a teacher."

The Band-Aid was coming loose from my thumb. I turned to reach for the box. "What did I have to show to my parents? To compare with those things?"

"Let me do that." Jenny came and stopped my hands, holding the one down that needed re-bandaging. "They were your parents. They loved you. Your Dad loves you."

Lifting my other hand, I wiped a tear from my cheek. "Why?"

"Because you're his daughter."

We were quiet for a while, finishing the dishes, waiting for the timer to go off. Finally, I said, "I was thinking about taking Dad to church. Do you think he'd be okay with that? Being around a lot of people?"

Would she make a big deal about me going to church?

She didn't. "I think he'd be fine. People with dementia still need to get out in public. It's good for them."

"Sam said he's probably bored, just sitting around the house with me."

"I didn't say that."

I patted her shoulder. "That's what Sam is good for."

~

"APPLE PIE. I think I'm in love."

I smiled and perched on one of Mr. Blackstone's porch chairs. "Oh sure. That's probably what you say to all the ladies who bring you pie."

He laughed and rocked his chair. Lifting the pie to his nose, he made a loud sniff. "That's what I used to say to your mama when she brought me pies. And cupcakes. And cookies."

"I don't want to disappoint you, but I'm not a baker like my mom. The only reason we have pie is because my friend Jenny came over to make them with me."

"You can learn. You're young yet. And just keep me in mind as a tester. I'm very skilled at tasting goodies."

He made me smile. "You'd do that for me?"

"Sure. What are neighbors for?"

I studied Mr. Blackstone. He looked ninety-one, I guess. His face sagged. His body slumped in the chair. Still, he looked good. He had a bright, laughing twinkle in his eye. He made me want so much more for my Dad.

"You know, lady, you should bring your Dad over sometime."

I jumped. Could he read my mind? "Dad?"

"Yes. He and I used to play checkers not too many years ago. I miss those evenings."

"Really? I don't remember Dad playing checkers."

"He's pretty good." He rocked his chair a few times. "Not as good as me, though."

"Is that right?"

"Yes, ma'am."

I waited to see if he'd say anything else to stretch out his brag, but he didn't. "Maybe you'll have to teach me, too."

"Maybe. If you're serious about it."

"Serious, huh?" We sat quiet a minute. "Maybe I'll just bring Dad over. And watch."

"That would be a good place to start."

CHAPTER 8

"Good morning, Jesse. Hello, Beth. Is it okay if I sit here with you?"

Dave?

"Sure. Sit down." Dad smiled and patted the pew beside him.

I blinked at Dave and shook my head. "You go to church now, too?"

He grinned at me. "And I'm a science teacher."

"Did you two go to school together?" Dad looked back and forth between us.

I nodded. "Yes. We graduated together."

"Beth used to help me study for science tests."

I snorted. "How do you guys know each other, anyway?"

"From church," Dad said.

Of course.

The organ struck a long note, and Dad picked up a hymnbook. I took one too, so I wouldn't feel any more out of place than I already did.

Dad sang out in a sweet tenor voice. It came to me then that he'd sung around the house when I was a kid. I didn't remember if he'd sung hymns or what, but he'd always had a nice voice. He smiled now.

What really surprised me was that Dave also appeared familiar with the hymns. "So I'll cling to the old rugged cross." "Holy, holy, holy, Lord God Almighty." "Great is Thy faithfulness, oh God my Father." He didn't have so much a nice voice as a willing one. He sang out, strong and . . . sure of himself.

What is all of this?

"YOU OKAY?" Dave stood beside me after the service.

My shoulders lifted. "I didn't know so many people would come to talk to us before we could leave." Dad was talking with yet another couple I didn't recognize, but they'd called me by name. "Dad seems more comfortable with it than I am."

Dave chuckled. "He's always been a social guy."

I looked down at my hands. "I feel bad."

"Why?" He touched my shoulder.

"I've been keeping him at home alone." I chewed my lip. "I didn't know if he'd be okay out with people. I guess I'm still not sure how he might be. I mean, if he'll always be able to handle it. I know so little about dementia. But I should have had him out sooner. He enjoys people . . ." I closed my mouth.

Dave moved so he could face me better. "Take it easy on yourself. No one knows a lot about dementia. And you haven't been with him that long. It's not like you've wasted a lot of his opportunities. Take it one day at a time." He tapped my shoulder. "Don't expect you'll have everything figured out tomorrow."

My cheeks grew hot. "I guess I've always been like that, haven't I?"

The corner of his mouth lifted. "Best I remember. Try to relax a little." He stepped toward Dad. "Jesse, I'm going to stop by your house later, if that's okay. I'd like to talk with your daughter a few minutes."

"What?" I frowned at him. "Why don't you ask me?"

"It's politeness. Between men," Dad said.

"That's right." Dave's face held a wide smile.

"Huh." Picking up my purse, I headed for the door.

"WHERE'S YOUR DAD?" Dave stepped inside the front door.

My hands gripped together so tight, my nails dug in. "In his room, looking at a photo album. What do you want to talk to me about?"

"Sure, I'll have a seat. Yes, I would like a cup of coffee. Thanks for asking."

I groaned. "All right. I'll get you some coffee. But you've made me nervous. Please, tell me."

Dave sat at the dining room table and moved another chair out with his foot. "Forget the coffee. Sit down. I'm not trying to make you nervous." He stopped and rubbed his face. "I wanted to offer you something. As a friend."

Sitting, I picked up a napkin and twisted it between my hands. "Okay."

Dave leaned over and laid his hand on mine. "I'll try to make it quick. I told you that I've gone to A.A."

I nodded.

"And you said you might be interested . . . you mentioned alcohol rehab."

"Yeah."

"I just wanted to say that if you'd like to try out A.A., I'd be happy to go to meetings with you. For support."

My breath caught. "Why was that so hard for us?"

He squeezed my hand and sat back. "There's nothing easy about being an alcoholic."

I wrapped my arms around my stomach. "Do you go to, to meetings a lot?"

Dave stood and walked into the kitchen. "I think I'll have that coffee now. You want some?"

"No. I don't know. … Yeah. Why not?"

He laughed and came back with the coffee pot and two cups. "Good job. That's one of the first steps, making a decision."

Managing a small laugh, I folded my hands around the hot mug.

Dave sat with his coffee and took a drink. He kept his hands busy too. "I haven't gone to meetings much for the last year, but it's been thirty-one months since I've had a drink." He stirred sugar into his mug. "I still go once in a while though, and I'd be happy to go with you. If you'd like."

I gulped. "I don't want to go at all."

"I know."

My lip trembled, and I caught it between my teeth. "Please come with me," I whispered.

He reached to lift my chin. "You got it." His eyes were kind.

CHAPTER 9

"*H*ello across the street."

I chuckled. Six o'clock in the morning and Mr. Blackstone was already sitting outside. "Good morning, Mr. Blackstone." I stepped down from the porch and crossed toward him.

"How are you this fine fall morning?" His voice sounded full of energy.

"Is it fall already?"

"Oh, yes." He nodded. "I can see those trees over there just thinking about turning colors."

I laughed. "Is the grass thinking about not growing so much too? I'd love to be done mowing."

"Don't be in such a hurry, young lady. The grass will be covered with snow soon enough."

"Oh, that's true. Snow to shovel." Leaning against the rail, I smiled at him. "How are you this morning?"

"Fine. Just fine." He rocked a couple times. "I was happy to see you in church the other day."

"In church? You go to church too?"

"Sure. I've always gone to church. Why is that a surprise?"

"It's not." I toyed with the rubber band on the newspaper. "I don't know. It seems like everybody I know is going to church these days."

"Good. The Lord knows how to draw you in."

"I don't know that the Lord wants much to do with me."

He shook his head. "Don't be so sure of that. The Lord wants you, trust me."

"Hmmm." I was quiet for a minute then straightened. "I guess I'd better head back."

"Don't forget to bring Jesse over here for some checkers."

"Yes, sir. We will do that."

"Good." He rocked. "Maybe you'll learn a thing or two."

"OOOHH, AREN'T THESE CUTE?" Jenny shoved a pair of shoes with heels at least three inches high into my hands. "I think they're your size."

"Yeah. We were needing somebody else at our house with a broken ankle."

Uncle Joe sat at the house with Dad while Jenny and I were at a thrift store, shopping for winter clothes for her kids.

"This is Half Price Day," she'd told me on the phone that morning with excitement in her voice. "And I've got the day off work."

"You don't need the kids to try on clothes before you buy them?"

"Nah. I know what size they wear." Jenny pushed some shirts along a rack. "Besides, at these prices, if it doesn't fit, we'll just give it away again. Yuck! Who would buy this?" She showed me a T-shirt with a large stain that could have been blood.

I wrinkled my nose. "Who would give it away?"

We moved over to look at pants.

"I thought we were here for clothes for the kids." I poked at some extra-large sweats. "I'm pretty sure these won't fit them."

"We'll get to that." Jenny scooted blue jeans along a rail. "So tell me. When you went to college, what did you want to study? What kind of job were you interested in?"

"You mean, besides cleaning toilets in gas stations?"

Jenny scrunched her face at me.

"That's what I did for a long time." I bent to pick up a pair of dress slacks that had fallen on the floor. "Truly? I wanted to be a librarian."

"Did you?" Jenny pushed through the pants, checking sizes.

"Yeah. I've always loved libraries. And books. All kinds of books. Don't you remember? Even when I was a kid, I enjoyed going to the library to look up information for school projects."

"I do remember that." Jenny held a pair of black jeans against her. "I used to make you look up stuff for my projects too."

"You didn't have to make me. But, if I remember right, you used to buy me an apple fritter for doing it. Extra incentive."

Jenny grinned. "You were too easy."

I lifted a pair of sweats covered with pink elephants. "You know, I don't really know Chris well yet, but maybe he'd like these for work. What do you think?"

She took the pants from me and hung them back on the rack. "Tell me about wanting to be a librarian."

"Right. When I didn't have much money, the library was the perfect free place for me to go and do so many exciting things. I even volunteered. Can you believe they let me read stories to little kids?"

"Imagine that." She threw a pair of orange sweats in our cart.

"Seriously. The kids liked me. I made up different voices for each of the characters." Standing still, I smiled, remembering.

"Come on, stay with me." Jenny had already moved far down the aisle.

"Huh? Oh." I hurried to join her.

She looked thoughtful. "You really enjoyed helping out at the library, huh?"

"I did."

"You could still do that, you know. You're not too old to become a librarian."

"I don't know, maybe." I picked up a hoodie from the cart and tugged on the string at the neck. "Right now I can't think about anything except taking care of Dad."

"I understand that." Jenny worked through some long sleeve T-shirts. "I just mean, neither your Dad's future or yours has to stay the way things are right now. There are other options, that's all. You could look into taking online classes from home." She shrugged. "It's something to think about."

"Maybe." Could I try college classes again? I wrinkled my nose. "How do you like this shirt?" I held up a green T-shirt that had a picture of a large black dog, gripping an entire pie in its mouth.

"Is that for Chris to wear to work too?"

"No." My face stayed serious. "I was thinking, for you. Maybe church."

"You are being such a help."

"I'm glad." Nodding, I placed the shirt with the dog in the cart.

Jenny returned it to the rack. "So, I saw Dave Marrow sitting with you guys in church the other day."

"Mmm hmmm. He and Dad seem to know each other pretty well."

"Yeah. And if I remember right, you and Dave used to hang out a lot too."

I bumped the cart into her. "Oops. So sorry. That was a long time ago. Before Dave got religion. And before he stopped drinking." I didn't meet her eyes. "And neither of us has a great record with relationships."

Jenny scooted the cart toward winter coats. "Things can change. Second chances. Give yourself some time. Who knows what might happen?"

"You've got a lot more faith in me than I've got in myself."

Jenny's face was serious too. "I'm sure I do. I also have faith in Jesus, for what He's going to do in your life."

"I have to admit . . ."

"Yes?"

I looked down then up again. "That comforts me."

CHAPTER 10

*D*ave directed his gaze straight at me. "So, how have you managed to keep from drinking since you got out of the hospital?"

"Wow. Is that the kind of question they're going to ask me at the meeting tonight?"

We sat in the diner with coffee before our first A.A. meeting together.

"No, they're not." Dave took a sip from his cup. "They'll be much more gentle with you. This is me, your friend Dave, also a drunk, talking."

Picking up my spoon, I turned it over and over in my hands. "Sam came to get me just a day or so after I got out of the hospital. Dad doesn't drink, so there's nothing in the house."

"You go shopping." He added more sugar to his coffee.

"I do." I closed my eyes. The day before, I'd stood in front of the wine at the grocery store, my hands trembling, my jaw tight, aching to pick up a bottle.

"So far I guess . . ." I took a breath. "I guess I've been too scared about Dad, wanting to keep an eye on him, I haven't had the nerve to drink."

"That won't last, you know."

"Thanks for the encouragement."

"Beth."

I laid down my spoon and looked up at him. "I know it won't. I'm not sure what will help, what can stop me from drinking."

"Good." He reached and covered my hands with one of his. "That means you really know where you are. And you're ready to listen tonight."

My teeth ground together. I didn't want to cry.

"I'll tell you one thing you've got."

"Yeah?" My eyes squeezed shut, and my nose ached from holding back tears.

Dave scooted his chair around the corner of the table and bumped it into mine. "Me. I'll stay right here. And I know what it's like."

"I BROUGHT YOU A COUPLE OF CASSEROLES." Joyce stood at the refrigerator, her back to me.

"I can cook, Joyce." Setting my purse on the counter, I searched for my car keys.

"I know. I just wanted—to help."

Her voice sounded unusual. Depressed? For the first time in a long time, I wished we were closer, so I could give her a hug and ask if she was okay.

"Thanks. I'm sure Dad will appreciate something besides my cooking." I laughed. "He doesn't seem to be getting tired of my meatloaf though."

"He does love meatloaf." Joyce walked over and sat at the table. "I brought some meatloaf too, so you'll have a little change of taste. A different recipe, I mean."

We were quiet for a minute.

She picked up a butter knife lying on the table. "I can't stay overnight this time. I'm sorry." She didn't look up at me.

"That's okay." I hesitated. "Is something wrong?"

She drew circles on the table with the knife. "No . . . I don't know. I just had a big fight with Ron last night. We still weren't speaking when I left this morning."

"I'm sorry." My fingers tapped on the table. "I guess I can't offer much advice when it comes to marriage."

"I don't know if I'm doing much better." She twisted her mouth.

"No, come on. You guys have been married for fifteen years. You've got a good marriage."

"I don't know sometimes." A tear dripped off her lashes.

"Hey, no." I came around the table to stand beside her. "You've got to stay together. Don't ruin my hopes that marriage really can work." I rubbed her shoulder.

Her laugh was shaky. "Don't worry. I'm just grumpy today. Get out of here. Get some fresh air."

"*A*h, Jesse, this is such a treat." Mr. Blackstone scrunched over the checkerboard at his kitchen table.

"You won't be saying that after I beat you." Dad leaned back in his chair and took a drink of coffee.

"Mmm hmmm. Better keep your eye on the board, sir."

"Keep an eye on the board yourself." Dad made a move. "Crown me."

I smirked. Dad still knew how to play checkers. I'd brought along a book to read, but watching them entertained me more.

"Don't get cocky, Jesse."

"I'm not cocky. I'm taking one of your men. Crown me again."

"Will you look at that, young lady?" Mr. Blackstone looked around at me. "Is that the way for your dad to treat an old friend?"

"I don't know if I would turn away from the board if I were you, Mr. Blackstone. I thought you were going to teach me how to play checkers."

"Smarty. And don't call me Mr. Blackstone. It makes me feel old. I'm Darryl."

"Well, Darryl." My father's voice held a smile. "I won't call you old, but I'm not sure you should be the one to teach my daughter to play checkers. You seem to be out of men."

The grin on my face hurt, but I tried to wipe it away when Mr. Blackstone looked my way.

"That's fine, missy. You can be proud of your papa. But the night's not over yet."

At the end of the evening, Dad had won four games and Mr. Blackstone, two.

"Ah, this was a good start." Mr. Blackstone rubbed his hands together. "Miss Beth, you should find one of your mama's cookie recipes and bring some next time."

"I think I'll buy some at the bakery. I want you guys to have a nice time." I hugged my middle and almost wanted to bounce. Dad had been so healthy this evening. *If I knew how to pray, God, I'd beg You to let him stay this way.*

"SURPRISE." I threw up my arms as Jenny opened the door. "Happy to see—hey. Are you okay?"

"What are you doing here?" Jenny stood still in her front door. Her face was taut, not at all glad to see me.

"Are you crying?" I laid my hand on her arm.

She turned her back to me and walked into the house. "Come on in."

I followed her to the kitchen. If Jenny was crying, who would be strong for me? "Do you want to talk?"

She rinsed dishes and put them in the dishwasher. "I didn't know you were coming over this morning." Her voice cracked.

"No, you didn't." I brought more dishes to her from the table. "Uncle Joe surprised us with a visit this morning, and I knew you had the day off today. I thought maybe I could help you, I don't know, clean the house or something. Maybe we could get pizza for lunch." I turned the water off. "Look at me. What's wrong?"

She walked to the counter. "Do you want some coffee?"

"Jenny, stop."

She turned to face me. Tears streamed down her cheeks.

"Come on." Taking hold of her arm, I led her to the couch in the living room. "Sit down." I wrapped my arms around her and held her for a few minutes as her shoulders shook.

Jenny finally pushed away from me and reached for a tissue from a box on the coffee table. "I'm sorry."

"What in the world for? Aren't we friends?"

She gave a shaky laugh. "Of course we are. Give me a minute." She blew her nose and groaned. "Oh, Beth."

"Yeah?"

She looked up. "Robby was caught stealing at school."

"Oh."

"Yeah. Oh." She took a deep breath. "I'm a mess."

"I guess so. You want to tell me about it?"

She leaned back on the couch. "It's not new. His stealing I mean." She picked up a coaster from the table and flipped it between her fingers. "He's stolen from me and Chris before. But yesterday he was caught taking money from his teacher's purse."

"Ouch, I'm sorry."

She laughed and wiped her nose. "I guess you aren't too impressed with me as a Christian mom, if I can't even keep my kid from stealing."

"Oh, honey." I put my hand on her shoulder. "Don't even start with that."

"Okay, sorry. I mean—oh—" She took another deep breath and grabbed more tissues.

"What's going to happen at school? Did he give all the money back?"

"Yeah. The principal said Robby dropped the money like it'd burned his hand when he realized he'd been caught."

"No doubt. So?"

"They said we should handle it at home for now. After all . . ." She sniffed. "He's just eight."

"That's true."

"Oh, oh." She slapped her hands on her legs. "I don't know what to do."

"What does Chris say?"

"He's so mad." She gulped. "He wants to ground Robby for a year. No TV, no playing at friends' houses."

Scrunching my face, I thought for a minute. "I want to tell you something, but I don't know if it will help much."

"What?"

"I used to steal money when I was little. From everybody at home, from the babysitter, from my grandparents."

"Did you?" She wiped her eyes. "For how long?"

"Until I was ten. Then I guess I got tired of it."

She stared at me. "So you think we should just ignore it?"

"Whoa, no." I held up my hands. "I'm no parent. I'm sure not telling you what to do." I grinned at her. "But he is just eight."

CHAPTER 12

"So, how was it tonight?" Dave rested his hand on my arm as we took a walk in the park after an A.A. meeting.

"I guess it was okay." My foot scuffed the ground. "Funny that they consider alcoholism a disease. Seems like that kind of takes the blame off of you."

Dave chuckled. "Do you feel better if you can blame yourself?"

We found a bench and sat down. "I guess so, in a way." I kicked at the grass. "That's always how I've felt anyway."

"I know what you mean. I feel that way a lot of the time too."

Keeping my head down, I shivered against the evening breeze. "They talk about God all the time."

"They do." He offered me a piece of gum. "They're not pushy though, and they don't suggest any particular belief."

"Yeah." Without unwrapping the gum, I folded it into a small lump. "Is that why you started going to church?"

He stood and reached for my hand. "Come on, let's go look at the fountain."

We didn't hurry. The traffic moved and honked at a distance. A bird sang nearby.

"Toby's mom started me going to church, right after he was

born." Dave still held my hand. "After the divorce, I just kept going. To a different church, though. It gave me something to hope for."

The gurgling sound of the fountain was close now.

"What do you think about going to church?" Dave asked. "I know your Dad likes it."

"I don't know." I laughed. "Jenny's praying that I'll become a Christian."

"Ah." He stopped me at the fountain, and a light spray reached my face as the wind picked up. "You're in then."

"She's that good, huh?"

"She's the first person I call when I have something to pray about." He dug in his pocket and handed me a nickel. "Toss it in. Toby and I always throw coins in the fountain."

"Should I make a wish? That might not go well with God."

"You make a wish. I'll say a prayer."

I didn't ask him what he prayed for. "What else do you and Toby like to do?"

He dropped in a coin. "We go to movies, or ball games." He paused. "Would you like to meet him sometime?"

Looking up, I could just see his face in the dim light at the pool. He didn't smile.

I licked my lips. "If you wouldn't mind . . . I would like to meet him."

"I think you're safe." He did smile then. "I'll introduce you guys."

THE PHONE RANG, and I sighed when I saw Caller ID. Sam.

"How are you, Beth?"

"I'm good. How are you doing?" Why did I always feel like I was under suspicion when my brother called?

"Fine." He sneezed. "Sorry. Have you and Dad been going to church?"

Fine, huh? "Yeah, he really likes it. I forgot what a nice singing voice he has."

"You're right. I remember that."

The clock on the wall made a loud tick-tock.

"He's been playing a lot of checkers with Mr. Blackstone. Did you know he was good at checkers?"

Sam laughed. "Yeah. He used to beat me all the time."

"I don't know if I should play with him. I wouldn't give him much competition."

"Oh, go ahead. He'll enjoy it." He cleared his throat. "So you're feeling okay?"

"I'm fine." I wasn't ready to tell him I'd been attending A.A. meetings with Dave. "You really need to not worry so much."

"Right." He did not sound convinced. "Thanks for what you're doing."

"You don't have to thank me, Sam. He's my father too."

I waited for him to say something like, "Well, you haven't shown much interest in him for a long time." But he didn't.

He sighed. "I know. But thanks still. I'm going to try to come there to visit sometime. It may not be until Christmas though."

It was mid-October now. Good. That gave me more than two months to get myself ready to face him again. "That'll be fun."

He snorted. "Try to curb that excitement a little."

"*Y*our dad and I are buddies," Dave told me as he joined us again the second week we went to church. After that, I expected him to sit with us every week. Occasionally Dad and Dave snickered together over something the minister said, and they shared a hymnbook so I could have one to myself.

One Sunday morning Mr. Blackstone stood next to our pew. "May I sit here, Miss Beth?"

"Sure." I scooted over so he could sit beside me. "We're going to start a little community here in the back row."

"I wanted to make sure you didn't fall asleep." For the first time, I noticed he used a cane. He leaned it between us. "I'll smack you with this if I see you nodding off."

"She does all right." Dad smiled across me at our neighbor. "I keep an eye on her."

"Hey, Darryl." Dave came up then on Dad's other side. "Thanks for joining our party."

"Mr. Blackstone wanted to sit by me so I could keep him awake," I told Dave.

"Watch it, missy." Mr. Blackstone nudged me with his cane. "Be quiet now. It's time to start."

I held my hymnbook so Mr. Blackstone could share it, but he didn't need it. With his eyes closed, he sang and smiled. "Standing on the promises of God."

All the men sitting with me looked happy. What was it in all this that touched them?

When the pastor started to speak, Mr. Blackstone elbowed me. "Listen to this now. It's God's Word."

I read what was written on the screen at the front of the auditorium.

Micah 7:7: "But as for me, I watch in hope for the LORD, I wait for God my Savior; my God will hear me."

I thought about believing in a God who cared enough to listen. Mr. Blackstone, Dave, even my father seemed to have that belief. Was it possible I could too?

JENNY STOPPED by after dinner the next night to have coffee. "I figured if you're going to keep going to church, you needed one of these." She handed me a Bible.

Chewing my tongue, I looked down at the book. "Thanks." I turned it in my hands then set it on the table at the end of the couch.

Jenny sat beside me. "I noticed you looked serious yesterday at church. What were you thinking?"

"I'm not sure." I pressed my fingers against my face. "I guess I was just wondering about the hope the pastor was talking about. If I could have hope like that."

"What is it you would hope for?" Jenny rested her back on the arm of the couch to face me better.

"Good question." My hand reached for a magazine Dad left on the floor. "I'm not sure." I tore at the front cover of the magazine. "I guess they're wishes as much as hopes."

"What are your wishes?"

I didn't look at Jenny. "I wish I could get rid of the garbage I've made of my life." The cover was off the magazine now, and I tore it into strips. "Maybe I wish I could hope for something better . . . to do something meaningful, to make more out of my future." My mouth grew dry. "I'm scared I can never be different." I bit my lip. "Different from the mess I am."

Jenny reached and took the magazine out of my hands. "Beth. Those are just the things Jesus wants to do for you. He wants to forgive and heal you from the past, and He wants to walk beside you and help you with the future."

Tears trickled down my face. "I don't know if I can believe that."

Jenny separated my twisting fingers. "He'll even help you with that. I'll pray that Jesus will help you to have faith. You can pray that too, even if you're not sure you believe it yet. He'll still hear you."

CHAPTER 14

*W*as that a knock at the front door?

Raising my head from the dining room table, I rubbed at the sleep in my eyes. Where was Dad?

This time I was sure I heard a knock.

How long had I been asleep at the table? I stood and stretched the kink in my back.

Dad lay on the couch, the newspaper on top of his face.

"Dad?"

The paper lifted a few inches. "Did you hear somebody knocking?"

My shoulders slumped with relief. He was okay. "Yeah. I'll get it."

The paper lowered again.

When I opened the front door, I blinked a couple of times before I could see.

"You're Beth, right?" A little boy stood on the porch.

"I told you he was sharp." Dave stood beside him.

My eyes squeezed closed. "I don't think I'm awake yet."

Dave laughed. "It's not a bad dream. We're really here."

I stepped back. "Come in."

Inside, Dave laid his hand on my shoulder and gave a little shake. "Beth, wake up."

"Yeah." I yawned. "Why are you here?"

Dave looked toward Dad on the couch. "Jesse, you okay?"

Dad lifted the newspaper again. "Sure. Was that you, banging on the door?"

Dave walked over and took hold of Dad's hand. "Nope. It was Toby."

"Oh." Dad cleared his throat, then with Dave's help, sat up.

"Dad, Uncle Joe's coming over in about half an hour."

"Why?"

"I don't know. He called last night and said he was coming. You want some coffee?"

"Yeah." He folded the paper on his lap. "Toby, why'd you bring your Dad?"

Toby laughed. "I can't drive, silly."

In the kitchen, I poured water into the coffeepot then stood still.

Dave had followed me. "Need some help?"

I turned from the sink. "I don't remember where the coffee is."

He took the carafe out of my hands. "Try the freezer."

"Why would it be in there?"

Dave's mouth tipped up on one side. "Are you always this cute first thing in the morning?"

"Usually only when I've slept all night at the dining room table." The coffee was in the freezer. "What does Toby want to drink?"

Dave took the bag from me. "Do you have any milk? Juice?"

Finding a chair, I sat down. "I don't think so."

Dave finished making the coffee and looked into the refrigerator. "Whew, this milk needs to go." He emptied the milk at the sink then tossed the plastic jug. "I'm pretty sure Toby wants water this morning."

"Why are you here?"

Dave pulled a chair next to mine. "You told me last night your uncle Joe was coming over today. I thought you might like to go out with Toby and me."

"Where are you going?"

"To get a dog."

A few minutes later, we were all sitting at the table. Dave passed a plate of toast to my dad, then to me and Toby.

"Toby, does your mom know you're getting a dog?" I picked up a piece of toast.

"Yep."

"It's a puppy, actually." Dave handed me the butter.

"Where is it going to live?"

"He, or she, is going to follow Toby wherever he goes. Except school."

"And your mom said that was okay?"

"She told me not to bring it home until it's housebroken."

I choked on a bite of toast. "Now, that, I believe."

"So you're coming with us?" Dave pounded on my back.

"Stop, stop." Coughing, I pushed his hand away. "Sure. Who's got the puppies?"

"Another teacher from work. She begged the rest of us yesterday at lunch to take one. She had tears in her eyes."

"Do you want a puppy, Mr. Drake?" Toby asked.

"I don't think so," I answered before Dad could open his mouth.

"I'm glad you guys got here." Jill, the math teacher with the puppies, led us to her back porch.

"Why?" Dave rested his hand on Toby's shoulder.

"There's only one puppy left."

We stood looking down at a box with a ball of black and brown fur inside.

"I think this one is yours, Toby." Dave nudged him closer to the box.

Toby knelt but just stared at the puppy.

"It's a girl, honey. And we didn't name her." Jill knelt beside him. "She's very sweet. You can touch her."

He gingerly laid his hand on the ball of fur. "Does she bite?"

"No." Jill smiled. "She does like to chew on pretty much everything, though."

As he stroked the puppy, she raised her head. I could almost see some eyes inside the fur.

"She's nice." Toby looked up at Dave.

"Pick her up." Dave knelt on the little boy's other side.

With some hesitation, Toby finally lifted the pup and cradled her against his chest. "Can I really have her, Daddy?"

"Yes." Dave ruffled the pup's fur. "Do you have a name for her?"

Toby rubbed his cheek against the pup. "Snuggle."

"Okay." Dave hugged him. "That'll be really good when she's as big as you are."

CHAPTER 15

"Scoot over." As church began the next Sunday morning, Jenny stood by our pew, waiting to sit between me and Darryl.

"Look at you, joining the back row straggly gang." I nudged Dad to move over. "Doesn't your family miss you?"

"Nah." Jenny set her purse down by her feet. She grinned and patted my knee.

"What a friend we have in Jesus." My father's and Darryl's voices rang out.

Moments later, Dave joined them with gusto. "Blessed assurance."

"Your dad's the only one with a nice voice," Jenny whispered to me.

"Mmm hmmm."

The Scripture on the screen at the front of the room read:

Jeremiah 29:11-13: "'For I know the plans I have for you' declares the LORD, 'plans to prosper you and not to harm you, plans to give you hope and a future. Then you will call on me and come and pray to me, and I will listen to you. You will seek me and find me when you seek me with all your heart.'"

With all my heart. I chewed my fingernail. For a future with hope? Would it be worth it? Could I do it?

Bill and Judy Branson, a couple with three college kids, stopped by after the service. "Beth." Judy turned to me. "We're having a little get-together at our house this afternoon. One last barbecue before it gets too cold. Would you and your dad like to come?"

A barbecue with a group of people I barely knew? Not me. "Sure." Whoa, how did that slip out?

Dad would love it.

"THERE'S a lot of cars here, Dad."

"Looks like fun." Dad smiled.

"Right." I parked my car down the street a couple of houses from the Bransons', hoping we would be able to get out quick and easy.

"Hey, guys, welcome." Judy grabbed my hand and pulled me into the kitchen where a bunch of women were setting out food and laughing. The last I saw of Dad, he and Bill were joining a group of men around the grill. How many men does it take to grill a few burgers?

"Beth, I'm glad you could come." One of the ladies gave me a hug. I had no idea who she was. "Could you help me finish this salad?"

That's how the next couple of hours ran. Groups scattered on the patio and through the backyard divided as his and hers. Women chattered at me non-stop.

"You look just like your sister."

"It's really good to have you home again. I'm sure your brother and sister feel so much better that you're here with your dad."

"Would you like to join our women's Bible study?"

Fortunately, they never gave me much of a chance to speak. I wouldn't have known what to say. They were a friendly lot.

Every time I saw Dad, he was smiling and laughing. The men crowded him the same way the ladies did me.

"Ho, Jesse, that's funny." One of the guys slapped Dad on the back. "You've always got the best jokes."

In a moment of unusual silence, I caught Dad's voice. "Rachel? Where's Rachel?"

My cheeks stung as the blood drained from my face. "Dad." I ran to catch him as he wandered away from the group. "Dad, where are you going?"

"Beth?" He looked at me but pulled away. "Where's your mother? I'm sure she said she'd be here by now."

He walked farther out toward the street. "Rachel? Oh, honey—" He turned back toward me. "Do you think she was in an accident?"

My breath caught, but I tried to keep my voice steady. "What are you talking about? Mom . . ."

Dad's hands shook. "She said she'd pick us up, remember?"

What should I say? "No. Dad . . ."

Bill and Judy hurried to join us. "Jesse." Bill put his hand on Dad's shoulder. "Why don't you sit down for a minute?"

"No." Dad shoved Bill away. "I want to go home. Rachel said she'd be here." Tears ran down his cheeks.

Judy rested her hand on my arm. "Can we give you a ride home?"

I wanted to shove her too. "No, thank you." My face ached, but I managed to keep back my own tears. "Daddy, please let me drive you home."

Dad let me take hold of his arm. His shoulders slumped, and his whole body shook. "Please. Take me home."

Opening the refrigerator, I stood for a minute, looking inside. The bottle of wine had only been there for a couple of days, since the last time Uncle Joe came over. It was a small bottle, almost half gone. Dad wasn't interested in it, and I'd wondered if I should throw it away. But maybe Uncle Joe would want it next time he came. I could handle it . . .

I laid my hand on the bottle and waited. Nothing traumatic happened, no flashes of lightning, no earthquakes. Picking up the bottle, I walked to the table.

Why am I crying?

Dad fell asleep soon after we got home. He'd been calm. It's like he forgot what happened at the barbecue.

Dad had been so upset tonight. My hands squeezed the bottle.

How will you feel at the next A.A. meeting, when you have to say how many days it's been since you had a drink?

Dad had shaken with tears. "Where is your mother? Do you think she was in an accident?"

I pulled the bottle closer. "I don't care. Are you A.A. guys going to help me comfort my dad?"

As I twisted the cork out of the bottle, the smell of the wine made more tears roll down my cheeks.

"How about You, God?" My voice rose. "Is this the plan You have for my future?"

The phone rang.

My hand jerked, knocking the bottle over, and the wine ran out onto the table.

I held the phone up to my ear.

"Hello? Beth? Are you there?"

"Sam."

"What's wrong? You sound funny."

"Do I?" I barked a laugh and splashed my hand in the spilled wine.

"Have you been drinking?"

"Now, why would you say that?"

"This isn't funny. I'm going to call Jenny and ask her to come over."

"Please don't call Jenny." I cleared my throat. "I'm okay."

"You have been drinking."

"I have not been drinking."

I could almost hear him grinding his teeth. "Then why do you sound so guilty?"

"Maybe . . ." I took a breath. "Maybe it's because you're always so good at making me feel like I'm doing something wrong." Picking up the wine bottle, I threw it against the wall. It made a satisfying crash.

"What was that?" Now Sam was yelling.

"I threw something and broke it. Are you happy? You can always do that to me."

"I can do that to you." He took a deep breath and growled. "Beth, this is not the time for you to feel sorry for yourself."

"Oh, of course. That's what I'm doing now."

I stopped. Dad stood in the doorway to his room, staring at me.

"I have to go. Don't call anybody. Just this once, Sam, don't be in charge." Dropping the phone, I laid my head on my arms and sobbed.

"Honey, what's wrong?" Dad stood beside me, patting my shoulder. "Come on now. Don't cry like that."

～

"I WISH Dad hadn't called you." I pressed my face in my hands as Dave sat down on the floor next to me.

The place in the house I'd chosen to hide was the laundry room in the basement. So there I sat, my back pressed against the dryer, surrounded by the mess spilled when I banged into the room and kicked the trash can over.

"He said mine was the only name on the list he recognized." Dave pulled my hands away from my face. "Besides, according to A.A., you should have called me."

"Is that how you think of me?" My voice squeaked. "Your A.A. assignment?"

"Oh, honey." He wrapped his arms around me and pulled me against his chest.

We sat for I don't know how long, Dave rubbing my back as I cried and shook and gulped.

When I'd quieted a little, Dave said, "I helped your Dad clean up the broken wine bottle upstairs, but I have to say, you don't smell like wine."

"I bumped the bottle and knocked it over before I could take a drink."

"Bummer."

I peeked up at him. That crooked smile could still make my heart skip. And what a sight I must look.

"Dad thought Mom was going to pick us up from the barbecue tonight." I gasped and hiccuped. "I couldn't think . . ."

"Shh." He pressed my head back down against his shoulder. "Just wait until you can get your breath. We're not in a hurry."

When I finally stopped shaking, Dave asked, "Are you asleep?"

I tried to laugh, but it came out a snort. Pushing myself away from him, I leaned against the dryer again.

"Maybe I shouldn't be alone with Dad anymore."

I reached to pick up trash, but Dave covered my hands with his. "It'll wait."

My hands clenched against my chest. "What if I'd gotten drunk tonight?"

Dave pushed hair out of my face. "You didn't. For today, that's one thing you don't need to worry about."

"Only because I knocked the bottle over." I sniffed. "And Sam called."

"Every time I don't get drunk, I thank God, no matter what stops me."

Looking down, I took a long breath.

Dave stood up and pulled on my hands. "Come on. Let's clean up this trash. We both need sleep." He bent to pick up used dryer sheets and balls of fuzz. "Tomorrow night, well, tonight I guess, I'm taking Toby to a costume party. If I can help you find someone to stay with your dad, will you come with us?"

I stood the trash can upright. "Do I have to wear a costume?"

"No." He grinned. "Unless you want to, of course."

"I think not." I brushed my hands together. "I'll call Uncle Joe and see if he can come over."

I clutched the phone in my hand. "Uncle Joe, I'm an alcoholic. Don't bring wine over here again."

"Oh, uh." Uncle Joe coughed on the other end of the line. "Sure, honey. Sorry about that." He cleared his throat. "I didn't know."

I guess I'd put that old man in his place. My eyes squeezed and I sucked in a breath. "It's okay. I, I actually called to ask a favor. Is it possible you could come stay with Dad tonight, this evening, for a few hours?"

"Oh, sure. Sure, I can do that." He chuckled. "You got a date for Halloween?"

"Not exactly. Kind of." Maybe I should dress up like a witch for the party. Maybe I didn't need to dress up.

"Thanks, Uncle Joe. For everything."

WHEN DAVE and Toby showed up, I stood in the door and looked at Toby. What was he supposed to be? He wore old clothes: a torn black and brown shirt, brown pants with patches on them, old brown shoes that were too big and floppy. Black flaps of construction paper were taped to his ears.

"I'm a dog," Toby said, impatience in his voice.

"Turn around." Dave laid his hand on his son's shoulder. "Let her see you from behind."

A longer strip of construction paper hung down from Toby's lower back.

"You are a dog." I smiled at Toby and tugged on one of his paper ears. "And you're brown and black, just like Snuggle. But sorry, buddy, you're not as cute as she is."

"Yeah, I know." Toby shrugged. "I wanted to buy her a whole bag of dog treats for Halloween, but Dad said it might make her stomach sick. Since she's just a puppy."

"Spoil sport." I frowned at Dave.

"I am." Dave nodded. "Toby's mom and I are going to hold on to his candy, too, and dole it out as we see fit."

"Uh huh. You'll probably eat it all. Toby, I'm sorry your dad's not being much fun. Why don't you go see Mr. Drake? I think he has a surprise for you."

"Sure." Toby moved past me, toward Dad on the couch. "Hi, Mr. Drake. Trick or treat."

Dave raised an eyebrow. "Let me in? It's getting cold out here."

"Sorry." I stepped back.

He came in and shut the door, then rested his hand on my arm and guided me to the kitchen. "So, what's your Dad got for Toby?"

"A roll of quarters."

"Nice."

"We didn't get any candy. I didn't know if Dad needed to see a bunch of kids dressed in weird costumes. When Uncle Joe gets here, we're going to turn off lights in the front of the house, and he and Dad are going to sit in Dad's bedroom and look at old motorcycle magazines."

"Good thought." Dave leaned against the counter. "I brought you a present."

He handed me a box, wrapped in aluminum foil.

"You are so fancy."

"Yep. Open it."

I was slow, peeling back the foil, to hold the suspense. I pulled out a large coffee mug with the following written on it: Matthew 6:34: "Therefore do not worry about tomorrow, for tomorrow will worry about itself. Each day has enough trouble of its own."

After reading the verse twice, I looked up at Dave.

He wasn't smiling. "I don't know the Bible as well as Jenny, but this verse is special to me. Maybe this is where we got the saying 'one day at a time.'" He ran his hand through his hair. "Sometimes, for me, it's ten minutes at a time."

As I looked back down at the mug, my eyes pricked. Dave did understand me.

He cleared his throat. "Look at me."

I raised my head.

He still looked serious. "I've been thinking about what you said last night, when you asked if I think of you as an A.A. Assignment."

My breath caught. "Dave, please, I'm sorry—"

He held up a hand. "No, listen." He looked around the room then brought his eyes back to mine. "I care very much for you. You're important to me."

A sense of cold washed over me. I waited for him to say, "But . . ."

He didn't. He took hold of my hand with a strong grip. "You and I both have a lot of junk from the past we need to work through." He paused. "And I have a son." His gaze stayed steady with mine. "You are important to me, honey, but we need to take it slow." His eyes held a question, a plea for understanding.

"I think." My voice cracked. I swallowed. "That sounds like a good idea to me."

The front door banged open. "Ho, anybody home?"

Uncle Joe.

Dave grinned and squeezed my hand. "Ready to party?"

"So, we have a new project?" Standing in the front door, I watched as Jenny set a second pumpkin on the front porch.

"It's November." Jenny headed back to her car. "I figured we could get started on pumpkin pies." She set two more down and closed her trunk. "And pumpkin bread. And pumpkin squares."

I bent down and picked up two of the orange monsters. "Let me guess. One of the patients in your office had a lot of extras in her garden."

Jenny grunted a laugh. "More than one patient. You should see how many I have at home."

"Did you grow all those pumpkins in your garden, Jenny?" Dad followed us into the kitchen.

"I don't have a garden." Jenny set her load on the counter then turned the oven on. "With Chris's mom and mine, plus all the people who bring me things at the office, I'll never need to learn to raise my own fresh produce."

Dad reached into the refrigerator and pulled out lunch meat and cheese. "Rachel tried to raise a garden the first few years after we bought this house."

"Really? I don't remember that." I took out a couple of pans and placed them on the counter. "First we bake the pumpkins, right?"

"Who said you couldn't cook?" Jenny drew a large knife from the block.

Dad found a loaf of bread and carried everything to the dining room table. "She gave up trying long before you were ever born." He came back into the kitchen for a plate. "Anybody else want a sandwich?"

I shook my head.

"Not right now, thanks." Jenny laid one of the pumpkins on a pan then raised the knife. "Stand back, everybody."

"Mom always had really pretty flowers though." From the top of the refrigerator, I lifted down Mom's recipe book.

"She did love her flowers." Dad sat at the table. "Is there any more coffee, Joyce?"

Catching Jenny's eye, I shook my head. "There's enough for one more cup. I need to make a new pot."

"I'M WHOOPED." Jenny pulled out a chair and sat down at the table. "Is your dad taking a nap?"

"Yeah." I yawned and sat across from her. "We were up most of last night."

"I'm sorry. I should have called before I came over."

"Oh sure, now you say that. After ten pies and two trucks-full of dirty dishes."

She grinned. "You loved it and you know it." She flipped through the recipe book. "Next Saturday, I'll teach you to make pumpkin rolls." She tapped her finger on the page. "How much cream cheese will we need?"

Fastening my eyes on the sugar bowl, I drew in a long breath. "I guess I didn't call you at all this week."

"No, and I didn't call you either." Jenny turned a few more pages. "I'm sorry. The kids had a busy week at school."

"You don't have to be sorry. I didn't mean that." I dug the spoon into the sugar. "I probably didn't call for a reason."

"Why's that?" She kept her eyes on the book.

"Dad was looking for Mom the other night."

She raised her head. "Beth, I'm sorry."

"So I tried to drink Uncle Joe's wine."

She came over and put her arms around me. "Oh, sweetie."

I laid my head against her chest. "I'm such a loser."

"Shh." She squeezed me. "You're not. You're precious."

"What would I do without you?" I drew back and wiped my nose with my hand.

"You'll never have to again." She handed me a napkin. "I'm sorry. I'm sorry I stayed away from you for so many years."

I sniffed and picked up my coffee. "You are so funny. I'm the one who was gone."

She went back and sat down across from me, wiping her cheeks with her hands. "I know. Loser."

Spluttering, I set down my cup. "You're a goofhead."

"Thanks. Oops, there goes the timer. Pies nine and ten are done."

A warm, cinnamon aroma filled the house.

~

"KNOCK, KNOCK. ANYBODY HOME?" Opening Mr. Blackstone's door, I stepped inside. He told me he'd leave the door unlocked during the day when it got too cold for him to sit out on the porch. "Hello?"

"In the kitchen."

"I'm a burglar, storming right in to steal everything you have." I moved toward his voice, looking around the living room. No trash on the floor, no empty cups, no half-eaten bowls of food. Who was the housekeeper here?

"Oh great. Where did I put my gun?" He turned from the sink

and smiled as big as Christmas. "Bless you, girl, you look more like your mother every day."

"Uh huh, you're just saying that because I brought you a pie." I set the pan on the table. "It's safe to eat. Jenny was here today to give me more baking lessons."

"I need to marry that girl." He dried his hands and took a seat at the table. "Have a cup of coffee. Make yourself at home."

The coffeepot was already in my hand, so I waved it at him. "You need yours filled?"

"Not yet. Thanks for the offer." He lifted the foil off the pie and sniffed. "Mmm, mmm. Grab us both a plate. Why are you being so bashful?"

"Not for me, thanks." Pulling out a plate, I searched for a knife. "I had two pieces already. Do you have whipped cream?"

"Of course. Oh, it's still warm. Hurry up, will you?"

As he picked up his fork and dug in, I sat across from him. "Can I tell you a secret?"

"You couldn't honor me more." He took a bite and smacked his lips.

"I'm an alcoholic."

"Are you? My wife was too. That's tough." He took another bite.

Swallowing, I looked down at my cup of coffee. "Was she able to stop drinking?"

"Thirty-five years clean. It was never easy."

"Thanks for the encouragement."

"Welcome," he mumbled through a mouthful.

"Will you still sit by me at church tomorrow?"

"You keep bringing me pies, and I'll take you to the church and marry you. Jenny's already spoken for."

An unfamiliar warmth snuck into my chest. None of these Christians pushed me away.

～

149

"HELLO, BETH." Sam's voice on the phone that night.

"I'll get Dad."

"Hold it a second. Talk to me. How are you?"

"I'm fine. Thanks for the concern."

He sighed. "You don't always have to be so rude."

I braced myself against the counter. "Would you recognize me if I wasn't?"

Was that a laugh?

I cleared my throat. "Thanks for not calling Jenny, or Joyce, the other night."

"Don't thank me. I called the house again that night and talked to Dad. He said Dave was there with you."

"Oh. I guess that makes sense."

The phone stayed quiet, and I shifted on my feet. "Do you want to talk to Dad now?"

"Sure. Beth?"

"Yeah?"

"Take care of yourself, would you?"

Was that kindness in his voice?

CHAPTER 19

*B*y the day before Thanksgiving, after all my baking lessons, I decided I could make pumpkin pies by myself for Joyce and her brood.

And Dave.

And Uncle Joe.

That evening, Dave brought the turkey dinner I'd ordered from Tommy's Diner.

I watched as he loaded everything into the refrigerator. "I can't believe I let myself get talked in to this."

Dave turned to me. "You want me not to come?"

My eyes popped open wide. "Are you kidding? I need you here to keep me sane."

He rested his hand on my shoulder. "You'll be fine. We'll have fun."

I snorted. "Fun. Right. Have you ever been around all of Joyce's crew?"

"I have." Dave took hold of my elbow and walked us into the living room. "Don't you like Joyce's husband and kids?"

"I like them fine. In ones and twos. But all together?" I shuddered. "And with Uncle Joe too."

"Sounds like a blast." He shrugged into his coat.

"You better show up." I wrinkled my nose at him then hesitated. "So what is Toby doing tomorrow?"

Dave took hold of the door knob. "Going to his stepdad's folks." He lifted a shoulder. "That's part of divorce, not getting to be together on holidays." He grinned. "I get Toby for Christmas."

"Nice." Touching his arm, I stepped back. "Joyce said they'd be here by eleven. Feel free to come earlier."

HOW LONG HAD it been since I'd seen Joyce's family? More than three years? I shook my head. Where had I been all that time?

I stood back as Joyce and the kids gathered around Dad.

Johnny, twelve, shook Dad's hand. "Hey, Grandpa. Happy Thanksgiving."

Lora, who I believed was ten, gave him a tight hug. "I've missed you, Grandpa."

Scott, maybe nine, was more shy. He stood back a little, but he had a nice smile. "Grandpa, are we going to watch the game?"

I remembered them being small, loud, always on the move. Today, they were not the same gang.

Ron joined me and hugged my shoulders. "They've grown up a little, haven't they?"

Dad brought out one of Mom's photo albums to show them. Joyce and all three kids leaned their heads close to his and were pointing and laughing. Nobody shoved or yelled, "My turn, get back."

I pursed my lips. "Are you sure you didn't pick up somebody else's kids?"

Ron laughed. "We had a long talk about not being too crazy around Grandpa. A couple of long talks."

"And they listened. Unbelievable. I congratulate you guys on your parenting skills."

"We just got here, remember. We'll see how the day goes." He moved in front of me so we were focused on each other. "How are you, Sis?"

I increased the distance between us. "You mean, how is my alcoholic rehab?"

"Beth, that's not fair."

Sighing, I looked down. "Sorry. I figured that's how you all discuss me."

He raised an eyebrow. "That's really what you expect from Joyce?"

"I guess not. Not really. She's been pretty decent to me. I guess she's always been good to me. I'm the one who's not made myself part of the family."

"You're here now. And we're all glad." He touched my hand.

Turning, I hurried away so he wouldn't see the tears that sprang to my eyes. "I'd better make sure Dave doesn't need any help with dinner."

The doorbell rang.

"That'll be Uncle Joe," I called over my shoulder to Ron. "Could you get it?"

I ran into the kitchen and grabbed Dave's arm. "Please come out here with me."

"Whoa." Dave closed the oven door and took hold of my hands. "Slow down. What's wrong?"

"Nothing. I . . . ." I gasped and squeezed his hands. "They're all being really nice."

He lifted one corner of his mouth. "I see. Should we sneak out the back door?"

I pulled my hands away and covered my face. "Dave, I don't know how to be with my family."

He wrapped an arm around my shoulders and squeezed. "It's okay. You're okay. I'll stay with you now."

~

"DAD'S ASLEEP." Joyce walked into the kitchen later that evening, carrying a load of plates from the table.

I dropped silverware into the dishwasher. "He and Lora were the only ones who didn't zone out after we finished eating."

Joyce smiled. "She loved looking at the photo albums with Dad. I never knew Mom kept so many pictures."

Plates went in next. "It's kind of fun looking through her old stuff in the attic. I've even found some pictures from when she and Uncle Joe were little kids."

"Ooohh, I'd like to look at those." Joyce picked up the coffee pot. "Will you drink more if I make a fresh pot?"

"I will."

Joyce scooped coffee grounds into the basket. "I have to say, I am so impressed with your pumpkin pie baking." She rubbed her stomach. "I think I may almost be ready for another piece."

"Thank Jenny." I closed the dishwasher and turned it on. "She's a good teacher."

Joyce leaned against the counter, waiting for the coffee to perk. "That was awfully nice of Uncle Joe to take everybody to a movie."

"He misses his grandchildren. They're so far away. It'll do his heart good to have the kids go to a holiday movie with him."

As Joyce found a couple clean mugs, she laughed. "What Ron didn't know is that this is an animated show. He'll hate it."

"Nice."

We sat across the table from each other, sipping coffee and not speaking for a minute. I scratched at a glob of gravy stuck on the table. "So things are better with you and Ron?"

"Huh?" Joyce took a swallow and set the cup down. "Better? What do you mean?"

"Well, you'd had a rough morning the last time you came here."

"Oh." She shrugged. "I forgot about that. We're fine. Just marriage, you know. Sometimes, you have bad days." She took another sip. "We're fine."

"That's good."

After a pause, Joyce reached over and laid her hand on mine. "Honey, I'm sorry."

"What are you talking about?"

She puckered her face. "I'm sorry. I wish I'd made an effort to, to spend some time with you after your divorce."

Sucking in a breath, I looked away. We'd never talked about this. "What could you have done?"

"I don't know. Talked to you. Listened to you. Taken you shopping." She sighed. "Just not left you alone."

My hands clenched together, and I still couldn't look at her. "There's so much I didn't do. So many times I didn't step in for you all. Especially for Mom and Dad, but for you and Sam too." I pressed my hands over my cheeks and didn't try to stop the tears. "And there's no way to fix that now. Not, not for Mom."

Joyce pushed back her chair and hurried around the table. She hugged me close, pressing her face against mine. Her lashes were wet too.

CHAPTER 20

"What time is it? Dad?" My chin rested on my arms at the dining room table. Through bleary eyes, I saw Dad's Bible open in front of me. I blinked. "I guess I fell asleep." I stretched and yawned. "Dad?"

The clock on the wall read 11:12. "Whoa, that late? It's almost noon, and we didn't have breakfast yet."

At 2:00 that morning I'd heard Dad moving around in the kitchen and come in to see if he needed anything. Where had all those hours gone? I shoved back my chair and stood up. "Dad."

I walked into the living room, but he wasn't on the couch. If he'd gone back to bed, I didn't want to wake him. I opened his bedroom door.

He wasn't in his room.

A cold blade stabbed my back. "Dad?"

I rushed through the house, starting with the laundry room in the basement, moving up to the attic. Yanking open the door, I turned on the light. "Daddy, are you looking for photo albums?" I stumbled up the narrow stairs, holding tight to the shaky rail. "Dad."

He wasn't up there. He wasn't in the house. A heavy weight fell in my stomach.

"Joyce, he didn't take his coat. It's twenty-five degrees out there." My teeth chattered as I leaned against the kitchen counter.

"Okay." Joyce took a long breath. "Let's stay calm. Who else have you called?"

"The police. They said they'd keep an eye out for him." I gulped and squeezed my hand around the phone. "Uncle Joe. Mr. Blackstone. Jenny and Dave." I tapped a pen on the counter. "Jenny and Dave said they'll both figure out how they can get away from work to go look for him. I called the minister, and he said he'd call a few people from church he knows Dad is close to." I took a breath. "Everybody says I should stay home. I want to go out looking for him too."

"No. Stay there. He'll probably come home, and somebody's got to be there."

How could she sound so calm? "Maybe Uncle Joe could come over."

"Beth, please slow down. I know this is driving you crazy, but we have to be sensible. Everybody can't be out looking for him. What if he goes to Uncle Joe's house, and he's not home?"

"I don't know what I should have done differently. At least I hid the keys to his car." I circled the table. "So he's walking. Where could he go? He doesn't have a coat."

"Sit down." Joyce used the same tone she did when directing her kids. "Tell me again what happened."

Pulling out a chair, I spun it around and straddled it backwards. "I told you. I woke up around two and heard him in the kitchen. I asked if he needed anything, and he said he couldn't sleep. Nothing new."

"Go on."

"I made some tea. I thought coffee'd just keep him awake." I drew circles with my finger on the chair back. "He had his Bible on the table, and we sat down, and he read it out loud. He's got such a nice reading voice, you know? Do you remember when he used to read to us when we were little?"

"I do remember that."

"He was reading in the Bible about a woman named Rachel. He said it reminded him of Mom." I shuddered, and my eyes ached. "Then he started crying. He talked about Mom for a long time. About when they were just kids. How Uncle Joe didn't like him back then and tried to keep him away from Mom." I wiped my nose.

"I know he and Uncle Joe never seemed to get along really well." Joyce's voice carried a smile.

I wrapped my arms around the back of the chair. "He talked about when they were first married, when we were all little." I gulped. "He seemed to go on for hours. I remember my eyes getting really sleepy, resting my head on my arms. I must have fallen asleep. I don't know when that was. When he left. How long he's been gone." I choked on a cough.

"It's okay, honey. You didn't do anything wrong. It's going to be okay."

My throat grew so tight, I struggled to push out words. I stood up. "I've got to go."

"Stay at home." Her stern mother's voice again. "Call me when you know something. I'll come if you need me."

My eyes squeezed tight. "Are you going to call Sam?"

"I have to call Sam." She softened her voice. "It's okay. It's going to be okay."

Laying the phone down, I pressed my hands against my face. "Oh, I don't think so. I don't know how it can ever be okay."

CHAPTER 21

"*B*eth, hello. It's Darryl Blackstone across the street." His voice sounded slow and calm through the phone. "Why don't you come on over here? Your dad and I are playing some checkers."

I grabbed Dad's coat and ran across the street.

Dad sat across the kitchen table from Mr. Blackstone, head bent over the checker board. When I banged into the room, he raised his head.

"Hi, honey. Oh, you brought my coat. Thanks." His face scrunched with a question. "How come you don't have your coat on? It's cold out there."

"My . . ." My hands and legs shook, but I managed to sink into one of the chairs at the table. "Dad? Where've you been?"

Dad looked back at the board. "Darryl and I are playing checkers."

It was a struggle to slow my breathing. I stared at Dad then turned to Mr. Blackstone. "How long has he been here?"

"Jesse came in a little bit ago. Wanted to play checkers." He nodded and watched Dad as he made a move. "We're both a little cold, so I made some fresh coffee. I think it's ready. You want to get us all some?"

"Coffee." The time on the TV read 7:03 p.m. "Dad? Where were you all day?"

"Where?" Dad rubbed his hand over his face. "I don't know." He looked at Darryl. "You gonna move?"

"Just you be patient." Darryl rested his chin in his hand. "I'm considering."

I boosted myself to my feet and made it to the coffee pot, then stood with my hands on the counter. What am I supposed to do now?

"Pretty sure there are three clean cups in the dish drainer." Mr. Blackstone's voice came from behind me.

I breathed deep and poured the coffee. After delivering the drinks, I walked into the next room to call Joyce.

"I talked to Sam earlier," Joyce said. "He's arranging things so he can fly home tomorrow morning. I'll come in a day or two." She hesitated. "Are you there?"

"Yeah." My voice cracked. I cleared my throat and tried again. "I'm here." Standing at the window, I watched as a car passed by on the street. "He doesn't know where he was all day."

Joyce sighed. "I talked to Uncle Joe. He said he'd come over and sleep at the house tonight. So you're not alone."

I forced breath in and out.

"Beth? Are you okay?"

Mr. Jeffers from up the street walked by on the sidewalk, pulled along by his yellow lab.

"Beth."

"I'm okay." I pushed through quicksand to make my way into the kitchen for my coffee cup. "I'll talk to you later."

Uncle Joe was coming. Sam. Me taking care of Dad had not been the right idea.

S AM WALKED into the kitchen the next morning. "Looks like Dad and Uncle Joe are playing some serious checkers."

I kept my back to him as I emptied the dishwasher. "They've been at it all morning."

Sam's suitcase landed on the floor behind me. "My flight was early. I need more coffee."

My hands shook as I lifted plates to the cabinet. "I turned the coffee off, but there's still plenty. Want me to heat some for you?"

"I've got it." He turned on the microwave. "Beth?"

I turned around.

Sam leaned against the counter by the microwave. "Look." He rubbed his hand over his face. "We've got to talk."

Putting my back to the sink, I lifted my chin. "I'm glad you're here. Obviously, this hasn't worked."

He moved away from the counter. "Wait a minute."

I raised my hands. "No. I'm not having a pity party this time. I mean it. I wasn't what Dad needed. We've got to figure out something better for him."

The microwave beeped, and Sam turned to get his coffee.

My teeth ground. Do not cry. "I'm sorry."

He turned toward me again, his shoulders slumped. "I'm going to call Dad's doctor, his insurance company. Check about home health and adult daycare." His jaw worked. "See what kind of options we have."

My stomach clenched. "Sounds like a good idea." I moved away from the sink. "I'm going to go out for a while. Maybe I'll call Jenny."

"Okay." He took a step toward me. "Beth?"

I walked out of the kitchen. "Let's leave it for now."

"*P*lease, no more coffee. I'll throw up again." Resting my elbows on Dave's kitchen table, I buried my face in my hands.

"You need more coffee." Dave pulled my hands away from my face and gave me a cracker. "Eat this."

I took a bite and managed to chew it. My head pounded.

Dave wrapped my other hand around a cup of coffee. "Try to drink more of this." He sat down next to me. "Eat more crackers, and I'll give you some aspirin for your head."

I picked up another cracker from the plate in front of me and took a bite. "I drove for hours before I ended up at the bar."

"Sam said you were going to call Jenny."

"I didn't." I rubbed my eyes. "I'm glad my head hurts. I wish it hurt more."

Dave handed me another cracker. "Take a swallow of coffee."

"Stupid. Stupid. I am an idiot."

He pushed the cup toward my mouth. "Drink."

"I sat at the bar, ordered a beer, and started crying." My whole body shook. "I talked on and on to some guy I thought looked familiar and kept ordering more."

"How many?"

"I don't know." My chin dropped to my chest. "How'd you end up rescuing me?"

Dave pushed back his chair and went to the sink for a glass of water. "John called me, the guy you were talking to at the bar." He set the glass in front of me. "Drink this."

I downed the water. "Who is he?"

"You've met him a couple times at the A.A. meetings." Dave smoothed hair from my face with a gentle hand. "That's something good that came from tonight. You kept him from taking a drink."

I squeezed my eyes then jerked my head up. "I have to call Sam."

"I called him. It's okay. He knows you're with me."

A lump rose in my throat. "Now he'll probably kick me out of the house."

Dave clasped my hands in both of his. "Try not to start crying again. You'll just make your head hurt more."

He was right. My eyes teared up and I choked. "I messed up."

"I know, honey. Shh. Tomorrow's a new day."

CHAPTER 23

Somebody shook my shoulder. "You should probably wake up."

I forced my eyes open. "Jenny?" My mouth tasted sour.

"Right on the first try." Jenny pushed against my back. "Come on. Sit up. I have coffee." She helped me to a sitting position on Dave's couch.

"Coffee, huh?" Rubbing my hands over my face, I pushed tangled hair out of my eyes. "I bet I look pretty sharp."

Jenny handed me the coffee. "Don't worry. I already know you're beautiful."

The coffee burned my mouth, but I swallowed it down. "The room is spinning."

Jenny stood in front of me, waiting. After I drained the cup, she held out her hand. "I'll get you another."

Pushing to my feet, I followed her into the kitchen. "I can get coffee for myself. What are you doing here?"

"I wanted to have breakfast with you." Jenny took a couple of plates out of the cabinet then traded one for a bowl. "Oooh, look at all that sweet cereal."

"Not for me. I'll stick with coffee." I slumped in a chair at the table.

"Have a piece of dry toast anyway." Jenny moved about the kitchen. "Dave keeps this place pretty clean for a guy." She dropped bread into the toaster.

I wrapped my hands around the hot mug and let the steam soothe my face. "So, why aren't you at work?"

"Dave asked if I could spend some time with you." She set a plate with toast in front of me then found milk for her cereal. "Chris took me to get your car, and I drove it here and called off work for today."

I couldn't look at her. "You must be pretty disgusted with me."

"Oh, Beth." Jenny sighed and sat across from me. "Drink your coffee. Eat some toast."

"And shut up, right?"

She took a bite of cereal. "I think you're feeling a little sorry for yourself."

"You think?" I barked a laugh then pressed my hand against my forehead. "I told Sam I wasn't having a pity party, but I guess, in truth . . ." Tears poured down my cheeks.

Jenny scrunched her face. "Easy. Come on. Tell me about it."

"Sorry. I've always been a weepy drunk." Wiping my eyes, I picked up the toast. "I failed Dad. Again."

"He has dementia. That's such a hard thing to deal with." She set her spoon down. "You didn't fail any more than anyone might have. This is a horrible struggle for many families."

"But this isn't any other family." My throat refused to swallow the toast, and my face ached as I cried harder. "I always . . . fail." I coughed and wrapped my arms around my middle. "School. Work. My marriage. My family. Why did I think things would be any different this time?"

Jenny came around the table and pulled my hands into hers, rubbing warmth into them. "Let's go to my house. You can take a shower, dress in something of mine, pull yourself together before you go home. You've got to keep moving forward."

Blinking up at her, I licked my lips. "I don't think I can."

~

"HEY, girlie. You trying to sneak in?"

As I opened the back door, Uncle Joe stood right in front of me, holding a bag of trash.

I stepped back and held the door for him to come out. "Maybe. How are my chances?"

"Not too bad." He grinned as he passed by me. "Your Daddy's asleep on the couch, and Sam's been on the phone in the bedroom for hours, seems like."

"Okay then. Our secret." Managing a smile for him, I went through to peek in the living room. Dad lay snoring on the couch. No sign of Sam. I slipped into my room and closed the door without a sound.

Easing onto the bed, I glanced at the ceiling. "What now? Should I pack?"

Where could I go? My eyes teared.

Clamping my jaw, I forced myself to sit up. "Don't you dare start crying." I clenched my fists. "This time, it's not about Beth."

Someone knocked on the door.

"Yeah?"

"Beth? Can I come in?"

Sam.

Uncle Joe never could keep a secret.

"Come in." I sat on the bed, my head lowered. Should I act mean or sorry?

After the door opened and closed again, I looked up.

Sam leaned against the wall, his eyes red and tired.

"Sorry, I don't have a chair in here."

"If I sit, I'll probably fall asleep." Sam walked to the window and looked out. "Beth, I'm sorry."

"What?" His back was to me. Had I heard him right?

He turned to face me. He sighed and shook his head. "You heard me. I am really sorry."

"I don't . . ." I cleared my throat. "I don't know what you're talking about."

He walked between the window and door a couple of times without looking at me. "This whole dementia thing. We know so little about it. What to do with it. Maybe we made a mistake."

I gulped. "Look. Last night, I . . ."

Sam shook his head again. "No, that's not what I mean." He laid his hand on the doorknob. Did he want to bolt out of here as much as I did?

He gripped his hands together. "I'm not talking about last night.

That's not how you've been the last few months." He sucked in a breath and paced. "Maybe I asked too much of you. I know as little about alcohol rehab as I do about dementia."

He stopped in front of me. "Dave told me you've been doing A.A. That's good. You're trying to help yourself." He twisted his mouth then turned away. "Not like I've done anything to help you."

My mouth fell open. "Sam?" Standing, I walked around to face him, then stopped. What should I say?

He worked his shoulders then grasped my arm. "Let's sit down."

We moved to the bed and sat down. He rubbed his face, and behind his hands I heard, "I know it's been good for Dad, having you here."

I blinked.

He turned to face me. "I wanted Dad to be able to stay at home, but maybe that's not the best thing for him."

I jumped to my feet and moved away. "No. No, no." Tears poured from my eyes. "Not a nursing home. I want to help him. I really want to. I know, last night . . ."

Sam sprang up and wrapped his arms around me. "No, honey, shh."

Sam hadn't hugged me since we were kids. And friends.

Clutching his shirt, I gagged with sobs.

He led me back to the bed and sat us down. I leaned against him and gasped for breath. He stayed quiet, squeezing my shoulders until I'd calmed.

When I pushed back, Sam held onto my hands. "I'm not saying we're putting Dad in a nursing home right now." His voice cracked, and he cleared his throat. "We have to think. There's assisted living. Adult daycare. Home health aides. We have options."

I looked down. "Do you want me to move out?"

"No. Please, no." He raked his fingers through his hair. "I mean, unless you want to. Maybe you want something different for your life."

My throat worked. "Right now, all I want to do is help Dad." More tears. "I don't know if I can."

Sam stood up and paced again. "If you can stay, that's great. Whatever we decide, it'll help Dad if someone's here. But you can't do it by yourself."

He stopped at the window. "Uncle Joe said he'd stay here for now, so there are two people around, so everybody can get some sleep. The doctor mentioned putting alarms on the doors, so if Dad tries to go out, it would wake you guys up." He walked back to me. "We know so little about what's possible. We're just starting with this. We're not giving up."

He moved to turn away then stopped. "It's only a couple weeks till Christmas. Joyce and I will come back then, and we'll all figure out what to do next."

He rested his hand on my shoulder and managed a tired smile. "Maybe you can think of other things that you can do, besides hanging around the house all the time. I remember you used to talk about working in a library. Maybe you could start by volunteering." He shrugged. "You can have options too."

After Sam left, I sat on my bed and stared at the door. Why was he being so nice? My chest tightened, and my breathing became forced. "I've got to get out of here."

*C*hristmas-lit houses and unfamiliar streets flashed by my car window. When I braked to a stop at a red light, something fell from the dash.

I leaned to pick it up. The Bible Jenny had given me.

"Talk to God, Beth. I promise He's listening." How many times had Jenny said those words to me?

I stepped on the gas. "Sure, God. May as well talk to You. Otherwise I'm just yelling at myself."

Passing a yard with a figure of Big Bird loaded with Christmas lights, I pressed the horn with a long, rude honk. "Merry Christmas."

My car squealed around a corner. "Maybe I can get a speeding ticket. How about that, God? Or I could bang into something, maybe cause enough damage that I could spend the night in jail."

I slapped at the tears on my face. "No crying. I don't deserve self-pity. I am a loser."

I ran a red light then slammed on the brakes.

The car behind me blared its horn and passed me.

Watching the traffic around me, I started up again. "I guess I better be careful after all." Loser or not, I wasn't trying to hurt someone else. "And, I certainly don't need to end up in the hospital. How nice would Sam be to me then?"

I pulled into an almost filled parking lot of a well-lit school. They must be having a program of some sort. Maybe a winter concert or play. Nice for them.

"I'll stop so we can talk, God. I guess You deserve that much courtesy."

Letting my seatbelt loose, I sat back.

"I'll go first, okay?"

I couldn't stop crying.

"Just ignore my tears." I swallowed. "I've heard people say You don't make junk. No offense, God, but if You created me, You made a big mistake. I'm junk. A huge mess of junk."

Another car stopped in the lot, and two people hurried to the school entrance. I reached to press the horn at them, then drew back my hand.

"What am I supposed to do now? Sam's being nice to me. He's not mad at me about last night. Says I can stay."

I punched the button that lowered the window. Cold wind struck my face.

"What sense does that make?" My voice raised. "I can't be trusted. What if I run out on Dad when he's alone? What if he leaves the house to look for me? Or if I get drunk at the house, and he gets confused?"

Raising the window, I banged on the switch to lock and unlock the door.

"He has Uncle Joe, at least for a while. It'd probably be best if I just leave."

My hands clenched in my lap. "Where would I go? I've got nowhere to live. No job."

Pounding my fists against my chest, I choked and shouted. "Beth, you are the most selfish person I've ever met. If you had any guts, you'd kill yourself. Better for everybody."

A memory flashed through my mind. Dad's face the night he found me crying.

"No." My voice was gravel. "You're not going to do that to him." My chest dragged at breaths.

After a minute, I picked up Jenny's Bible. "I guess it's only fair to give You a turn to speak, God."

On the inside cover Jenny had left a note for me.

"What a terrible excuse for a friend I am. I've never even opened this Bible. I didn't know there was a note."

"Beth, I wanted to share some Bible verses with you that I pray will help you. Please, believe me that God knows about all the things in your life that have hurt you. He hurts with you. He loves you more than I can say, and He wants to lift you out of the muck you feel you're in right now. I love you. Jenny"

Psalm 56:8: "You keep track of all my sorrows. You have collected all my tears in your bottle. You have recorded each one in your book."

2 Corinthians 1:3-4: "Praise be to the God and Father of our Lord Jesus Christ, the Father of compassion and the God of all comfort, who comforts us in all our troubles, so that we can comfort those in any trouble with the comfort we ourselves receive from God."

I read the words through several times.

People began emptying out of the school, heading to cars, driving away. How long have I been here?

I pulled back onto the street and drove, not paying attention to what direction I headed. When I passed Big Bird the fifth time, I figured I needed to find somewhere to stop.

ONCE I PULLED in front of Dave's house, I didn't get out. I sent him a text.

"Second night in a row, asking for help. I'm right outside."

Folding my arms against the steering wheel, I rested my head on them. My heart ached with exhaustion.

The passenger door opened, and Dave climbed inside.

I didn't look up.

Dave touched my shoulder. "Beth?"

"I haven't been drinking." I pushed myself up straight in the seat but didn't look at him.

Dave wrapped his hand around mine, and neither of us spoke for a long while.

A car drove by on the street. Another. A van full of laughing singing teens emptied at the house next door.

"Dave?" My voice cracked. I licked my lips. "I am so messed up. I need, help."

Dave turned in the seat to face me. In the light coming from his front porch, his face held calm.

Swallowing, I tried to work moisture into my mouth. "You said A.A. has really helped you. I, I guess I haven't taken it too seriously up to this point."

I inhaled a deep breath, exhaled. "Last night . . . I want to help Dad. I just keep failing."

I was crying again. I gritted my teeth. "I can't do it on my own. I can't promise I won't drink again."

Dave nudged closer and wrapped an arm around my shoulders. "You're at exactly the right place where A.A. can help you."

Squeezing my eyes closed, I sucked in a few breaths. Dave pressed my head against his shoulder.

I gulped. "Were there still times when you drank, even after you started A.A., even after you tried not to?"

"Yeah." His voice scraped rough. "That's why we have to take it one day at a time. The Bible says that too. It says God's mercies are new every morning."

I rubbed my face against his coat. "I've read the A.A. literature. About the twelve steps. And, and it talks a lot about God too."

When I sat up, I clutched his hand in both of mine. "I know A.A.

doesn't push one certain religion." I shook my head from side to side. "But for you, the religion that Jenny talks about, the whole Christian thing, it works?"

Dave reached over and held my chin so he could look straight in my eyes. "Jesus makes sense to me. The people who love Him, they've loved me. He's given me a hope for what I can be for Toby. And more."

BEFORE I WENT TO BED, I looked again at the Bible verses Jenny had left me in her note.

"You keep track of all my sorrows. You have collected all my tears in your bottle. You have recorded each one in your book."

I hugged the Bible against me. "All my tears, God? So many. So many."

CHAPTER 26

*D*ad and I arrived early, but it didn't take long for the church to fill. I spread out our coats, Bibles, my purse. Anything to try and save seats for everyone in the backseat crowd.

"Dad. This is going to be a special service."

Dad thumbed through the hymnbook. "I know. It's Christmas Eve."

"Not just that." I took a breath. "Tonight I'm, the church, the Bible . . ."

God, I need to take a step forward. These people of Yours, they have taken me in, even with all my garbage. And weakness. I'm choosing to believe that You will too. That Jesus will stand by me.

"Dad." I stopped.

Dad looked up.

"I've talked to Jenny and Dave. And the minister."

A light turned on in my father's face. "Are you getting baptized?"

I gulped. "Yes. Tonight."

"It's about time, young lady." Mr. Blackstone took the seat next to Dad. "Did you want me to baptize you?" He thumped his cane against the floor.

175

I smiled. "No. Thank you. Dave and Jenny are going to do it."

"That's great. I want to see that." Dad patted my knee. "There's Joe and . . ." His eyes widened. "Joyce is here. And Sam. And all their families." He stood up. "I didn't know they were coming."

"It's Christmas, Dad. Remember? They've all come for Christmas."

"Christmas?" Dad shook his head. "Is it really?"

Before I had time to react, Uncle Joe, my brother, sister, and all that went with them, crowded around and in front of us, reaching to hug Dad. And me.

In the aisle, Dave and Jenny beckoned to me. "Come on." "It's time."

I wormed my way out and took hold of each of their hands. Looking back, I saw Dad's face, beaming at me. Mr. Blackstone grinned, and Joyce threw me a thumbs-up. Sam raised an eyebrow then winked.

My throat tightened.

Jenny leaned close and spoke in my ear. "It's your party. Look at the crowd."

We exited the auditorium and found the door to enter the baptistery.

My party.

"A new beginning, Beth." Dave squeezed my hand.

A new beginning. A new start every day.

I closed my eyes. Questions pressed against my mind.

What was going to happen with Dad?

With Dave and me?

Maybe a job at the library?

A.A.?

A life with Jesus. What would that mean?

For once, the pressure of tears behind my eyes spoke of hope.

Dear God, I do believe that You are with me.

I took in a long breath. *One step at a time.* I opened my eyes.

Dave gave me his crooked smile.

Jenny took my hand again. "Ready?"

My lips trembled, but I smiled. "Ready."

THE END

MY FAMILY

Psalm 68:6: "God sets the lonely in families."

CHAPTER 1

"*D*ear Lord, Daddy, is this all a mistake?"

Sitting on my bed, I looked through the door to the living room. All I could see of Kimmie was her back to me as she lay on the couch. Her shoulders still shook, but she kept her crying soft. I'd tried to hold her earlier, but she'd pulled away, saying in a rough voice, "I'm okay. I'm okay."

Dear God, of course she isn't okay. Neither am I.

Just over a week earlier, my brother John called and woke me up in the middle of the night. "Martie, I'm sorry. RuthAnne's dead. Anthony too."

Our sister and her husband had been killed in a car wreck on an icy road.

The next couple days went by in a haze as we were surrounded by family and friends and survived the funeral. The day after, I received another shock.

My mother stopped me as I came downstairs. "Martha, Ruth-Anne told me she and Anthony asked you to be Kim's guardian if anything happened to them. Have you made any plans for that?"

"Plans?" The room spun around me, and I sank onto the couch. "Mom, I . . . I forgot all about it."

"Honey." Mom sat down next to me. "We need to make some plans."

Kimmie was eight years old now. My sister, Miss Organize Everything, called to ask if I would be her daughter's guardian before the baby was a month old. Certainly, I said yes. It honored me that they would ask. But, of course, I never thought it would happen.

I doubted RuthAnne or Anthony thought it would happen either. When I finished college and moved to a city quite a distance away, they hadn't changed the part in their will that made me Kimmie's guardian.

KIMMIE WAS AT ANTHONY'S FOLKS' house the night of the accident, and she stayed on there until after the funeral.

After talking with my mother, I took a deep breath and called Anthony's mother. "Mrs. Warrick, could I come over to talk with you and Mr. Warrick?"

"All right." She didn't sound friendly, but then, she never had. "Come over in the morning at about ten."

Kimmie and Mr. Warrick were not at home when I arrived at their house. Mrs. Warrick's face held no smile, no welcome.

"I'll take your coat, Martha." She nodded toward the couch.

I sat down, but I was ready to spring up in a second. Anthony's mother sat on a chair facing me, back erect, hands clenched in her lap. Nothing about this situation offered promise for our discussion to go well.

"Mrs. Warrick, did you know Anthony and RuthAnne asked me to be Kimmie's guardian?"

"Yes." Her face was white. "But I never knew if you accepted. Of course, we would understand if you'd feel more comfortable with Kimmie staying with someone she knows better. Her grandparents, maybe."

Which grandparents might she be thinking of?

"Yes, I accepted." I forced myself not to clench my own hands. "My father has a copy of their will, and my name is on it as guardian."

"I see." She didn't say anything else.

Be kind. Remember, she's just lost her son.

"I was wondering if we could set up a time to tell Kimmie. Maybe you and Mr. Warrick and my parents. And me. How do you think would be the best way of handling it?"

"Jason and I can do it by ourselves."

"Okay, that sounds good." It took work to keep my voice calm. "But I would at least like to be in the house when you tell her. So I can talk to her afterwards."

"I will talk to Jason and let you know what we decide."

Dear God, help me not to lose my temper.

"Okay. Thank you." Mrs. Warrick didn't accompany me as I hurried to get out the door.

I didn't hear from them for two days. My father helped me file the will with the court and do all the necessary paperwork. When we came out of the courthouse, he took hold of my hand. "Martie, this is going to be okay. Don't expect it to be easy in a hurry."

Pressing my face against my father's shoulder, I shivered and not only from the cold January wind. "Oh, Dad, I'm afraid it will never be easy."

CHAPTER 2

$\mathcal{O}$n the third day, Mrs. Warrick called. "We're planning to talk to Kimmie tonight. You can come over to talk to her after, if you like."

I arrived ten minutes before the set time. Mr. Warrick answered the door. His face was kind but tired. "Why don't you have a seat here in the living room for now?"

"Where's Kimmie?"

"She's with her grandmother. In the kitchen. I'll come get you when . . . when we're ready."

My eyes squeezed tight. *Lord, give us all strength to make it through this. Give us wisdom.*

In the next room I heard soft voices. Then I heard Kimmie crying.

"Sweetie, please." Mrs. Warrick's words grew louder. "If you're not happy there, you can always come home to us."

Home.

My teeth ground together.

When I walked into the kitchen a few minutes later, Kimmie kept her head turned away from me. I wanted to hug her, but I was sure that wouldn't be accepted.

Sitting in the chair across from her, I took a deep breath. "Kimmie. Your mom and dad wanted me to take care of you. I want to. I'm going to do everything I can to . . ."

To what? Make her happy?

I shook my head and tried again. "I'm going to do my very best for you, honey."

She wouldn't look at me. It was time for me to leave.

God, please stay with us. There's nothing I can say that will help anyone in this house right now.

MY PARENTS and I decided the best thing for Kimmie would be for us to leave as soon as possible. I made plane reservations for two days later.

The day after I'd been at the Warricks' house, my mother decided to take Kimmie to her house to pack. "Come with us, Martha."

"I don't know. I think that will just make it harder for Kimmie."

"And for you?"

I bit my lip. "Mama, she doesn't want me around."

Mom put her arms around me. "I know, honey. But you two are going to have to be together in a couple days anyway." She handed me my coat. "Besides, you are her guardian now. You need to be part of everything in her life."

Our plan was to pack two suitcases. My parents, John, and the Warricks, if they chose, would go through everything in the house and ship more to Kimmie in the next couple of months.

I held back as my mother worked with my niece. Mom was kind but practical. She made sure Kimmie had the clothes and school supplies she'd be needing.

"What else do you want to take, sweetheart?"

Kimmie scrunched her face. "I don't want to go."

Mom knelt in front of her granddaughter. "You're going, honey. You need to take some of the things you like best." She hugged her close. "Please find some of your favorite toys, something to make you feel at home there."

Kimmie jerked away and ran to her bed. She pulled a bedraggled stuffed teddy bear out from under the blanket and hugged it to her chest as a tear rolled down her cheek. "This is all I need. I'm not staying long."

CHAPTER 3

$\mathcal{O}$n the plane, I decided I needed to force Kimmie to talk to me. She was sitting next to the window, her head turned to look out.

"Kimmie, we need to talk."

"My parents called me Kimmie. Nobody else."

I knew that wasn't true. Over the past week, I'd heard family and everybody call her Kimmie.

I guess that's not going to be my privilege right now.

"Okay. Kim. Will you look at me?"

"I don't have to look at you to talk."

Okay. Deep breath. Remember, Martie, she's just lost both of her parents.

A flight attendant stopped by. "What would you ladies like to drink?"

"I'll have coffee. Kim, what about you?"

"Soda I guess, like Sprite." Her head stayed turned away.

Taking another deep breath, I tried again. "All right. Kimmie— Kim, you understand that your parents asked me to take care of you?"

"That's what Grandma Warrick said. I don't know why. I hardly even know you."

"What do you mean, honey? Of course, you know me."

"Not very much. You hardly ever came to visit, except Christmas."

I couldn't argue about that. After I graduated from college, I'd accepted a job several states away from my family. I wanted to be independent. New surroundings, new friends, a new church. I needed to know if I could take care of myself.

"You're right." Move forward, Martie. "But your mom and I always kept in touch. We were really close. We talked on the phone or emailed each other every day. Didn't she ever tell you?"

"I guess. But I didn't know you. You didn't talk to me on the phone."

That was obviously a mistake. But how could I know?

"And besides, you didn't like my dad."

"What? What are you talking about? Of course, I liked … I loved your dad."

"That's not what Mommy said."

Ruthie, what in the world did you say?

"One time I heard Mommy and Daddy talking about when they were dating. Mommy said that you didn't even like Daddy back then."

"Oh, Kim." I wished she would look at me. I put my face in my hands. "Honey, when your Mom and Dad started dating, your Mom was sixteen and I was seventeen. I was the older sister, and I had never dated anybody. And here was my younger sister with a serious boyfriend. I was, I was jealous. I was hurt. I felt left out."

This child was eight years old. Why did I think she could understand any of that?

"Here you go, ladies." The flight attendant brought by our drinks and some tiny bags of peanuts.

"Kim?"

She didn't answer, didn't turn toward me.

I swallowed some coffee. "But soon, I promise you, I got to like your dad. How could I help it? How could anybody not like Anthony? He was so much fun. So smart. He loved Ruthie so much." My voice came out scratchy. I cleared my throat. "And by the time they got married, I promise you, I loved him. Please look at me. Do you believe me?"

No response.

Oh, Ruthie, why did you think I could do this?

Dear Lord, I don't think I can be a parent. Why did Anthony and RuthAnne do this to us?

JESSICA, a good friend from work, agreed, with very little notice, to spruce up my place and make it more comfortable for Kim. I lived in a decent one-bedroom apartment. It wouldn't be perfect, but I thought, until I found something better, we could manage there, with Kim sleeping in the living room.

When we walked into the apartment, I looked around and said a quick, silent "Thank you" to Jessica.

She had found a small dresser and moved it in next to the couch. A basket of fruit sat atop the dresser. Two of the shelves on my bookcase were open, welcoming Kim. The couch held unopened packages with a brightly colored pillow and sheets.

I couldn't see anything on Kim's face. She kept her thoughts hidden.

"Kim, the couch makes into a bed. I'll get some blankets and make it up for you."

"You don't have to. I'll just sleep on the couch like it is."

"Okay. But I'm at least going to get you a couple blankets, and we have a new pillow and sheets here."

We'd stopped on the way home from the airport to eat some supper. The best thing for us now was to go to bed. I fixed up the couch as much as Kim would let me.

"This is your dresser," I told her. "And the open shelves on the bookcase are yours. Would you like me to help you unpack?"

"No."

"Okay, is there anything I can do to help you before you go to bed?"

"No."

Her small frame and bent head held so much need, and I'd never felt more useless.

After checking the front door to make sure all the locks and bolts were secure, I walked toward my bedroom then turned back. I decided I probably shouldn't keep Taffy a secret.

"Oh, by the way, I have a dog. She's a little part beagle, part something else, and her name is Taffy. Grandma Stevens told me you always played with their dog when you came to visit."

"Dogs are okay." Kim kept her head down.

"Good." What else to say? "She's been staying with a friend. She should be home tomorrow. She usually sleeps in my room, and I'll take her out for a walk and everything."

"I can help take care of the dog."

"Thanks, Kim. And after a day or so, we can talk about what other chores you can help with around the house." I felt mean for saying this, but my mom said it would be important to set some rules right away.

"Okay." Kim turned her back on me.

I left the door between my room and the living room open. When I woke in the morning, it was closed.

CHAPTER 4

*I*n the morning, I searched for something to offer for breakfast. "Did you sleep okay, Kim?"

"Fine."

Right.

My own sleep had been restless. There'd been no noise from the living room, but then, she'd closed the door.

"I have some corn flakes. Oh, but I don't have any milk. I can make orange juice."

"I don't like orange juice."

"Would you like some toast?"

"Okay."

I worked in the IT department of a large high school. When I explained the situation to my boss, he'd told me to take whatever time I needed for getting Kim settled in.

My parents said I should get Kim into school and starting on her new routine as soon as possible, so we headed out after breakfast the first day. I thought I might as well get Kim used to using the city bus right away.

"I used to have a car, and I'm hoping to be able to get another one soon. But for now, I pretty much use the bus for everything."

"Whatever."

My parents had collected paperwork from Kim's old school, so we were able to get her registered in the new school without any difficulty. The principal, Mr. Johnson, offered us a tour. He was kind, explaining everything. He stopped us first by a line of doors leading outside. "This is how you'll go out to the playground. You'll get very familiar with this."

Next, we stopped at a window which looked inside a large room. "We won't go inside the library, but you can see we have many books to go through." Mr. Johnson smiled. "And a lot of computers."

Kim didn't have any questions, no comments.

We ended at the door to the third grade classroom that would be Kim's. Mr. Johnson turned to face us. "Kim, you are of course welcome to start today if you like."

Kim's eyes grew large, and she glanced between me and Mr. Johnson, her lower lip caught between her teeth.

This kid must feel amazingly lost, in a new place, without her parents. Whether she likes it or not, I'm going to give her a hug.

I did, and Kim stiffened but didn't pull away. It was work to keep my voice light. "Why don't we go home today? Tomorrow is Thursday, and you can have a nice short two-day week to start."

Kim trembled a little then relaxed. "Okay." She pulled back.

Mr. Johnson walked outside with us to show us where the buses dropped off and picked up. "I'll let the bus driver know that you'll be starting tomorrow," he told Kim.

AT THE GROCERY STORE, I stopped us in the fresh fruit and veggie section. "What kind of fruit do you like?"

"Apples I guess."

A memory popped in my mind of RuthAnne saying she gave Kim milk at every meal. I wouldn't drink it, but I got some without asking Kim.

"Is there any particular kind of meat you like?"

"No."

"How about cookies?"

"It doesn't matter."

My favorite was chocolate covered graham crackers, so that's what landed in our cart.

Kim gave me no help about what else she would like to eat, so I did the best I could from things RuthAnne and my mom told me.

As I got ready to cook dinner, the doorbell rang. When I opened the door, Taffy rushed in, did a run twice around the entire apartment, then stopped in front of Kim on the couch.

Kim hesitated then held out her hand. Taffy sniffed, wagged her tail, licked Kim's hand, then jumped up on her lap. Kim smiled before lowering her face to the dog.

"Can I come in too?" Jessica asked.

"Please." I stepped back. "Kim, this is my good friend Jessica. Taffy has been staying at her house. Jessica, this is my niece Kim."

Jessica didn't make a big deal of the introduction. "Hey, Kim, glad you like dogs."

"Yeah. Hi." Kim gave Jessica a quick glance then returned her face to the dog.

I shook my head at Jessica. She smiled, knowing I needed help.

"I hope I caught you guys before you cooked dinner."

"Just barely."

"Good thing, because I ordered pizza, and it should be arriving any minute."

CHAPTER 5

I walked down with Kim to the bus stop the next morning but stood back as she joined the group of kids already waiting there. I knew I shouldn't give her a goodbye hug, but she looked so lonely, scuffing her feet, her head down. Then I noticed a couple of the other kids smiling at her and saying hello. *Father, let this be a good day.*

Kim's first couple of days at school did go well.

The first night, she handed me a sheet of paper out of her backpack. "This is from Mrs. Wallace. She's my teacher."

Reading down the list of supplies, I noticed a few things Kim hadn't already brought from home. "We'll go tonight, right after dinner, and get these."

Kim nodded. "There's a girl in my class who lives in this building. And another one who lives just down the street." She sat on the floor beside Taffy. "Mrs. Wallace is nice, and nobody in the class was mean to me because I'm a new kid."

My chest swelled with hope. Kim had enjoyed her day.

After we finished the dinner dishes on Friday night, I sat down in a chair in the living room. "Kim, I know you and your parents read the Bible together every day. I like to read at night after dinner. Will you read with me?"

"That sounds okay." She looked down at her lap, not at me.

Reaching for the Bible on the table between me and the couch, I asked, "Is there any special book you'd like to read?" Don't ask what she and her parents were reading, Martie.

She shook her head. "It doesn't matter."

"How about John? I like reading one of the gospels every so often. Or would you like to read one of the other gospels instead?"

"John is good." She still didn't look up at me, but this was one step forward.

THE NEXT MORNING, I asked, "Would you like to go to the mall? Just to look around?"

I caught her smile before she turned her head. "Sure. That'd be okay."

We didn't buy anything, but it was fun, looking at the different stores.

"Kim, would you like to look at any clothes? Or shoes?"

"No. Let's go in this jewelry store."

Kim stood for quite a while looking at the earrings. Sneaking a peek, I noticed her ears weren't pierced. Hmmm.

I touched her shoulder. "How about the toy store?"

"Okay."

We walked along the aisles of dolls and stuffed animals. "Would you like one of these?"

She shook her head. "I've got my bear." She headed back out into the mall. "Let's look at this music store."

She did allow me to buy her a CD. The singer was no one I'd ever listened to, but I remembered kids at school talking about her.

Afterward, we went to my favorite restaurant for lunch. The older couple who managed the place, Mr. and Mrs. Glover, knew my name, and they remembered I liked the bacon burger plate with tater tots instead of fries.

"Mrs. Glover, this is my niece, Kim."

"Hello, Kim." Mrs. Glover sat down beside Kim for a minute and shook her hand. "What kind of sandwich do you like?"

"Just a hamburger."

"All right." Mr. Glover offered Kim his friendliest smile. "Do you want fries, chips, or onion rings with that?"

"Chips, please."

"And, since it's your first time, you get free ice cream." Mrs. Glover gave me a stern frown. "Not your aunt. She already had her first time free dessert."

Kim grinned at that.

WE HAD A NICE MORNING. Not wanting to push my luck, I didn't ask Kim to help me with the laundry that afternoon. I brought up her stuff and laid it on the couch. "You'd better put these away yourself. I don't know what drawer you want to put what in."

"I'll just put them back in my suitcase." She didn't look at me. "I don't know how long I'll be here."

"Oh." She might as well have slugged me in the stomach.

Turning away, I hurried into my room and shut the door. I sat down on the bed and drew in a few deep breaths.

"Well, Martie, why are you surprised? Do you think that just after a few days, and one not so bad morning, she'll already be comfortable here?"

Why did her few words hurt me so? She was so cold and unaccepting of me, but she treated new people, the Glovers and Jessica, with genuine friendliness. Why did she dislike me?

"Okay, sweetheart, remember not everything's about you."

Kim had to be overwhelmed. She found herself in this new,

strange situation, and she was expected to go along with it. Nobody asked her opinion or gave her a choice.

"And she's just lost her parents."

I hugged my arms around my middle. "Yes, Father, I understand I need to stop thinking about myself, and remember what a terrible time this is for Kim. But I get my feelings hurt too. I'm still me, You know? Martie."

I rolled onto my belly and clutched my pillow.

"This is all quite a surprise to me too. I know. She's the eight-year-old, and I'm the twenty-nine-year-old. But this isn't an easy thing for me either." My breath shook, and I pressed my face into my pillow. "Please, please help me to swallow my hurts and move on. I want to be the parent this child needs, but I don't have any idea how to do it." Pushing myself up, I wiped tears from my face. "Daddy, You'll have to help me every minute."

*R*uthAnne and Anthony had always taken Kim to church, so it was a relief not to have an argument with her about going the next day. A group of kids her age gathered around her, showing her where to go, making a big deal of welcoming her. She smiled, enjoying the attention. My shoulders relaxed. *Thank you, Father.*

Later that afternoon, I came upstairs with laundry again and heard something from our apartment. I hurried. "Kim, are you crying?"

Pushing the door open, I stopped and stared. Not crying. She was laughing! She and Taffy rolled together on the floor. The dog was growling then licking Kim on the face, and Kim laughed so hard, she screamed.

As soon as Kim saw me, she stopped laughing and lay still on the carpet. I shook my head, picked up the laundry basket, and went into my room.

It's too bad she loses her joy when she sees me, but I'm glad she's able to have a good time.

Taffy came into my room and jumped on my bed. I bent down and hugged her. "You little troublemaker."

OVER THE NEXT couple of weeks, Kim made several friends at school and church. Lizzie, a seventeen-year-old who lived on the second floor of our building, agreed to stay with Kim after school until I came home from work. They discovered they liked the same music. Jessica joined us several times for dinner and movies.

One evening when Jessica came over, I took Taffy outside for a bathroom break. When I came back in, Jessica sat on the couch by Kim, and they were both laughing. Why is it easy for other people to get Kim to warm up to them and not me?

After Jessica went home, I couldn't stop myself. I asked Kim, "Why don't you like me?"

She jumped and looked up. "I, I guess I like you."

"Why is it . . ." *Oh Father, why am I trying to talk about this with an eight-year-old?* "Why is it you seem happy with everybody except me?"

Kim stared at me then lowered her head. "I don't know what you mean." She picked at her finger nails. "I just don't know why I have to go away from home and live with someone I don't even know."

"I didn't force that on you." My voice was harsh, but I went on. "I'm just trying to do what my sister asked me to do. Are you mad at me for that?"

She jerked her head up. "Should I be mad at my Mom and Dad?" Her mouth trembled, and tears rolled down her face.

"Of course not." I sat down beside her. This is a stupid conversation. Why did I even start it?

Kim turned her face from me. "Mom and Dad asked you to take care of me when I was a baby. Maybe, maybe if they'd really thought about it now, they might've changed their mind. They might have let me stay with someone I know better. Back home."

"But we do know each other, Kim."

I stopped.

Maybe she's right.

When I first learned that RuthAnne was pregnant, I'd been so excited. We'd worked together to paint the nursery and spent long hours shopping for baby clothes. "I'm so scared, Martie. I'm, I'm so happy." RuthAnne's eyes poured out tears. "You're going to be such a fun aunt."

I'd loved sitting for Kim when she was a baby, holding the warm, sweet-smelling bundle, being amazed at this tiny soul.

When Kim was one year old, I moved away for my new job. Every time I came home to visit, she'd changed and grown so much. I became shy with her. Never spending much time with kids, I didn't know what to say to her, how to interact.

And, of course, since I was shy and uncomfortable, so was Kim.

Shaking my head, I reached my hand to touch her, then drew it back. "But don't we need to try to get to know each other better? I love you, honey. I want to take care of you. I want to do what your parents asked."

Oh no. Maybe that wasn't the right thing to say.

"Kim?"

She'd turned her whole body away from me. She wasn't talking any more that night.

Oh, Daddy, please help me. Please help both of us.

CHAPTER 7

*N*ot long after this, Jerry called. "I wondered if you'd like to go out this Friday night."

"Go out? Friday?"

Whoa. How am I going to handle this?

Jerry taught history at the high school. We'd been on a couple of dates. The relationship didn't seem to be going anywhere far, but guys weren't pounding my door down. I didn't think I should turn one away in a hurry.

But this is too soon for me to be going out and leaving Kim with a babysitter for an evening.

"You're going to do what?" Jessica asked me the next day at work.

"I thought we'd just stay at home and have pizza and watch a video."

"With Kim?" She leaned across my desk and planted her hands in front of me.

"Yeah."

"Bad idea."

I leaned back in my chair. "It doesn't seem right for me to go out and have fun on the town yet."

"If this goes badly, you're going to resent her." Jessica stood back. "You don't want to start your relationship with her that way."

"I'm not going to resent her. I think this is the best way to handle it."

Please, God.

I DIDN'T TELL Kim about Jerry coming over until the night before.

"You mean, you're going to have like a date?"

"Well, yeah, kind of."

"And I'm going to be here?"

"Yes. Look, he's just a friend. It's not a big deal."

She shook her head and didn't say anything else.

When the doorbell rang the next night, Kim yelled, "I'll get it," and ran to the door. "Hi, Jerry, I'm Kim, Martie's niece. You knew I was gonna be here, right?"

"Um, yes, I did. It's good to meet you, Kim."

"Oh look, you brought flowers. How nice. I'll take them and put them in water." She snatched them out of his hand and ran to the kitchen.

"Hi, Jerry." My laugh was nervous. "Thanks for coming. And for the flowers."

"Sure. Listen, I haven't had a chance to talk to you since, well, since your sister … passed away. I'm really sorry about that."

"That was my mom. Did you know that?" Kim ran back into the room with a soda bottle filled with the flowers. "My dad died, too. Nice vase you have here, Aunt Martie."

That was probably the first time she'd called me Aunt Martie since she'd moved in with me. The first time she'd called me anything. We'd have to make a decision about that.

I didn't know who this Kim was. She ran around the apartment and chattered nonstop. "I'll set the table." She giggled. "Fancy china." She got out paper plates and cups, and when the pizza arrived she shouted, "Dinner is served."

Jerry and I didn't have a chance to talk to each other. Through mouthfuls of pizza, Kim asked Jerry a ton of questions.

"So, Jerry, have you ever been married?

"Do you have any kids?

"Has anybody close to you ever died?" Loud burp. "Whoa, that was rude."

As soon as I choked down a slice of pizza, I jumped up. "Let's watch the movie."

I have no memory of what movie I chose. Putting it in the DVD player, I turned it up loud, hoping it would make Kim be quiet. Jerry and I sat on the couch, Kim and Taffy on the beanbag.

At least they started on the beanbag. But soon they were chasing each other around the room, running between us and the TV. Kim squealed, so of course, Taffy barked.

Then they ran close enough to us that Kim "accidentally" shoved Taffy against Jerry's legs. And his cup of soda.

"Whoops," Kim yelled and caught the cup before all of the soda spilled on the carpet. This made it possible for her to spill the rest on his lap when she tried to hand it back to him.

"Martie, I think I'd better go." Jerry stood up. "I'm sorry about the mess."

"No problem." I turned off the TV. "Kim's going to clean it all up right now. Carpet cleaner under the kitchen sink, Kim. I'll walk down with you, Jerry. Come on, Taffy."

This was one time I was glad we didn't have an elevator in our apartment building. Jerry and I didn't have to stand right next to each other and try to talk for the seventy seconds it would have taken to get down. Instead, I talked to Taffy as she ran down the stairs in front of me. "Taffy, I'm gonna kill her."

When we were outside the front door of the building, Jerry and I stopped and turned to face each other.

"Jerry—"

KATHY MCKINSEY

"Martie—"

We both stopped. Clearing my throat, I tried again. "I'm sorry. I've never seen her act like that."

"It's okay. She's obviously having a hard time with her parents' death. Of course, she is. And I know that's what's most important to you right now." He stepped back. "Maybe we shouldn't try to see each other again until she's feeling a little more stable."

"Yeah. That makes sense." I couldn't meet his eyes. "Thanks for being so understanding. And I'm sorry about all the soda on your clothes."

"It's okay." He touched my shoulder. "Take care of yourself. And her."

Jessica said I would resent Kim if this night went bad. I didn't resent her. I was crazy mad. Except when I wanted to laugh. These emotions went back and forth inside me as I climbed the stairs. I ended up back at the apartment with crazy mad.

Slamming the door, I threw my keys on the end table. "What in the world did you think you were doing? Who are you?"

The apartment was clean, the stain on the carpet gone, and everything cleared or thrown away from the kitchen table. Kim was sitting on the couch when I came in, but she jumped up.

"Why'd you think I wanted to go on your date with you and your boyfriend?" she yelled back at me.

"What? He's not my boyfriend." I hung Taffy's leash on the doorknob. "Never mind, I just, I didn't feel right going out and having fun and leaving you."

She opened her mouth, then closed it again and turned her back to me.

I wasn't done being mad yet, so I yelled again. "Everything you did was rude. I know you didn't learn all that from my sister."

Kim's shoulders slumped.

I covered my face with my hands. "Oh, honey, I'm sorry. I didn't mean to say that."

She sat back down on the couch and kept her head down. "I'll tell him I'm sorry if you want me to."

"No, no. You don't have to. Honey . . ." I stopped.

Kim's shoulders shook.

"Please, Kim, I'm sorry."

She wouldn't look at me.

I walked into my room and threw myself face down on my bed. "Dear God, what on earth was I thinking?"

*S*itting at my desk at work, I looked out the window into the parking lot. Kim and I hadn't talked much the last few days. "What can I do to change things, Father?"

The phone rang, and I reached for it.

"Martie, this is Lizzie!" She was crying. I could hardly understand her. "Kim didn't come home on the school bus. I called all her friends I could think of, and I called the school. No one knows where she is."

"Lizzie." My lips were numb, and I felt cold all over. "How long ago did the bus come?"

"I don't know. About twenty-five minutes ago maybe. I called everybody I could think of."

I hung up and called 911. Four minutes later, a police car pulled into the parking lot of the high school. The officer leaned over and opened the passenger door. "Miss Stevens? I'm Will Ranger. Why don't you ride with me and tell me what you know?"

We went by our apartment first to see if it looked like Kim stopped there, if she'd taken anything. Nothing looked different from that morning.

"I wish she'd come by." My teeth chattered. "Then she'd have less time to, to get farther away."

Officer Ranger nodded. "Let's go talk to the babysitter, to people at school. Any friends you can think of."

My head buzzed, so I didn't hear much of the conversation he had with anyone. He asked questions, but I didn't catch any of the answers. I could hardly breathe.

Back in the car, the police radio cackled. Officer Ranger asked me a few more things, and I know I said more than only what could have been helpful with Kim being lost.

Everything poured out of my mouth. How RuthAnne and Anthony died and made me Kim's guardian. "Anthony's parents don't like it."

I told him how Kim was so cold and angry with me and didn't want to stay here. "I don't know how to make things right between us."

I kept talking, not thinking about how this was a stranger I was dumping all my troubles onto.

He must have known it was healthy for me to get it out because he would ask another question when I ran out of something to say.

Then the voice on the radio sounded clear.

"Will, I think we've found the little girl. We got a call from the airport that they have a child by herself there, blond hair, black jeans, red and white sweater."

Will looked at me. I nodded, all at once unable to talk.

"Let them know we're on our way," he said on the radio. "I wonder how she learned how to find her way to the airport." This time it sounded like he was talking to himself.

"I showed her how to use the city bus." My lips were numb again. "I don't have a car, so we use the bus a lot. She was always getting schedules and taking them home to look at."

We drove in silence for a while.

"Is that your cell phone?" Will asked.

I hadn't even noticed it ringing. "Hello . . ." My voice croaked. Clearing my throat, I tried again, "Hello?"

"Martha, this is Julie Warrick."

Kim's grandmother.

"Martha, can you hear me?"

"Yes."

"I just got a call from Kimmie a little while ago. She said she was at the airport and wanted to come home to us."

My stomach clenched.

"Martha, are you still there?"

"Yes. Yes, I'm here."

"I told Kimmie we'll be there as soon as we can. I called the airport security, but fortunately, they said they're already keeping an eye on her. I thought you might want to pick her up and take her back to your place. It will be some hours before we can get there."

"Yes. I'm on my way." My tongue plowed through sand in my mouth.

"Tonight we will take Kimmie to a hotel with us." Mrs. Warrick still spoke, and my head throbbed. "Then we can all talk tomorrow." She didn't wait for me to say anything else before she hung up.

For the first time that afternoon, I cried. When I cry, I'm not pretty. I cry big, loud, shaking sobs.

Will pulled off the road and parked the car. While I cried, he sat beside me, quiet, his hand on my back.

CHAPTER 9

*K*im sat on a bench in the airport, her head down, her hands worrying the straps of her backpack.

"Kim? Hi." I worked to keep my voice soft, calm.

She jumped then hugged her backpack, not getting up from her seat. "Grandma Julie and Grandpa Jason are coming."

"I know." I sat down beside her. "Grandma Julie called me. They're not going to be here until late this evening, so they wanted you to come home right now. They said you could stay with them tonight in a hotel."

Kim didn't respond but got up and walked with me out of the airport. She stopped and pulled her bottom lip between her teeth when she saw Will standing beside the police car.

"Kim, this is Will. He's going to give us a ride home."

We all kept quiet on the ride back to the apartment. Without asking if he should, Will came upstairs with us. Kim ran straight to the bathroom and locked the door.

"Are you guys going to be okay?" Will asked.

"I think so." I sighed. "Since we live on the fourth floor, I don't think she'll try to climb out the bathroom window, even to get away from me."

He smiled and gave me his card. "I think you'll be okay. Let me know if I can do anything to help."

Kim didn't try to stay in the bathroom all night, but while she did, I paced and let the pressure grow inside me. I wanted to explode with anger and hurt, but when she finally came out, all I said was, "Kim, you thought you could take a plane to your grandparents?"

"Yes." She sat on the couch, keeping her face turned away from me. "But then somebody from security stopped me, and they wouldn't let me fly by myself."

I wanted to shake her. "How were you going to pay for it?"

"Grandma Julie gave me a credit card."

"She gave you a—" Anger boiled inside me, and my chest squeezed. Closing my eyes, I inhaled and exhaled several deep breaths. When I thought I could talk again without screaming, I looked at Kim. "Please give it to me." I held out my hand.

She looked at me, every part of her face frowning. Neither of us said anything for a minute, then she pulled the card out of her pocket and tossed it on the couch. Maybe she saw something in my face she decided not to argue with.

Kim was asleep by the time the Warricks got there. Even so, I'd decided not to argue with them about waking her and taking her with them to a hotel.

As I met Julie Warrick's eyes, I thought it would be best if I didn't say much. "I'll call Kim's school in the morning and let them know she'll be late." I held out Kim's overnight bag. "When she's gotten up, and when you've had time to have breakfast, come on over here. I'll take the morning off from work and take her to school. Then we can talk."

Mrs. Warrick's face stiffened. She wanted to disagree, but Mr. Warrick spoke up first. "That sounds good, Martha. We'll see you in the morning."

Maybe he, too, saw something in my face he decided not to argue with.

AFTER THEY LEFT, I went to bed, but I didn't expect to sleep.

"Dear God, I am so mad at Julie Warrick."

Turning over, I punched at my pillow. "Why in the world did she think it was okay to give Kim a credit card? I wanted to punch her tonight."

Turning over again, I was quiet for a minute. "Thank You that I didn't punch her." My face ached with tears, and my breath caught. "I really don't want to get mad when I talk to them in the morning. Please, Daddy. Help me."

CHAPTER 10

$\mathcal{B}$y morning, I was no longer afraid I'd punch Kim's grandmother.

I rode in the Warricks' cab to take Kim to school, and then we went to a restaurant to talk. As soon as we'd ordered coffee, I took the credit card out of my purse and handed it to Julie Warrick.

"I am Kim's guardian." It still took effort not to scream at her. "I will handle her financial needs."

She sputtered. "You're her guardian . . . Well, I don't know . . ."

"I am her guardian."

"She told me you yelled at her." Her hand shook as she tried to pick up her coffee.

"She told you—" I took a deep breath and almost laughed. "Yes, I yelled at her. I think that probably happens in most families."

Mrs. Warrick squeezed the cup in her hands. "She's going through a terrible time right now. And you yelled at her."

"She behaved pretty bad."

"She'll no doubt behave badly again. She's just a child. Are you always going to yell at her?"

"No."

"How do you know? You're not a parent. You don't have any experience with—"

Mr. Warrick put his hand over his wife's. "I think that's all we have to discuss right now, Julie." His voice was calm, soothing.

"But, Jason?" Her face was red, her eyes filling.

I almost felt sorry for her. Almost. I stood up. "I think you're right, Mr. Warrick. I need to get to work, and you probably need to get to the airport. Mrs. Warrick, please believe me that I am working very hard to take good care of Kim. I know she usually calls you on the weekend. I'm sure she will this weekend, too, if not sooner."

THAT NIGHT I saw Kim's face crumple as she was getting ready for bed. As she lay down on the couch, her back to me, her shoulders shook.

Dear God, I miss RuthAnne so much. Help me be able to take care of her baby.

Up to now, I'd been careful not to force affection on Kim, but tonight I decided to give her whatever comfort I could.

"Kim, honey, your parents are gone, and I'm guessing you feel pretty horrible." I had to stop to force a lump out of my throat. My eyes stung. "Well, my sister is gone, and my brother-in-law, my close friend, is gone too, and I'm pretty sick about it. I think I have some idea how bad you feel."

Lying on the couch beside Kim, I wrapped my arms around her. I held her until she finally stopped shaking and fell asleep. By that time, my cheeks were drenched.

I reached for the phone ringing on my desk, my mind on the work in front of me. "Hello?"

"Miss Stevens. Martie, isn't it?"

The voice sounded familiar. "Yes."

"This is Will Ranger. I'm the police officer who drove you to the airport the other day."

Well, he'd done much more than that.

"Yes, Officer Ranger. Will." I jerked upright. "Is anything wrong with Kim? Did something happen—"

"No, no. I'm so sorry. I didn't mean to startle you." He cleared his throat. "I was wondering if I could come over and have coffee with you during your break. Or at lunch."

"Today? You're sure nothing's wrong with Kim?"

"Absolutely nothing. I just wanted a chance to talk to you."

"Okay." I looked at the clock. Eleven-sixteen. "How about noon?"

Jessica grinned when I told her. "I meant to tell you the other day he is pretty cute. I thought you might not have noticed."

"Yeah, probably not. I wonder what he wants."

Her smile spread. "I guess you'll find out at lunch."

My office was the only empty spot where we could meet at lunchtime, so I asked Will to join me there.

"How is Kim doing?" He accepted a cup of the terrible coffee we had in the teachers' lounge and managed not to make a face when he took a swallow.

"She's okay." I shook my head. "I never really know how she is, but I guess she's okay."

He took another sip of the coffee. My respect for him went up. "I noticed a Bible in your living room. You're a Christian?"

I nodded.

"Me too. I wanted to let you know that I'm praying for you. For you and Kim."

"Thank you." My throat tightened.

"I also wanted to ask you something." He squirmed in his chair and took a sip. "And I hope I'm not being out of line."

I squirmed a little too. "Go ahead."

He set down his coffee and looked straight at me. "Would it be okay if I asked you on a date sometime?"

I certainly hadn't expected that. Wait till I tell Jessica.

"No." I stopped, inhaled. "I mean, no, it's not out of line. And yes, it would be okay for you to ask me on a date."

He smiled and took in a long breath. "Then I'll call you soon."

I looked forward to it.

"*H*ey, Kim," I called to her after we'd finished dishes one night. "Did you ever clean a bathroom before?"

She scrunched up her nose and shook her head.

"Well, as Grandma Stevens used to tell me, you'll never learn any younger."

She didn't answer.

After a short pause, I added, "We could go get ice cream afterwards."

She tried to turn her head away in a hurry, but I glimpsed her smile anyway.

After Kim's failed attempt to run away, I had the impression things improved between us. Maybe I just grew stronger, more confident. Especially after I'd handed that credit card back to Julie Warrick.

Besides chores, I gave Kim more rules, too, and stuck to them.

One night we sat in the living room, each with our own book, not talking.

"Kim, it's bedtime."

"It's only nine o'clock."

"What time did your parents tell you to go to bed?"

She didn't answer, but she went to bed.

When I wanted her to stop something, I said "stop" and tried not to worry it would hurt her feelings. I didn't ask so much if she wanted to do something. I told her to do it.

"All right, Kim, here's your laundry." I set the basket on the floor in front of the couch. "Please fold these and put them away in your dresser."

My growing confidence as a parent told me ... well, maybe not. But somehow I was sure Kim was more comfortable with this change in our lives. I'd heard kids do better if their parents set rules and boundaries. Maybe Kim didn't like me any better, but I hadn't always liked my parents much as a kid either.

A COUPLE of nights after Will came to see me at school, he stopped by our apartment. Of course, we were doing dishes when he showed up. My hair fell damp in my face, and I carried the dish rag to the door when I opened it.

I twisted my mouth when I saw him, and he grinned at me.

The mixture of flowers he handed me smelled wonderful.

"The florist told me these are spring flowers. I figured we could all use a little hope that spring is on the way, so I thought I'd bring these for you ladies."

Taffy sniffed around him, trying to jump for the flowers.

"She wants to chew on them." I took them, glad they already had a vase, so Kim couldn't point out what I used to hold flowers.

"Hi, Kim." Will looked past me. "How are you?"

"Fine." Kim frowned and walked back to the kitchen.

I raised my eyebrows and shrugged.

He shrugged, too, and cleared his throat. "I was wondering if you'd like to go out for dinner this weekend. Maybe Friday night."

With my nose in the flowers, I didn't meet his eyes. "That would be nice. Yes, thanks."

He took a deep breath. "Okay then. How about I pick you up at six?"

I nodded. We were both nervous.

He shifted on his feet. "I'm on duty in a few minutes, so I have to go. Bye, Kim," he called into the kitchen.

There was no answer.

"Good night, Martie."

"Good night." He was still smiling, so I did too. "Thanks for the flowers."

"Why is he hanging around?" Kim barked when I'd barely stepped into the kitchen. "Is he trying to make sure I don't run away?"

"No, actually, I think he likes me." I risked a quick glance at the mirror. "Messed up hair and everything."

"Do I have to go with you on your date?"

"No. Absolutely not. How would you like to spend the evening with Jessica?"

Her face lit up. "That would be fun."

"What would you like to talk about?" Will pulled out my chair from the table at the restaurant.

"Tell me what it's like to be a cop."

"Not what you'd think." He took a drink of water. "Not so exciting. More routine kinds of things than you might expect."

"No scary stories?"

"Hmmm. You want scary stories?"

"I don't know. Probably not."

He reached across and opened my menu for me. "I'll tell you the scariest thing that ever happened to me. On the job or, or any time."

I looked up from the menu. "Okay."

"We had a call one time to go to a house where a lady had fallen and needed help." He unwrapped his silverware. "She was okay. I mean, she called 911 herself. She was still conscious and everything."

I picked up my glass of water. "Yeah?"

"She told us the front door was unlocked. When we opened it, I was knocked down by the biggest, loudest black dog I've ever seen."

Choking on the water I was drinking, I grabbed my napkin and coughed. "Was he dangerous?" I asked when I could talk.

KATHY MCKINSEY

"Nah. He just wanted to play."

I held my napkin to my lips and cleared my throat. "Did that really happen?"

He nodded. "Sure as shootin'."

When I could breathe normally again, I said, "I don't think I'm going to believe anything else you say."

"Too bad." He turned a page in his menu. "I've got some great stories."

He went on to tell me about some of the people he worked with and some of the interesting and funny folks he'd met. He made being a policeman sound like a funny job much of the time. Of course, I was finding out that almost everything was funny for Will. He was easy to laugh with.

"Your turn." He leaned back. "Tell me about your job."

"It's probably what you might expect. People spilling food or drinks onto their computers, kids logging onto websites that they shouldn't, people needing help with a project due yesterday."

"Oh, come on. You must have a goofy story."

"Goofy, huh?" I laid down my fork and rested my chin on my hand. "Well, there was the time my boss lost his report."

"Sounds good. Go on."

"He calls me in and says he's got a report due that day, and he accidentally deleted the document, and I have to find it."

"No pressure there."

"None. Now often, if you delete a file, I can get it back. But he didn't delete it. He'd never saved it. He erased what he was working on before saving it."

"Ouch. So what did you do?" Will set his fork beside his plate.

"I thought to check his email. Of course, he didn't mention to me that he had worked on the report at home the night before and emailed it to himself at work. Almost the entire document was there, in his inbox."

"Nice. He must have been impressed when you found it."

"Mmm." My nose wrinkled. "He doesn't impress easily."

220

Will grinned. "He doesn't sound like the brightest guy."

"It seems like that. But I don't like to think so because he is the one who hired me."

"Okay." He laughed. "He had one really good day."

With his encouragement, I thought of other interesting details and people at work to talk about, and dinner was over way too fast. We drove around for a while afterward and continued to talk.

"So, you want to know the story of my life?"

I laughed. "I do."

"I'm an only child, and I live five minutes from the house where I grew up. My parents still live there."

"So you're the adventurous type."

"You got it. Your turn."

"I was a tomboy."

"I don't believe it."

"Yep. I followed my brother and his friends around all the time and pestered them."

He turned onto a different street. "Go on."

I swallowed. "I told you about my sister."

Will reached over and squeezed my hand.

"We were so different." My fingers trembled. "She was the pretty, feminine one, and I—" Will grunted, and I hurried on. "But even though we were so different, and even though we fought a lot, we were really close."

We were both quiet for a minute. Will finally said, "I think I envy you. If that makes sense."

I looked over at him. "It does, actually."

In the light of a neon sign, I saw Will smile. "Guess what church I go to."

"Oh, I'm not going to be able to figure this out." I tapped my fingers on the door handle. "Let's see. The same one you grew up in?"

"You are sharp." He squeezed my hand again. "And I became a

Christian when I was ten. What about you? Tell me about your faith."

"I always went to church, too, when I was growing up. But I didn't become a Christian until I was in college." I stared out the window for a minute. "I still feel like a really young Christian a lot of the time."

We talked about college, books we liked, movies, even people we'd dated. I was afraid he'd never ask me out again because there wouldn't be anything more to talk about.

But when we got to my front door, he said, "I'll call you soon, okay?"

"Okay." I sighed. And smiled.

He stood there for a minute, resting one hand against the wall of the building and looking down at me. "I forgot to tell you what my mom told me today."

"What was that?"

"That Christians can kiss on the first date." He put his other hand on the side of my face and kissed me. "Good night, Martie."

I stood still for a minute after Will walked away. His kiss was gentle, but my heart pounded against my chest.

CHAPTER 14

*W*ill called the next evening after Kim was in bed.

"So how was your day?" he asked.

You mean, after you kissed me last night? I smiled. "Good. How about yours?"

"Excellent." His voice carried a smile too.

He called every evening he didn't work.

One evening he asked, "What are you three girls doing?"

"Three? What do you—oh yeah, Taffy too." I peeked through my open bedroom door. "Actually, right now, Kim and Taffy are both asleep on the couch."

"Aww, that's cute."

"Taffy used to sleep with me."

"Don't be jealous. Things have to change."

"Easy for you to say."

"I do say. Happily."

We always laughed as we talked, and his calls guaranteed I smiled all the next day too.

And we went out again.

"I want to show you all of my favorite places in the city," Will told me.

A hamburger joint. A fountain in the park. An ice cream shop.

"This is my absolute favorite place." Will reached over and rubbed ice cream from my chin with his palm.

"Oh yeah." I licked at the watermelon chocolate dripping from my cone. "When the weather gets warmer, let's come here every night. Forty-three flavors. Yummy."

"Yeah." He wrinkled his nose. "And who'd guess you'd pick the only one I don't care for our first time?"

I took a big bite. "Mmm. No sharing." I grinned at him. "Maybe next time."

He wiped more ice cream from my face with a napkin. "You're a messy date."

Licking my lips, I stuck my tongue out at him. "But, speaking of dates, I only want to go out once a week for now. I don't want to take too much time away from Kim." My shoulders lifted. "Even though she does seem to have a lot of fun with Jessica when we're out."

Will touched my hand. "I'm having fun too."

"Hmmm." I thought a minute. "You can come over other times in the week to visit, if you want."

His eyes crinkled. "That'll make Kim happy."

I smiled back at him. "You're growing on her."

He tilted his head. "How about you?" He flicked my nose with his thumb. "Am I growing on you?"

MY HEART LIFTED NOT ONLY because of Will. Kim was relaxing. She talked more with me.

We took walks with Taffy almost every evening.

"Oh, hold the leash tight, Kim. Here comes somebody with another dog."

Kim sat down and put Taffy on her lap. "I'll just hold her until they're gone."

"She's going to lick your face, you know."

Already Taffy was on her hind legs, washing Kim's face.

Kim smiled up at me. "I don't mind."

When we read the Bible in the evening, we took turns reading out loud. One night I asked Kim if she'd like to read other books together too.

"I think that would be okay." She bit her lip. "Mama and Daddy used to read books with me a lot."

"What was the last book you were reading together?" I held my breath, praying she would answer.

Kim looked down. "*Little House on the Prairie.*"

"That's one of my favorites." My breath eased out. "Grandma Stevens read that to us too."

Kim looked up. A tear rolled down her face. "Mama told me that."

"Would you like to read it with me?"

"Could we start at the beginning?" Another tear leaked out of her eye. "I'm not sure where we left off."

"I'd like that." I leaned over and kissed the top of her head.

I gave Kim a goodnight kiss every night now. Sometimes, she smiled at me.

CHAPTER 15

I took off from work the week of spring break and looked for fun things to do with Kim. We took in a couple movies and visited a nearby park.

Will took us to the ice cream parlor.

"So, Kim, I'm supposing you want chocolate and watermelon, like your aunt."

"What?" Kim scrunched her face. "No way. Yuck. I want chocolate mint."

Will gave her a high five. "I knew you were the smart one in the family."

We made another trip to the mall.

When we passed an ear-piercing booth, Kim asked, "How old do you think I have to be before I can get my ears pierced?"

How am I going to handle this one?

"What did your mom say?"

"I thought you were my guardian now."

"I am, and as your guardian, I'd like to know what your mom said."

Kim surprised me by giggling. "Sixteen."

"Sounds good to me." I patted her back.

On Friday, Will asked if we wanted to go to the zoo.

"I've probably been to this zoo more than a hundred times." Will took hold of my hand. "Today it seems brand new."

Kim kept running ahead of us then back toward us, her eyes getting bigger all the time. We had to hurry to keep her in our sight.

"The zoo at home wasn't this big," she told us. "Oh, there's the elephants!" She was off again.

"I don't think she's ever going to wear out."

"Me neither." Will stopped for a minute. "My feet are not as young as hers."

When at last Kim showed signs of winding down, Will asked, "Kim, would you like to see my two favorite spots at the zoo?"

"Sure."

First he took us to a large aquarium area. We stood in the middle of glass walls. Behind the walls were so many kinds of fish. Scores of colors, dozens of sizes.

"This is beautiful," I murmured.

Kim didn't speak. She walked around the area and stared, not wanting to miss anything.

"Okay," Will said after a few minutes. "Let's go to my favorite place now."

This was another area surrounded by glass walls. Behind the walls was an unbelievable variety of snakes, most of them moving. I felt like I might be sick to my stomach. Will stood still and grinned. Kim circled the walls, eyes huge, repeating, "This is so cool."

"You two are the weirdest people I have ever met." I hurried to walk outside.

KIM PLANNED a sleepover that night with Jenny, the girl in her class who lived in our building. Will and I brought home Chinese food and a couple of movies.

When the first movie climbed to an exciting point, I clicked Stop on the remote and said, "Time for popcorn."

"Not arguing." Will stood from the couch. "Sit. I'll fix it."

A knock came at the door.

"Who could that be?" I pushed myself off the couch and moved to open the door. "Beth? What is it?"

Jenny's mom stood in the hall, her eyes wide, her face drained of color.

My chest squeezed. "Beth?"

Will walked to stand by me, wrapping an arm around my shoulders. "Beth, come in. Tell us." His voice held calm.

Beth didn't come in. "Oh, Martie, I'm sorry. Kim is gone."

CHAPTER 16

*M*y body washed cold, and I stumbled back.

"When?" Will's voice tensed, and he tightened his arm around me.

"I don't know." Beth's entire body shook. "I'm so sorry. They had dinner, then they were watching a movie. I heard them laughing. They seemed to be doing well, so I just left them alone."

"How long since you've seen Kim?" Will reached a hand to steady Beth.

"Maybe two hours. Jenny says she doesn't know where Kim planned to go. She's crying. She won't tell me anything. She says she doesn't know." Beth gulped and wiped at tears. "You can come talk to her if you want to."

"No." Will shook his head. "I'd just scare her. All right. Go back to Jenny. We'll take care of things."

When she was gone, Will helped me to the couch. He sat close beside me and talked into his phone. "This is Officer Ranger. We've got an eight-year-old girl missing, Kim Warrick, again. Please ask everyone to start searching for her." He gave Kim's description. "Call the airport and the Greyhound station and call me back after you talk to them."

Will held me close and didn't say anything more. I shook with terror and pressed myself tight against him. In a fog, I heard Will's phone ring.

"Okay. We're on the way."

Will knelt in front of me and held both my hands. "She's at the Greyhound station, Martie. One of the officers was close by, and she's staying there to keep an eye on Kim. We'll go get her." He laid his hand on my cheek. "It's going to be okay, honey."

It was a struggle to find breath, and there was a roaring in my ears. "No. No, it's not."

THE POLICE OFFICER sat on a bench beside Kim when we got to the bus station. She kept her head down, not looking at us, not speaking.

Will sat on Kim's other side and wrapped her in a hug.

I stood back. I couldn't think of anything to say either.

IT WAS the next morning before Julie and Jason Warrick could get there. Julie pushed past me at the door and walked straight to where Kim lay on the couch. I opened the door wider for Jason then turned to follow Julie.

"Get up and pack, Kimmie," Julie said. "We're going home."

Julie grabbed my arm and pulled me into my bedroom, slamming the door. "I'm taking this to court, Martha." She pressed her lips together. "If you can't keep her safe, I'm asking for the guardianship to be changed."

I faced her, my hands limp at my sides. "I won't fight you," I said through numb lips. "If she's so unhappy with me, I guess she shouldn't be here."

My stomach clenched, and my head swam. What would I do without Kim?

CHAPTER 17

*F*or the next two weeks, I was lost.

Will sat on my desk at work and grasped my hand. "Honey, talk to me."

I looked away from him. There were no words. Why couldn't he leave me alone?

"Oh, no." He pressed his hand on my cheek, turning my face so that I had to meet his gaze. "You can't get rid of me that easy. You may as well talk to me."

Could he read my mind already?

"Martie."

"I—" I cleared my throat and grabbed his hand in both of mine. "I thought she was starting to warm up to me." My mouth trembled. "I thought she was more, more comfortable being here."

"I did too." He leaned close to me. "I'm so sorry."

Another day Jessica found me at my desk, staring out the window. She shook my shoulder. "Martie, you have to snap out of this."

I blinked then looked up at her. "I guess I didn't realize how much I depended on, how much I loved, having her with me. It was such a short time she was here." I covered my face with my hands. "I feel like there's a big hole in my life."

Jessica knelt on the floor and wrapped her arms around me.

I thanked God Will and Jessica were in my life. They got me through the days, but the nights were hard. No one to talk to. To read with. No one playing with Taffy, or complaining about chores. "Daddy, I wasn't this lonely by myself, before Kim came."

My sleep was restless and hard to come by, so I started lying down right after dinner. When the knock came at the door, I thought it was a dream.

A louder knock.

Kim and her Grandma Julie stood outside in the hall.

Kim ran into the bathroom and locked the door. Julie stayed in the hall, holding her face in her hands.

"Mrs. Warrick?" My voice was gravelly with sleep, with shock. I cleared my throat. "Come in."

She came in but didn't sit down. Grasping her purse with white knuckles, she forced herself to look me straight in the eye. "Kimmie wasn't happy at our house." Her lips trembled, but words poured out. "She lay on her bed all the time and cried. When I tried to get her to talk to me about what was wrong, she just cried harder."

She stopped and swallowed, then went on. "There didn't seem to be anything we could do to help her. Jason has always thought I was wrong to try to get Kim to be with us, to go against what Anthony and RuthAnne wanted. He's convinced me . . ." She stopped again and took a shaky breath. "We agree now that it's right for Kimmie to be here with you." She pulled a tissue from her purse and wiped her face. "I don't know how to take care of a child anymore. I didn't even know how to start with her, to help her."

"She's grieving." My mouth was dry, and my heart thudded a slow, hard beat. "It's going to be hard for anyone to help her right now."

"It's kind of you to say that." Julie reached for the door. "Jason is waiting in a cab downstairs. It's probably best if I leave now."

$\mathcal{A}$s I stood outside the bathroom door, my nails dug into my palms. "Kim, please come out here."

She came out and lay on the couch, burying her face in her pillow. Kneeling beside her, I laid my head down next to hers.

"Grandma and Grandpa didn't want me either." Her voice muffled into the pillow.

"Oh, Kim, that's not it." I swallowed. "They love you. I love you. We're all just trying to do what's best for you."

She turned her face toward me. "You were probably happy I was gone."

"Honey. Come on." I leaned back and rubbed my face. "Of course I wasn't happy you were gone. I want you here with me." Taking a deep breath, I cleared my throat. "We'll talk about all this tomorrow, but I need to ask you, did you have enough money for a bus ticket?"

"No." Her face trembled. "I thought I might. I'd saved a lot, some from before I moved here, and some money you'd given me to buy stuff that I didn't spend. I thought it might be enough, but it wasn't."

She blinked and tried to turn away again, but I stopped her. Grasping her hands, I searched for the right words to say.

"Honey, please listen. The bus station isn't a safe place for you to be by yourself. You're eight. You need an adult with you. I want to help you be safe. If anything had happened to you . . ." I stopped and bit my lip. "Please, sweetheart, if you ever feel like you have to go away again, promise me you'll talk to me instead. I'll do my very best to be fair. Please, promise me."

"I promise."

For the first time I could remember, she didn't turn away from me when she cried. I pulled her closer and laid my head on hers.

NEITHER KIM nor I felt like eating breakfast the next morning. So I came over to where she lay on the couch and did something I probably hadn't done since she was three. I picked her up and sat with her on my lap.

"Kim, will you—can you tell me what's going on? Why did you run away from me?"

She turned her head away. "I thought you'd probably be better without me."

"Why in the world would you think that?"

"Will." She picked up her pillow and hugged it. "Maybe he'll want to marry you. But maybe he won't want to, since you have me to take care of."

"Are you . . ." I stopped and took a breath. "Are you serious? That's why you left?"

She nodded.

I sat still, my chest aching. *I've failed, Father. How can I show her how important she is to me?*

"Kim—"

"You can call me Kimmie." She still didn't look at me.

This kid is going to break my heart.

"Thank you, sweetie." I squeezed her and forced my voice to stay calm. "Kimmie. You need to understand that if Will or anyone else wants to marry me, they have to understand, they have to know, that you and I come together."

"Somebody you have to take care of because my parents said so."

"Yeah." I inhaled a deep breath. "I think maybe I've said that too much. Of course, it's important to want to do what your parents asked. That will always be important." I turned her face to look at me. "But that's not all. It's not even the biggest thing. I love you, honey. You're my family. If anybody else wants to be in my family, then they need to know that you are part of that family too."

"Family." She turned on my lap to better meet my eyes. "Like Uncle Johnnie is our family, and Grandpa and Grandma Stevens, and my cousins?"

"You bet. They are all part of our family, and we love them." My throat stuck, and I swallowed. "But there's another family, Kimmie. Special, closer. You and me. Because, even though I'm not your mom, I'm your parent, and you're my little girl."

Thank You, Father. Thank You that I finally got that out.

I was her parent. No more of this guardian business.

Kimmie's eyes opened wide, but she didn't say anything.

I liked the sound of it, so I said it again. "We are each other's special family."

We sat quiet for a few minutes. Then I asked, "I can really call you Kimmie?"

She nodded. There were tears in her eyes, and her voice came out rough. "Yes."

"Good." Smiling, I rubbed her back. "Then let's talk about what you call me. Aunt Martie is too formal. And my friends call me Martie. I'm not your friend. I'm your parent. What would be a good name for you to call me?"

She squirmed and turned away again. "Mommy said she used to call you MayMay when she was really little. Could I call you MayMay?"

RuthAnne's little girl nickname for me. I hadn't thought about it in years. "Of course you can." My voice was rough now too.

CHAPTER 19

immie let me touch her all the time now, not only when she was upset or crying. She often hugged me too. I tried not to expect too much too soon, but it was hard not to be hopeful.

One evening, Will and I sat at a small table outside the ice cream shop. Jessica and Kimmie were at a movie.

"I wish I had just given Kimmie more hugs and been more affectionate with her all along," I told Will. "Maybe she'd have been more comfortable with me sooner."

"And maybe not." Will pushed several napkins across the table to me. "We don't have a lot of experience being parents. We don't really know what would have happened."

"We." My heart skipped a beat. "Parents."

He grinned. "You are going to marry me, aren't you? You're going to let me be her parent too?"

My spoon fell from my fingers. "Will? What . . ."

He picked up a napkin and leaned across to wipe my face. "I love you, Martie. Will you marry me?"

My face tingled as the blood drained. "Marry you?"

237

He nodded. "You know, become husband and wife. Like people do when they love each other."

My head spun. Covering my face with my hands, I squeezed my eyes. *Father, can we do this? Would it work?*

Will tapped my head with his fingers. "Hey, you. Are you going to finish your ice cream?"

I opened my eyes and looked down at my bowl. "I don't think so."

He pulled it toward him. "What flavor is this? Some weird mixture again?"

"Just plain chocolate."

He picked up my spoon. "I'll finish it for you."

My mouth was dry. "Will?"

"Honey." He leaned closer to me. "I'm not trying to scare you." His eyes were warm, and …Was that what love looked like?

Will took hold of my hand in both of his. "I know things have been crazy for you lately. I'm not rushing you. I just want you to know where I am. I love you. And I love Kim." He smiled and touched his spoon to my nose. "I'm here when you're ready."

Was I crying?

Will came around to my side of the table and wrapped me in his arms. "You don't have to give me an answer now. Maybe I was wrong to say anything. I don't mean to pressure you—"

"No." My head shook back and forth against his chest. "I don't want to push you away. Please." I grasped his shirt in my hands. Maybe I wasn't ready to talk about marriage, but I needed him. "Please, stay with me."

Will knelt on the ground in front of me and clasped my hands again. His smile was huge. Nothing but promise showed in his face. "Oh, don't worry. I'm not going anywhere."

CHAPTER 20

*A*s the end of the school year drew near, I asked for permission to work from home as much as possible during the summer. I was more comfortable when Kimmie was with me.

"You're going to have to let her be with other people without you," Jessica told me one day. "And not just me."

"I know."

But I was scared.

Standing in front of my bathroom mirror later, I saw the fear in my eyes.

"This isn't what Kim needs, Daddy. I need to trust that You will work things out for us. That You will keep her safe. Help me, Father."

Kimmie's ninth birthday was near the end of June. One night I asked her if she'd like to have a party. "A sleepover maybe? You can invite anybody you want, from school and church. Jessica . . . Kimmie?"

Her face crumpled, and she looked away. It was the first time in quite a while that she'd cried.

"Hey." I knelt down in front of her. "What is it? Sweetie?"

She shook with sobs.

Sitting beside her on the couch, I pulled her onto my lap. What had I said? We rocked and didn't talk for a long time.

When she lifted her face toward me, it was covered with tears. "Mommy and I had been planning a big ninth birthday party. Probably a sleepover, but a lot more. We were going to keep talking about it." Her mouth trembled.

Oh, Father. What could I say? I wiped her eyes and rubbed her face with my hands.

"I don't want a party," she whispered. "Maybe not for a long time."

Holding her closer, I pressed her head to my shoulder. After a few minutes, she pushed back to look up at me. "MayMay, I love you."

My heart squeezed. It was the first time she'd said that.

FOR KIMMIE'S BIRTHDAY, Will and Jessica and I took her to a fancy restaurant for dinner. "Whoa." Will stopped when he saw all the wrapped gifts waiting for us on the table as we arrived. "Who are all these for?"

Kimmie squealed. "Let me see." She reached for the packages.

"Not yet," Jessica pushed Kimmie's hands back. "First dinner. Then you have to pick out a really creamy, messy dessert."

"Oh, yes." Kimmie grabbed the dessert menu. "Let me look at this."

"Good idea." Will looked at the dessert menu too. "Who needs dinner? We could all just have two desserts."

Kimmie giggled. "Or maybe three."

"Oh yeah?" I looked up from the menu. "Maybe I'll just skip dessert and open the gifts myself."

"No, no." Kimmie jumped up and went to cover the pile of gifts with her arms. "Will, you're a policeman. Don't let her steal my gifts."

"That's right, ma'am." Will made his face serious and grasped my hands. "Don't make me drag you down to the station."

The server arrived then and stopped, looking confused. Will still wore his uniform, having just come from work.

Jessica and Kimmie burst out laughing.

I didn't know if we'd ever have a party, but I knew, with all of us together, this was a good evening.

CHAPTER 21

*W*hat gave me the most hope for Kimmie was that she acted more like a little kid. She played kickball with the kids in the neighborhood in the alley behind our building. She rolled on the living room floor with Taffy, giggling.

Jenny and other school and church friends came over to our place often. The kids watched movies, played computer games, threw pillows, and shrieked with laughter.

One night Beth, Jenny's mom, knocked on the front door. "Martie, is it okay for Kim to come up to our place and watch a movie with Jenny?" She met my eyes with a straight gaze, and her mouth only shook a little.

It felt like a punch to my gut. *Daddy, give me the courage to trust You.*

I swallowed. "Of—of course. Sure."

My parents sent Kimmie's bike to us, all taken apart. Will came over one night, and he and Kimmie got down on the floor and put it back together.

"Kim, hand me that goofy-looking tool, the one by your foot."

"Goofy looking?" Kim pursed her lips. "Is that its nickname?"

"Nope." Will squeezed her hand as he reached for the tool. "Official."

"I think it's a wrench," I suggested, trying to help.

"Bor-ring," Kim and Will said in unison.

I smiled. *They can make a good family together, Father, can't they?*

"Where's your bike, Martie?" Will smoothed his hands along the front tire.

"Locked up down behind the building."

Kimmie looked up at me, surprised. "You have a bike?"

"And a helmet."

The next evening, Will brought over his bike, and the three of us rode to the park. Several of Kimmie's friends met us there, and the kids rode around the bicycle track.

Will took hold of my hand and led me to a bench where we could sit and still see the kids. "Let's sit here and be like lazy old people."

I leaned against him and buried my face in his shoulder. "I love you, Will."

"I know you do."

WILL and I were watching a movie one evening when we heard footsteps running out in the hall. The door banged open. "MayMay, MayMay." Kimmie gasped. "There's an ice cream truck coming. Come on, quick. Can we get ice cream?"

Grabbing my purse in one hand and Will's hand in the other, I stood up. "Come on, honey. Let's hurry. We need to start this as a regular tradition for our family."

THE END

I BELIEVE IT'S TRUE

CHAPTER 1

The front door slammed, and Alex's voice rang through the house. "I got a promotion." His shoes thudded to the floor as he took them off just inside the door. "Kathleen, kids, where is everybody? I got a promotion."

The knife I was cutting potatoes with fell to the table as I sprang up. "What? I'm in the kitchen. What did you say?"

Alex almost crashed into me as he came into the room. He grabbed me and spun me in circles, his smile huge. "Why are you cooking? We're going out to celebrate. Where are the kids?"

I laughed and planted my hands against his chest. "Slow down. Stop. You're making me dizzy."

He sat me back in the chair where I'd been working. "Where are the kids?"

I grabbed his hands. "They're in the yard playing with the dog. Did you say promotion?"

He leaned against the table, and if possible, his smile grew wider. "I did."

I shook his arm. "Come on, tell me. What's the deal?"

Alex pulled away from me and walked to the sink. "You want a drink of water?"

I stomped my feet under the table. "Alex, I want to know what happened."

He filled a glass with water, then came back and sat across the table from me. "I've been transferred to the office in Grant City."

I stared at him, sure I hadn't heard him right. "Grant City?"

"Yes, Kathleen." His face held no smile now, and he met my gaze straight on. "Grant City."

My head swam, and my mouth went dry. This didn't make sense. "They offered you the job?"

"Yes, a promotion, higher salary."

"When do you have to let them know?"

He rested his hand on mine. "I did let them know, honey. I accepted the job."

My ears pounded. "You, you what?"

He stood up and came around the table to stand by me. "I accepted, honey."

My throat tightened, and I raised my hand to my neck. "Without talking to me about it."

He reached for my hand again. "Please listen to me."

I pulled away from him and pushed back from the table. "Now you want to talk?" My voice squeaked, and my eyes pricked with tears.

Alex paced from one side of the room to the other. "Please listen to me. You know how unhappy I am at work. Ever since Ron was promoted to be my supervisor." He kicked a chair then caught it before it fell. "He's always breathing down my neck. Everything I do is wrong. You know how hard that's been." He stopped across the table from me. "And there's no way now for me to move any higher here. Honey, please." He raked his hand across his face. "I thought, I thought you might be happy for me."

I stood up. "But you didn't talk to me."

"That's right." His voice rose too. "Because I knew there would be no talking. You would have just said no. You wouldn't have listened to me."

"I would say no ... I do say no." Taking a breath, I steadied my voice. "I'm not going."

"But I am." His voice was softer too. "I'm taking the new job."

We stared at each other.

I didn't know this person.

CHAPTER 2

"Where are you going?" Alex called to me from the front porch as I hurried down the sidewalk.

I didn't answer.

"Kathleen?" he called again, almost a shout.

On the porch next door, Mrs. Roberts looked up from her book as I rushed past.

"I need some time." My voice came out a croak, but I didn't try to speak again.

Behind me, I heard Alex call the dog to come back to him. My legs pumped faster.

The park was only a couple of blocks from our house. I wanted to get into the wooded area, away from anybody who might hear me scream.

I didn't stop running until I tripped over a tree root. Sprawling in dry leaves left from last fall, I banged my face against a tree trunk. Good. Now I had something to cry about.

Wrapping my arms around the trunk, I yelled. "Okay, God, what is this all about?"

My voice was hoarse, but I kept yelling. "What are You doing here? I thought we were settled. We both have jobs. The kids are at a good school. We are involved with our church. We've got close friends, and so do the kids. This is so wrong. Why are You letting this happen?"

The side of my head stung. I sat up and pushed hair out of my face. "Ouch." My fingers found a bloody scrape on my temple. With my other hand, I wiped at my nose and eyes. "Father?" My voice was soft now, but it still croaked. "You know how hard this is for me. I don't understand."

THE HOUSE WAS dark when I climbed the front steps, except for a small lamp in the living room. Taking a deep breath, I opened the front door and walked inside.

"Kathleen." Alex's voice came soft from the living room.

I walked in and stopped a few steps in front of him. He sat on the couch, the newspaper spread out on his lap, his hands folded on top.

Swallowing, I worked moisture into my mouth. "Did you guys eat?"

"The kids did. Come here a second."

I moved a couple of steps closer but didn't sit down.

"Honey, what happened to your face?"

I raised my hand to my cheek. "I just bumped it. It's okay."

He leaned closer. "You look . . . Where have you been?"

For the first time, I looked down at myself. My hands were scraped, and my clothes were rumpled and stained with dried mud. I licked my lips. "I was at the park." After crying myself to sleep, I'd leaned against the tree and slept for several hours.

Alex made a move to stand up.

"No." I backed up and sat in a chair. "I'm okay."

He slumped back against the couch. "We need to talk."

"Y-yes."

Who was going to start?

Silence.

"I don't . . ." My mouth went dry. Leaning down, I picked up Alex's coffee cup from the floor. It was cold, but I gulped a couple swallows. "I don't understand."

Alex bunched the newspaper between his hands. He didn't meet my eyes. "I need to do this."

I pressed the coffee cup against my chest. "But this, this is our home. Summersville is our home."

"It's your home, Kathleen."

My eyes opened wide. "We've lived here ever since we got married. I thought you liked it here. I thought you were happy."

Alex got up and paced to the television, his back to me. "It's a fine town. But we settled here because this was where you grew up, and you wanted to live here. I wanted you to be happy, and I was able to find a good job." He stopped. "It's not good anymore." He turned to face me.

I stared into the empty coffee cup. Sure, I'd known Alex wasn't happy with his job lately. But . . . My shoulders shuddered. I didn't know what to say.

Alex walked back to the couch and sat down. "I'm sorry." He rested his elbows on his knees and covered his face with his hands. "I'm sorry, but I'm going to move to Grant City."

What I wanted to do was yell at him again, but I couldn't even make myself mad at him. My lips were cold. "I can't move there."

We held each other's eyes. This was my husband. We'd been so close, but a great distance widened out between us.

"We've got to tell the kids tomorrow," Alex whispered.

CHAPTER 3

"*M*ama, Jason stuck out his tongue at me."

Jason grinned at Sherri from across the table and stuck out his tongue again.

"Okay, guys." Alex looked up from his plate. "Finish your dinner and put your dishes in the sink. We need to talk."

I looked down at my plate. Most of the food was still there. My stomach clenched. Looking over at Alex, I saw his plate was still full too.

"I'll race you to the sink." Jason pulled Sherri out of her chair, and they ran out of the dining room, giggling.

"Let me take yours." Alex reached for my plate but didn't meet my eyes.

My legs shook as I stood. "Come on, guys," I called over the noise the kids were making in the kitchen. "Into the living room."

Alex and I found seats a good distance apart from each other. Jason flopped on his belly, and Sherri sat on his back and bounced. She was seven. He was almost twelve.

"All right, guys." Alex cleared his throat. "Sit up now and listen."

They sat up on the floor. I flinched as Jason reached over to tickle Sherri. How could we do this?

Alex leaned forward and clasped his hands tight together. "Sherri, Jason." He had to clear his throat again. "We've got a little bit of, of strange news."

The kids stopped touching each other and pointed their faces straight at their dad.

"I've got a new job in Grant City."

"A new job?" Jason's face flashed with excitement. "Is it a promotion?"

Sherri's eyes widened. "Are we moving?"

I wrapped my arms tight around my stomach.

Alex's jaw twitched. "I'm moving, sweetie, but not you guys yet."

Jason jerked back. "What are you talking about? Why aren't we moving?"

My heart thudded, and my hands were clammy. "I'm not, I'm not ready to move to the city."

"But Daddy's going?" Sherri's lips trembled.

"Yes."

"Then why aren't you?" Jason's eyes were slits. He reached over and put his arm around Sherri. "We're a family. We all have to go."

Resting my face in my hands, I choked back tears. "Jason, this is just how it has to be right now."

"No way." Jason jumped up. "I'm going with Dad."

My head shot up, and I looked over at Alex.

He sat back and took a breath. "Jason, wait."

"What? You don't want me to go with you?" Jason's fists clenched.

"Of course I want you to come, but—"

"I'm going. That's it." Jason turned and ran upstairs.

Sherri sat with her arms around her legs, her face buried on her knees.

I moved to kneel by her and wrapped my arms around her. "Sweetheart."

She jumped into my lap and pressed her face against my chest. "Mama? We're all not going to be together?" Her face wet my shirt.

Lifting my face, I looked over at Alex. Did my eyes look as sad as his? Jason was not even twelve. How could I let him go? I pressed my hands on my neck. He was so close to his dad. How could I make him stay?

CHAPTER 4

*A*lex and I decided he and Jason should leave as soon as
school was over in three weeks. A fog surrounded me for
those weeks. How could this be happening? We'd made promises,
Alex and I, about staying together for life.

I looked for support for my decision, from my mother and my
best friend Jodi.

"So, was he right?" Jodi asked as we sat together in the swing on
her front porch.

"Right about what?"

"Would you just have said no if he asked you? Not listened to
anything he had to say?"

"I, I don't know." I put down my feet to stop the swing's motion.
This wasn't what I expected her to say. "What if Ben told you he had
a job in another city, a five-hour drive away?"

"What if I told Ben I found a better job in another city? Maybe in
a cancer center. You know that's always been my dream."

Jodi was a nurse. She had a passion for her work. She and Ben
had three little girls, and she was devoted to her role as a mother. But
her job was important to her, and she had taken only the necessary
short leave from her full-time job when each baby was born.

"You'd just move?" I shook my head. Summersville was where they'd both grown up. Their parents were getting older, and both of their mothers had health problems.

"Not just." Jodi turned to face me better. "Of course, it wouldn't be an easy decision to make, if either of us had another opportunity. But we'd sure talk about it. And yes, maybe we'd move."

This conversation was unbelievable. "He didn't talk about it."

"And of course, he should have." She laid her hand on my arm. "But can you just leave it at that? You're married, honey. When you got married, part of the vows weren't 'and we'll always live in my hometown.'"

"You're saying I should move." Tears pricked my eyes.

"I'm saying you should think about it." Her voice was soft, and there were tears in her eyes too. "Talk about it."

MY MOTHER SET a glass of iced tea on the picnic table and sat across from me. "Kathleen, aren't you afraid this will end in divorce?"

I set my glass of tea down before I choked. "Mom?"

Her eyes were kind but steady as they met mine. "I'm sorry, honey, but I mean it. Aren't you?"

Of course, I was afraid. I looked down at the table and didn't answer.

"Don't worry about what I think." Mom picked up her glass of tea. "Tell me what you believe. From the Bible. What about that women's group you were a part of in college? What did they teach about divorce?"

A fist slammed me in the stomach.

My mother knew how important that group was to me. Thirteen years after I graduated, I still talked about it. Wives of ministers and leaders in the church led the study. As a student, I saw them as wise, full of knowledge about the Bible, and understanding of where I was in my life. We studied the Bible, but we also talked about issues important to young women.

Because of them, I believed the Bible was true and still relevant for today. And yes, we'd discussed divorce.

Looking up at my mother, I couldn't find anything to say.

She pried my fingers off the glass of tea and held my hand in hers. She didn't speak either.

The discussions we'd had in the women's group still sounded clear and sharp in my memory. The ladies warned us to be gentle toward people who were divorced. It happened to Christians, and most of the time, we wouldn't know the painful secrets in their lives. We needed to be merciful where God was merciful.

But they told us that God still hated divorce. He knew how it tore people up inside, the pain it caused families. We needed to work hard to keep our marriages strong and together.

"God hates divorce," I whispered to my mother.

"Yes, sweetheart."

I wiped at my eyes. "We're not getting divorced. We're just separating for now."

"Did you talk about getting counseling?"

My jaw tightened. "We didn't talk, Mom. He accepted the job without saying anything to me about it."

She squeezed my hand. "Honey, you know I don't think that's right. But someone needs to talk. This is your marriage, your children."

"I have to be the one who gives?" With my head in my hands, my body shook. I cried all the time these days. Mom came around the table to sit on my bench and held me.

~

WE SHOULD TALK ABOUT IT.

But Alex hadn't talked about it. Was I just being stubborn?

Father, Alex was wrong when he made this decision for our family without discussing it with me. I'm not the one who's wrong here.

Mom and Jodi told me I should take the first step. *Father, please forgive me.* I didn't plan to be the one to take the first step.

CHAPTER 5

*J*ason sat in the front seat of the pickup close to Alex. Neither of them looked at me as they pulled away. Leaning against the post on the front porch, I watched until they turned the corner, and the moving trailer disappeared from sight.

My face tingled as blood drained out. I squeezed my arms around my middle and tried to catch my breath.

Father, I'm scared.

Inside the house, I forced my legs up the stairs and into Sherri's room. She lay on her bed, her face buried in her arms, and sobbed.

I lay down beside her and held her tight against me. Jason hadn't spoken to me in days. Would she close herself off too?

Sherri turned toward me. Her face was red and puffy and wet. "Mama, are they gone?"

"Yes, sweetheart." My voice croaked.

She put her arms around my neck and her face against my shoulder. If possible, her body shook even harder.

Squeezing her closer, I choked to keep back my own sobs. *Dear God, what have I done?*

~

"Hey, Kathleen, I just wanted you to know we got here safe." Alex's voice on the phone came out loud and fast.

"Good. I'm glad you called." I didn't sound any better.

Silence.

"Can I talk to Sherri?"

My husband and I didn't know how to talk to each other, the tension between us stiff. And I knew better than to even ask if Jason would talk to me.

I walked out on the porch, leaving Sherri alone to talk to her dad. Sitting on the steps, I wrapped my arms around the dog. "What's next, Springer?"

"Mama?" Sherri's voice trembled behind me.

I turned and reached out to her. "Come here, sweetie."

Sherri sat on my lap, and I buried my face in her hair.

"Mama?" She turned her wet face up to look at me. "Will I ever see Daddy or Jason again?"

"Of course you will, honey." My stomach clenched, and my voice choked.

"When?"

"I'm not sure." Alex and I still needed to discuss that. "Soon."

She laid her head against my shoulder. "I miss them, Mama."

"Me too."

Reaching out my arm, I pulled Springer close to us, and neither of us said anything else.

CHAPTER 6

a couple of days after Alex and Jason left, Jodi showed up in the evening with doughnuts. "Is Sherri already in bed?"

"Yes."

"Excellent." She set the box on the table. "The kids are asleep, the mothers can pig out. Do you have coffee?"

I managed a smile. "I do." Opening the box of doughnuts, I grabbed one before going to get the coffee. "Yum, you got plenty of chocolate ones."

We sat and munched, not speaking for a couple of minutes.

"Kat, why don't you want to move to the city with Alex?"

My hand shook, so I hurried to set my cup down. "Nothing like jumping right in."

"Come on. It's me. Talk to me."

With my head lowered, I drew circles on the table with my finger. "I guess I'm just selfish. Of course I am. I want to stay in my hometown, near my parents, near you, in the job I've always loved. And I don't seem to mind hurting the rest of my family to get my way."

Jodi reached her hand across the table and placed it over mine. "Okay. This is Jodi here. Your best friend. I've known you since you were four years old. All that selfishness stuff is fine. We're all selfish and want things our own way. But come on now. Tell me why you really don't want to go."

I hesitated, looking down at my doughnut. "I'm scared," I whispered.

She sat back, taking her hand away from mine. "That's better. Now you're talking about real stuff. Scared of what, honey?"

My eyes teared. How could I explain?

Jodi leaned forward again. "Is it because of what happened when you were seventeen?"

"I guess. Part of it, sure." My hands gripped into fists. "Remember how I called Dad instead of the police?"

Jodi smiled. "That was cute."

I spent the summer between my junior and senior years of high school with my aunt and uncle in the city, babysitting my two small cousins. One weekend, my aunt and uncle decided they could trust me alone with the kids and went to a cabin on the lake.

"It was terrifying," I told Jodi. My lips trembled.

In the middle of the night, the girls crawled into my bed and woke me with a hand over my mouth. "Kathleen, somebody's trying to get into the house."

I heard it then too. A muffled banging on the back door.

My breath stopped. What should I do?

After lying paralyzed for a minute, I called my father, several hours' drive away. "Daddy, I think somebody's trying to break into the house."

He was gentle with me. "Sweetie, hang up now and call 911."

Mom told me later that Dad hung up the phone, called the police long distance himself, then paced through the entire house.

"The girls buried themselves under the sheet with me. We were so scared." I looked at Jodi, the memory still fresh in my mind. "I wanted to get up and look out the window, to move around. But I couldn't have pried the girls' hands off me."

I closed my eyes. "It seemed like the sound got louder, the girls pressed themselves tighter to me." My breath quaked. "I don't know. The 911 operator stayed on the phone with me until the police got there and found the robbers, still trying to get the back door open." I opened my eyes.

"I know." Jodi took hold of my hands and forced my fingers open. "I know that was scary. Sure it was." She paused for a moment. "But I know that's not all that's bothering you."

Blinking, I looked down at my empty coffee cup. I pulled my hand from Jodi and started drawing circles on the table again. "I've always been part of a small-town community. Would I even be able to find a place for myself in a city? Would I be able to get to know people? Make friends?"

Getting up, I went to refill my coffee cup. Now I couldn't stop talking. "Would I be able to find a job? All I've ever done is work at a florist shop. Could we find a church where they really teach about Jesus? Where I'd feel comfortable raising the kids?"

Jodi nodded. "Okay. I can understand all of that. What other fears do you have?"

Laughing, I coughed. "You dig deep."

"Hey, if your best friend can't dig until it hurts, who can?"

My hands pressed against my face. "What if Alex finds someone more interesting?"

Jodi didn't interrupt. She let me say it all.

"There'll be a lot of attractive women around, more cultured than I could ever be, with jobs more exciting than an assistant manager in a small-town florist shop." My teeth chattered on my coffee cup. "What if we couldn't afford a house in a good neighborhood? Because yeah, there's a lot of crime in the city. What if someone broke into the house, or the car? There are people who steal kids. What if, what if someone kidnapped one of the kids?"

Tears streamed down my cheeks. Angry, I rubbed my knuckles against my eyes and looked up. Jodi leaned with her elbows on the table. Her eyes bore into mine.

"Go ahead, tell me." My jaws ached. "I'm crazy. I'm out of control."

Jodi came around the table and pulled a chair up beside mine. She wrapped her arms around me and held me tight. "No, honey. You're scared."

CHAPTER 7

$\mathcal{M}$y cell phone rang as I walked toward the front door of Gloria's Blooms the next morning.

"Good morning. Are you at work yet?" Jodi. Awake and energetic.

"I'm just walking in the door."

"Is Gloria already there?"

"Probably." Stepping inside the shop, I made sure the *CLOSED* sign was still showing.

Jodi chuckled. "I just wanted to tell you to have a good day. I love you."

"That's important to me." I closed the phone as I went to the back to drop off my purse and lunch.

"Good morning, Kathleen." Gloria stood on a stool in the back room, lifting a box to a high shelf in the closet.

"Can I help you with something?" Closing the refrigerator door, I moved toward her.

"Nope. I'm done." Gloria dropped down from the stool and pushed it into the closet. "Lucy had fresh chocolate muffins this morning. Grab one. They're by the coffeepot."

In the early years, I'd tried a few times to show up at the shop before Gloria got there in the morning. I didn't bother anymore.

"Chocolate muffins, huh?" She didn't have to tell me twice. "Do you need coffee?"

"Sure, I could use a second shot." Gloria walked forward into the shop. "Thanks. My cup's there by the coffeepot."

As if I wouldn't recognize it. Gloria's mug had a picture of a robin on it, singing, "Good morning, Grandma." She'd used that cup eighteen years ago, when I'd started working in the shop as a high school senior.

I poured our coffee, with four added sugars in hers, and went into the front room.

"Thank you, dear." Gloria sat at her desk, checking the list for deliveries we had scheduled that morning. "So it's Grant City where Alex is starting a new job?"

My hands stilled before opening the cash register, and I kept my back to her. "Yes. Grant City." I took a breath. "He started yesterday."

Gloria opened a drawer and rummaged for a pen. "And what's Jason doing while he's at work?"

Thanks for reminding me what a bad mother I am. "There's a church there with summer day care for younger kids. Jason's going to be there as a helper for the teachers."

"That's a good idea." She stood up. "Twelve's still a little young to be staying by himself. Especially in the city."

My jaw twitched.

Gloria walked around the front of the counter and faced me. "I've got some good friends in Grant City."

I kept my eyes down as I organized the cash register. "Really?"

"Mm hmm. They've got a good-sized florist operation there." She paused.

My hands trembled as I counted out a roll of quarters. Why was she telling me this?

"I think they have three different locations now."

"Sounds nice." I bent down to pick up a quarter I'd dropped.

"Yeah, Russ always has been a good businessman." She checked the box that held her business cards. "Sue said he wants to start a nursery next."

"Hmm."

"Yep. He never slows down." She turned to walk toward the front door. "She said they'd be needing more help in the flower shops if they do start the nursery. Probably somebody as a manager for at least a couple of them."

Closing the cash register, I didn't respond.

"You know I'd give you an excellent recommendation." Her back was still toward me as she flipped the sign to *OPEN* and unlocked the door.

I grabbed the back of my chair to steady myself. "Gloria, thank you . . ."

She turned back toward me and grinned. "Course, you know I've always thought you'd take over this shop when I retire." She moved toward the back room. "That could be soon, you know."

Yes. She'd been saying that ever since I'd graduated from high school.

An hour later I called back to Gloria. "I need to go make deliveries. Josh isn't going to be here until one o'clock today, remember?"

"I'll be right out."

It relieved me that Josh, the high school student who usually ran deliveries for us, wasn't in yet. I needed some time by myself.

AFTER DROPPING off daisies and geraniums for centerpieces at Rolley's Diner, I headed to the hospital.

Last night, I'd told Jodi I loved my job. My fingers tapped the steering wheel. I do love it.

It was the only job I'd ever had. After high school, I'd continued working there on breaks from college. Many weekends too, since the city where I went to school was only a half-hour drive away.

"And then there was you, Alex."

We'd met in college, and since his major was accounting and mine business, we shared a number of classes. He graduated a year before I did and took a job at a law firm in the same town where I was still in college.

"It all seemed so right."

The lady crossing the street in front of my stopped car looked at me with a question on her face.

Was I yelling?

I pressed the button to close the windows. "It all seemed so right." Yep, yelling.

We married as soon as I graduated. Alex told me, "Of course, we can live in Summersville, if you like. It's such an easy commute to my job."

The car behind me honked and I hurried through the intersection. My face ached, and I blinked at tears.

After we'd moved home, I went to work at Gloria's full-time, taking on some of the administrative tasks. Gloria shortened her hours to more like forty a week.

When Jason was born, I went back to part-time and continued, with differing numbers of hours, until Sherri started school two years ago.

When I went back to work full-time, Gloria gave me the title Assistant Manager and diminished her hours as before.

"She's going to retire sometime, God." I swerved and honked at a squirrel. "She's told me for a long time she'd make me manager when she does."

Pulling into the parking lot at the hospital, I sat, twisting my keys in my hands. "I thought I'd spend my life running Gloria's Blooms. Alex knows that, Father."

Climbing out of the car, I got out the shopping basket I used to carry deliveries from the trunk.

We attended the church where I'd grown up. Some of Jason and Sherri's school teachers were ones I'd had in grade school. Alex and I joined the PTA and helped out with many school field trips and activities. We taught Sunday school and helped with the nursing home ministry at church.

"We've got a good life." My voice had lowered, but my eyes blinked at tears.

"But Alex hasn't been happy at his job for a long time, Lord. I know that."

Straightening my shoulders, I pushed the cart toward a side entrance of the hospital.

"This is home," I whispered. "And now Gloria says she'll give me an excellent reference if I want to apply to be manager in her friends' floral business in Grant City. What am I supposed to think about that, God?"

CHAPTER 8

*T*hat evening Jodi called me as I was getting ready for bed. "Hey, I'm sending you an email."

"Well, thanks for letting me know, but with the wonder of today's technology, I probably would have figured that out pretty soon anyway."

"Don't be sarcastic. Listen, I'm sending you some Bible verses. Please read them, and don't be too mad at me."

"Okay. I'll try not to." I hesitated. "Jodi?"

"It's okay. I, I know how important the Bible is for you, for guiding your life." She sighed. "Just look at them for a couple days and call me. Okay?"

"Sure. I will."

Hanging up, I wondered what she was sending me. "Why does she sound so worried?"

A few minutes later, her email showed up on my computer. I looked through it, resting my chin on my hand. There was quite a list of verses, from a bunch of books: Psalms, Jeremiah, Romans, 2 Corinthians, more.

After reading through the entire list a couple of times, I sat, pondering, wondering. Trust in God. Obedience. Sure, it was the

Bible. I believed it was true. But I couldn't understand what it all meant to me right now.

I called Jodi. "I read the verses. Thank you. But I'm not sure what you mean, what it means for me."

"That's okay." Her voice sounded a little shaky. "Read them some more, tomorrow or the next day, or the next, a little at a time. Just think about it and pray about it. I'm praying for you, honey."

"Okay." My nose wrinkled. "I'll read it some more."

"ALEX. HI. I'LL GET SHERRI."

Before I could set the phone down, Alex's voice stopped me. "Wait. Honey, Kathleen, wait. I need to talk to you for a minute."

"Oh, okay."

The guys had been gone for almost two weeks, and Alex called every night to talk to Sherri. These calls cheered her, but Alex and I still didn't know what to say to each other.

Silence.

I cleared my throat. "What's up?"

"We need to see each other." Alex hesitated. "All of us."

"Okay." Where was this leading?

"Could you and Sherri come visit us next weekend?"

"Us? Visit you?" My heart jumped.

"Listen." Alex went on before I could say anything else. "We want to show you guys everything, where we live, the park, the church, my office. Just everything."

"But—"

"I know you're not crazy about coming to the city, but this is where we live, Kathleen. And we're family." He took a breath. "And I may have to work a little late, so it would be hard for us to visit you next weekend. Please."

"Where is Jason while you work late?" My voice rose.

"I bring him to my office. He's always safe. I promise."

How could he be sure of that? Biting my tongue, I managed not to say it out loud.

I looked at Sherri. She didn't know what he had asked, but her eyes were big. She wanted to know what we were talking about. "Sweetie, would you like to go visit Dad and Jason next weekend?"

"Yes." She squealed. "Yes, yes. Let's go." She danced a circle around me.

"I think we're coming," I told Alex and gave the phone to Sherri.

MY INSIDES TWISTED with worry as the week went by. I wanted to back out, but Sherri was too excited. When Jodi called, I dumped.

"I can't handle this. What are Alex and I going to say to each other? Will Jason even talk to me?" I squeezed the phone in my hand.

"You and Alex have been married for thirteen years." Jodi's voice was calm. "You'll be able to talk to each other."

"We really haven't much lately."

"You will."

Where did she get her confidence? "And Jason. I don't know how to make up with my son." My voice squeaked.

"Honey, you're getting yourself all wrapped up in worries. Everything probably isn't going to be solved this weekend." Jodi's voice held a smile. "Try to think about making this visit fun. For the kids anyway."

"Fun. Right."

CHAPTER 9

*N*ot wanting to chance driving after dark, I took off work after lunch on Friday. My nerves were taut as I started the long drive.

Sherri bounced in the backseat and sang one song after another. "Row, row, row your boat, gently down the stream. If an alligator gets ya, don't forget to scream."

I kept checking to make sure her seatbelt was on, then the speedometer to make sure I wasn't speeding.

"Mama, can't you go any faster?"

"No. I cannot."

"Do you think Daddy and Jason will like the pictures I drew for them? Maybe they can hang them on their refrigerator."

"I know they'll love them." My only gift was a few dishes Alex asked me to bring. "Honey, please stop bouncing."

"Sure, Mama. Sorry."

She tried, but she was so excited about this trip. As the hours passed and we drew closer, I had to bite my tongue to keep from scolding Sherri for her excitement. This needed to be a fun trip, for the kids, but my heart was filled with a jangle of fear and anxiety.

When we reached the city, I started to panic. My phone had GPS, but I couldn't trust that I'd be able to find their apartment. Even though I didn't want Sherri to see how scared I was, I locked all the doors and sneaked glances at every stoplight to make sure no one was trying to break in.

When the GPS said, "Your destination is on your right," I still didn't believe it. I called Alex to see if we were at the right place. In less than a minute, he and Jason ran out of the front door.

"There they are," Sherri squealed. She had the door open the second I unlocked the car. She didn't know who to hug first. Jason picked her up and spun her in a circle.

Alex walked over and reached to hug me then drew back. "How was the trip?"

My heart squeezed at the sight of him. "Good," I lied.

Finally Jason looked over toward the car. "Didn't you bring Springer? I asked the apartment manager, and he said we could have a dog here."

I kicked myself. It hadn't even occurred to me to bring the dog. Of course, Jason wanted to see him.

"I'm sorry, honey." I took a step toward him. "He stayed at home. I asked Mrs. Roberts to stop in and feed him and let him out a couple times every day."

"Oh." Jason turned his back to me and took Sherri's hand. "Come on. I'll race you up the stairs."

"Don't worry about it." Alex touched my shoulder. "He'll warm up soon."

"I'm not sure." My throat worked to swallow.

We stood for a minute, awkward, quiet, not meeting each other's eyes.

"Let's go on in, honey. It's not much, but it's nice enough."

"Okay." My shoulders lifted, and I raised my head. "There are two boxes in back, with your pans and dishes."

"Good. Thanks." Alex got the boxes then walked beside me to

the front door. We climbed the stairs to the third floor in silence. When we reached the top, I could hear Sherri and Jason laughing inside the apartment.

"Here we are." Alex opened the door and stepped back to let me go in first.

Moving inside, I looked around. This was their home.

Alex followed me in and set the dishes on the counter. "Let me show you around." He laid his hand on my elbow.

It didn't take long. Two small bedrooms, one bathroom, and a little kitchen off a living/dining room area. They hadn't taken much furniture: just what Jason needed from his room, the smaller TV, and an air mattress for Alex.

They'd only been here a few weeks, and I didn't expect them to decorate. But the apartment gave off no air of being lived in. No messy piles in Jason's room, no towels on the floor in the bathroom, no dirty dishes in the sink.

"Did you guys clean up before we came?"

"A little, I guess." Alex shuffled from one foot to the other. "We're not really here that much to make a mess."

"I see that." We walked back into the living room. Not even any newspapers scattered anywhere.

"You see we've acquired some new stuff." Alex gave a crooked smile and pointed to a used couch and a card table with two folding chairs.

"So are you guys comfortable?" I rested my hand on the back of the couch.

"Ah, sure. We're guys. We don't need much." He patted one of the boxes he'd carried in from the car. "These will help though. Thanks." He cleared his throat. "You and Sherri can have my mattress. This couch is plenty big for me."

My heart squeezed. "Alex, I, but . . ."

He touched my hand. "I'll be fine." His voice was rough.

Sherri decided to sleep in Jason's room instead. It took a while for them to quiet down. They were so happy to be together.

When everyone finally fell silent, my tears dripped onto Alex's pillow. *He's sleeping on the couch, dear Lord. Please help us.*

CHAPTER 10

"*T*his is our favorite restaurant." In the back seat, Jason played tour guide for Sherri. This was the fifth restaurant he'd shown us. I looked across at Alex in the driver's seat. How often did they eat out?

"Here's where I'm going to school in the fall. Do you see the baseball field?"

Stealing a quick peek over my shoulder, I caught the big smile on Jason's face.

"I'm going to try out for the middle school baseball team. Oh, and there's the museum we took the kids from daycare to last week."

A lump caught in my throat. He sounded so grown up. And happy.

"That's our church. Dad said we could have a picnic there for lunch, so I can show you the playground where I help out with the kids."

"Are you a teacher?" Sherri sounded impressed.

"Kind of a teacher's assistant."

"Here's my office." Alex pulled into a parking lot. "Come on in. There may be people here I can introduce you to."

We walked into quiet, empty halls. "This office is a lot bigger than where you used to work, Daddy," Sherri whispered.

Alex gave her a squeeze. "You don't have to whisper, sweetie. It is bigger. And a lot more people."

"I think I'd get lost." Sherri's eyes grew large as she turned her head to look at all the hallways and offices we passed.

"Nah." Jason put his arm around her shoulders. "I get around fine. I'll show you." He stopped and opened a door just enough to peek inside. "Dad, there's no one in the library. Can I show Sherri where I use the computer? And all the books," he added, bouncing from foot to foot. *He's so excited to share with his sister, Father.*

"Sure. I'll show Mom my office."

When we reached Alex's office, I stopped to look back before we went in. "This isn't really close to the library. Is that where Jason always stays when you work late?"

Alex opened the door and stepped inside. "Come on in, Kathleen. Yes, he stays in the library." He walked to the window then turned around. "He's fine. I check on him often. He's got his own cell phone, and we text a lot back and forth. There are always plenty of people around. He's really okay."

Joining him at the window, I looked down at the traffic. Constant, fast traffic. "This is a busy area."

"Yes, it is."

I swallowed. *Stop nagging him with all your fears, Kathleen.*

He touched my arm. "So this is it. The first time I've had an office to myself."

It took effort, but I turned my back to the window and looked around, trying to focus on Alex's pride in his office. "Nice. Big desk, fancy new computer. Whoa, snazzy chair. Can you fall asleep in that?"

"Not hardly. Too much to do."

As I circled around to the front of the desk, I stopped. Right in front he had the family picture we had taken for last year's Christmas card. I picked it up, set it down, picked up a stapler. "So, do you like it? Your job here?"

"I do." He sat down in his chair, picked up a pen, and twisted it between his fingers. "I've got a lot to do, a lot to learn. It'll get easier."

Continuing my inspection of the office, I smiled. "Smart, putting up your diploma right away. And your certification." I turned back around. "So you have to work late most nights?"

Alex stood up. "Right now I do. It's not best." He rubbed his face with his hands. "But when Jason starts school, he can study here as easy as anywhere. And I really think it won't be too long, and I won't have to work as many nights."

His eyes were pleading. For understanding? For me to be here with him, to help? I wrapped my arms tight around my middle and turned to the door. "We should go see what the kids are doing."

CHAPTER 11

"This is a nice playground."

Alex and I sat at a picnic table as Jason chased Sherri around a jungle gym, then up and down a slide.

"It is." Alex tore at bread left from his sandwich. "I think this is good for Jason. He feels like he's needed, an important part of what goes on with the younger kids."

"That's good." Picking up a chip, I crushed it in my fingers. I had to tell him. "Gloria has some friends with a florist business here in Grant City."

"Does she?" He looked at me, a question in his eyes.

"Beacon Florist, I think it's called." My mouth was dry.

Alex kept his gaze right on me, waiting.

I took a drink of my soda and cleared my throat. "She said they might be looking to hire a new manager. They're expanding, I guess."

He blinked.

Not wanting to meet his eyes, I looked away. "She said she'd give me a good recommendation if I wanted to apply." My hand crushed another chip.

"Okay."

"She also reminded me that she's always expected me to take over Gloria's Blooms when she retires."

Alex chuckled. "Probably in the very next breath. That sounds like Gloria." He touched my hand. "Look at me."

Taking a breath, I lifted my eyes to his face.

"Kathleen." He hesitated. Was he as confused, as tormented, as I was? He sighed. "I know Beacon Florist." His voice was soft. "We can go by and look at it sometime if you want. It doesn't have to be this weekend, though."

I bit my lip. Jodi said not everything would be fixed this weekend.

"Higher, higher," Sherri shrieked.

I looked over at the kids. Jason was pushing her on the swing, and they were both laughing. Covering my face with my hands, I didn't try to stop the tears. The kids missed each other so much. What had I done to us?

Alex covered my hands with his, and neither of us spoke.

ALEX STOOD next to the car, resting his hand on the open window. It was time for Sherri and me to start home. I sat in the driver's seat, but we still needed to get Sherri in the car.

Alex cleared his throat. "It's Jason's birthday in three weeks."

"I know it is." I pulled my lower lip between my teeth.

The kids chased each other around the car. Sherri did not want to leave.

"Jason," I called. "Would you like to come home and have a birthday party?"

He stood still, glanced over at me, then looked away. "I don't know."

"Grandpa and Grandma would love to see you. Jodi's family. Tell me who else you want me to invite."

He scuffed his foot. "I talked to some of the guys I've met here about having a birthday dinner in the buffet restaurant we like." He looked at Sherri. "They have a chocolate fountain."

My eyes pricked as I looked down at my lap.

"We'll talk about it." Alex laid his hand on my shoulder. "Come on, Sherri. Get in the car now. Let me give you a hug."

I couldn't look at Alex or Jason. "Thanks, you guys. It was a nice weekend."

When we got home, Sherri ran to her room and slammed the door. She'd been trying not to cry for most of the drive.

Wrapping my arms around Springer, I buried my face in his fur. "I'm sorry, buddy. I know you would have liked to see Jason." Springer whined and licked my face. He didn't know why I was crying. "Dear Lord, what are we going to do?"

*A*fter Sherri fell asleep, I sat down at my computer and opened Jodi's email with the Bible verses. Before I could look at it, my eyes filled with tears. I rested my elbows on the desk and my face in my hands.

"Father, I miss them so much. Alex wanted to hold me, I think, but he was afraid, afraid I wouldn't accept him, maybe? I don't know. Jason still doesn't want to talk to me. Sherri was so happy to be with them. Now she just cried herself to sleep. I hurt so much, we all hurt so much."

My nose was runny, so I sat back in my chair and found a tissue. "What's happened to me, Daddy? My heart feels like a hard block. My stomach's tied up in knots."

I pressed my palms against my eyes. "I think, I'm so far away from You. I don't know how to come back. Please, help me."

After a few deep breaths, I sat up and opened Jodi's email.

Psalm 46:1: "God is our refuge and strength, an ever-present help in trouble."

Turning off the computer, I flopped onto my lonely bed and muffled my cries into the pillow. "We are in so much trouble. We need You, Father. Help us."

THE NEXT DAY AFTER WORK, when I went to pick up Sherri at my parents' house, Mom laid her hand on my shoulder. "Stay for dinner, honey. Talk to me a little."

No, I want to go home. I don't want to talk.

Taking a deep breath, I straightened my shoulders. "Okay."

"Dad's home from work already too." Mom took my hand and drew me with her. "He's got Sherri in the living room talking about baseball. Come in the kitchen and help me finish dinner."

Mom turned to the stove. "How was your weekend with the guys?"

Nothing like jumping right into it, Mom.

At the sink, I washed my hands and grabbed a towel. "Hard. Really hard."

Mom lifted a lid from a pot. "Set the table, will you? It's so hot, I just have salads and sandwiches. But I made some mac and cheese for Sherri." She stirred the pot. "She sure seemed to have a nice time. She talked about it all day."

"She and Jason had a great time together." I laid plates and silverware on the table and waited for Mom to start with the questions.

"So, you went with them to church."

"Yes."

"How was that? Sherri said it's a big church."

"It is. It was nice, actually. A lot of people seem to already know Alex and Jason, and they were really friendly to us."

I'd been afraid Alex might have told them about our problems or that people would ask how soon Sherri and I would be joining them. No one said anything like that. Swallowing, I shook my head and reminded myself I should have had better faith in Alex.

Mom emptied the macaroni into a bowl. "What did you think about the teaching? The worship?"

I poured lemonade into glasses. "It was nice. The minister is going through a study of Acts. I liked it. He made it personal." The pitcher was empty, so I set it next to the sink. "The worship was a mixture of hymns and newer praise songs. There were people of all ages, and everybody seemed to really get into it."

After laying napkins on the plates, I turned to face Mom. "A lady made an announcement about needing help with a new ministry they're starting."

"Really? What?"

I looked down at my fingers, weaving them in and out of each other. "She said they are planning to do after school homework help for kids. Most of them are from families who have just recently moved here from other countries, so they need lots of help. Their parents don't always speak much English yet."

"What do you think about that?"

Looking up at her, I blinked hard. "I thought it sounded kind of exciting. Mom, I, I don't know what to do." My lips trembled.

Mom reached over and clasped my hands in hers. "I know, honey." She raised her voice. "Jeff, Sherri, come on in for supper."

Dad sat directly across the table from Sherri. "How was work today, Bubbles?"

Bubbles was Dad's nickname for me. "Okay. Busy."

Dad stretched out his long legs and kicked at Sherri's feet.

Sherri giggled. "Grandpa, stop."

He found a straw on the table. Sticking one end in his nose, he aimed it toward Sherri, then sucked in a long breath.

"Grandpa, yuck. Stop." She giggled again. "I'm seven, not four."

As I looked around the table, I almost choked on a bite of my sandwich. My parents were such a big part of Sherri's life. How could I move her away from them?

～

LATER THAT NIGHT, I looked at the Bible verses from Jodi again.

James 1: 5: "If any of you lacks wisdom, you should ask God, who gives generously to all without finding fault, and it will be given to you."

Pressing my hands to my face, I cried out, "Father, what is the right answer for us?"

"I didn't get a chance to talk to you yesterday, we were so busy." Gloria stood beside me as I set up the cash register the next morning. "How was your weekend?"

My hands jerked, and a roll of dimes spilled on the floor.

"Kathleen, I'm sorry. I didn't mean to startle you." Gloria rested her hand on my shoulder then started to bend down.

"My fault." Dropping to my knees, I scrambled for dimes. "I'm clumsy today."

When I stood, Gloria was still there. "Tell me about your weekend."

"Nice." I went back to setting up the cash register, avoiding eye contact.

"I talked to my friends Sunday, the ones who need to hire a manager for their business in Grant City."

She didn't need to tell me which friends she meant.

Gloria walked around to the front of the counter. "They're almost ready to start advertising the position."

Closing the drawer on the cash register with care, I walked to unlock the front door. "Uh-huh."

"I think you'd do well there." Gloria faced me when I turned around. "Of course, after yesterday, I don't know what I'd do without you around here."

My throat stuck, and I swallowed. "Summertime, I guess. Lots of weddings and birthday parties." I bent to pick up a brochure I'd knocked on the floor.

Gloria walked toward the back room. "This town is growing. Our business is growing." She stopped with her hand on the door. "I can see you really expanding this shop over the years."

My jaw clenched, and I stumbled to sit on the stool behind the counter. "I, I'm sure Gloria's Blooms is going to continue to do well." My back was turned to Gloria, and after a minute I heard her close the door to the back room.

Drawing in a long breath, I pressed my hands to my face. That had been my dream: taking over Gloria's Blooms, watching the business expand, opening another shop eventually. Alex had shared that dream with me. "It all seemed so right," I whispered. "Now what?"

WHEN ALEX CALLED that evening to talk with Sherri, he asked her to give me the phone when they finished.

"My boss told me today they're going to give me an intern next week." He hesitated. "I mean, I'm going to be his only supervisor."

"That's great."

"Maybe. I've never supervised anybody, Kathleen. I guess . . ." He cleared his throat. "I'm nervous."

Alex was asking for my encouragement. As I took a breath, I squeezed the phone in my hand. "You'll do fine."

"I'm not sure." He paused. "I want it to be a good experience for him. I'm afraid I don't know how to do that."

"Alex." I stopped then pushed on. "You're so good, teaching our kids, the kids at Sunday school. You'll do a good job. Because . . ." I swallowed. "Because you care."

Later as I sat at my computer, I pressed my face into my hands. "Father, my husband needs me."

Alex and I always talked about our jobs together, bounced ideas off one another. We asked advice, and gave suggestions, and we'd grown to trust each other's opinion. Each of us leaned and depended on the other.

We still needed that, and we were separated. Not only by miles. We'd pulled away from each other. "Tonight I didn't feel like I was any help to him, Father."

As I lifted my face, I scrolled through the verses from Jodi.

Jeremiah 16:19: "Lord, my strength and my fortress, my refuge in time of distress."

Romans 8:15: "The Spirit you received does not make you slaves, so that you live in fear again; rather, the Spirit you received brought about your adoption to sonship. And by him we cry, 'Abba, Father.'"

"Abba. Oh." My eyes squeezed shut. "I get to call You Daddy." I wiped at tears. "Why am I so messed up? Why am I so scared?" I groaned. "My family needs You, Daddy. Thank You that You're with us, that You'll continue to help us." Maybe I didn't believe it yet, but I was sure it was right to reach for it, to thank God for this help.

*A*fter that, Alex talked to me every night. I realized how much I'd missed talking to him.

"Alex, how is Jason? He won't talk to me."

"He's good. He's making a lot of friends." He sighed. "He's just a kid, honey. Give him time. He'll come around."

My eyes teared. "I'm scared. What if I've pushed him too far away from me?"

"You're his mom, honey. He needs you, and he loves you. That hasn't changed."

ONE EVENING when I walked into Sherri's room, I found her lying on her stomach, her face buried in her arms, sobbing.

Kneeling on the floor beside her bed, I wrapped my arms around her. "What is it, sweetie?" My throat tightened. I knew what the answer would be.

"I miss Daddy and Jason so much, Mama. It hurts."

Later that night, I sat in front of my computer, my phone in my hand.

Psalm 18:6: "In my distress I called to the Lord; I cried to my God for help. From his temple he heard my voice; my cry came before him, into his ears."

My lips trembled. "Daddy, please."

I dialed Alex's number. "We need to come see you guys again. We'll come to the city on Jason's birthday."

"Okay." Alex paused. "Sure. That's great. Are you okay?"

I gulped. "And let Jason know Springer will be coming with us."

A LIGHT TURNED on in Sherri's face when she saw her dad and Jason. She stayed in Alex's arms for a long time, and my stomach felt sick. One of the verses Jodi sent me said, "God sets the lonely in families." *Lord, You mean for us to be together. I feel like I'm plowing through mud. Help me make a decision.*

Jason continued to trade hugs between Sherri and Springer. It had been a long time since I'd seen him smile like that. He barely looked at me.

CHAPTER 15

*F*or Jason's birthday dinner, we all went to the buffet restaurant he'd told us about. To my relief, he didn't invite any of his new friends to come with us.

"The salad bar looks great." I picked up a plate. "I'm going to start with this, I think."

Alex nodded. "Sounds good to me."

We sat down and started while Jason and Sherri were still filling their plates. Alex laid his hand on my arm. "Look," he said, smiling and pointing.

The restaurant had a chocolate fountain. Jason and Sherri carried plates with wings, meatballs, chunks of cheese, and a few raw vegetables as they approached the fountain. Shaking my head, I laughed. "I'm glad they're having a nice time together."

My throat squeezed. It was my fault they weren't together. I was hurting everybody, including myself.

The kids came to the table, laughing and elbowing each other. I looked at the chocolate covered assembly on their plates. "That looks —amazing."

"Yummy, yummy." Sherri scooted her chair up to the table.

"Happy birthday, honey." After hesitating, I rested my hand on Jason's shoulder.

He gazed down at his plate. "Thanks."

WHEN THE KIDS WERE ASLEEP, Alex moved around the apartment, picking things up and setting them down again. The coffee pot, a newspaper, a stuffed animal Sherri left on the floor. I stood in the middle of the living room and clutched my hands together.

Alex walked over to me and took my hand. "Sit on the couch with me."

My stomach dropped. What was he going to say? Was he going to ask me for a divorce? My breath caught in my chest.

Alex leaned his back against the arm of the couch and looked at me. His face was white. "Honey." His voice cracked. "I made a terrible mistake."

My gaze dropped to my lap. I gripped my hands together so hard, my nails dug into my palms.

Alex took hold of my hands and unclenched them. "I should never have accepted the job without talking to you. Of course, that's a decision we should have made together."

My eyes filled with tears, and I kept my face down. "You were right. I would have said no. I would have tried to make the decision for us."

I was shaking now, tears streaming down my face. Alex put his arms around me and pulled me against his chest. Taking a few deep breaths, I tried to calm myself. "Alex, what happened to us?"

He rubbed my back. "I don't know." He exhaled. "I think we got to where we just weren't as careful with each other anymore. I don't mean we got too comfortable." He held me tighter and gulped. "I guess we were comfortable together. But different from that, somehow. Just not taking each other's feelings into consideration as much, not as thoughtful with each other. I'm so sorry."

Raising my face to look at him, I saw a tear slide down his cheek too.

My chest squeezed. "Oh, I don't know if you have to be sorry. I have so much to be sorry for, keeping our family apart, hurting you, the kids." Resting my hands on his chest, I pulled back. "Do you think our marriage can survive this?"

He wiped tears from my face. "I don't know." His voice was hoarse. "Our marriage is a gift from God, and He can do anything. We have to figure out how to obey Him, how to put each other before ourselves. I guess I'm not so good at that."

I gasped a laugh. "I'm sure not." My gaze slid from his. "It's not just my job or . . . or being close to my family, you know." Sucking in a long breath, I said it. "I'm really scared of living in the city."

"I know you are." He laid his hand on my cheek.

My eyes widened. "You do?"

His laugh was shaky. "Don't you think I know you?"

Laying my head on his chest again, I whispered, "I love you."

"I love you too."

WHEN WE WERE ready to leave for home the next day, Alex forced Springer into the car and closed the door. "Call me when you get home tonight." After he hugged Sherri goodbye, I thought he would have to force her into the car too. Her face was already crumpling.

CHAPTER 16

The next night after work, I called Mom. "Can Sherri stay with you tonight? I have overdue spring cleaning I need to finish."

When I got home, I piled every cleaning supply I could find in the middle of the living room floor. "Father God, I know it's not the house that needs a thorough cleaning."

Grabbing a dust cloth, I moved pictures and books and gave the shelves a quick swipe, then shoved the objects back. "What have I even been talking about?" I screamed. No one was at home but me and Springer, and before I walked into the bathroom, I caught sight of the dog crawling under Sherri's bed.

In the bathroom, I sprayed cleanser over every surface in sight. "What's all this about Gloria's Blooms, and having a career? And living near my parents and Jodi? What am I going on and on about, living in a safe little town?"

I grabbed a sponge and scrubbed the sink with fury. "That's the life I've chosen, God. You never promised me all that."

Tears dripped down my cheeks.

Kneeling in front of the tub, I clenched the sponge between my hands. "You've placed me in a family with Alex and Jason and

Sherri, and we're supposed to be together. That's the place where I belong. All of us together. Wherever that is."

I pulled the vacuum cleaner out of the pile in the living room and turned it on, hoping I could drown out my voice. But verses Jodi'd given me from Psalm 91 had pushed their way into my mind.

"I will say of the Lord, 'He is my refuge and my fortress, my God, in whom I trust.' You will not fear the terror of night, nor the arrow that flies by day, nor the pestilence that stalks in the darkness, nor the plague that destroys at midday. ... 'Because he loves me,' says the Lord, 'I will rescue him; I will protect him, ... I will be with him in trouble.'"

These verses ran through my head again and again. After I'd vacuumed every room in the house enough to wear out the carpet, I stopped and parked myself on my bedroom floor. Wrapping my arms around my legs, I rested my face against my knees. "Lord, I know those verses don't mean we can never be hit by troubles, but where in the world did I think You would be?"

My breathing slowed. "I was fooling myself to think nothing bad could happen to us in a small town." I wiped at the wetness on my face. "Scary things do happen to Your people, but You're the daddy who promises to hold us."

As I sat still for long moments, quiet settled over me. When I knew I'd calmed enough not to yell anymore, I stood up and moved to the table beside my bed.

I picked up my Bible and quickly flipped through, looking at verses I had underlined. There was another promise in there that I wanted to remember right now.

1 Corinthians 2:9: "However, as it is written: 'What no eye has seen, what no ear has heard, and what no human mind has conceived'— the things God has prepared for those who love him."

"Father." My voice rasped, and my nose ran. "I keep forgetting all the exciting things You're going to bring to our lives."

My decision was made, and I was okay with it.

*T*he next evening after dinner, I picked up my phone to call Alex. Before I could dial, I heard Sherri screaming from the living room. "Daddy, it's Daddy." She slammed through the front door.

Walking to the door, I stood and watched as Alex and Jason climbed out of the pickup. Sherri threw herself into Alex's arms and squealed some more. Then she and Jason grabbed each other's hands and danced around the truck. Springer pushed past me through the door and ran to the kids, jumping on them. All three fell on the ground and rolled, screaming and growling and laughing.

Alex stood by the truck a minute watching, then turned and walked toward me. I couldn't move, couldn't talk. He came up on the porch, gently pushed me back inside the house, and followed me in.

For long seconds we stood still, staring at each other.

"Honey." His voice sounded hoarse. "We're coming home." He drew in a breath. "Ron told me when I left, he said I could talk to him if I wanted to come back to work at the old job. We, we all need to be together."

My mouth fell open, then I began to shake. Alex put his arms around me and pulled me close. Laying my face on his shoulder, I tried to catch my breath.

When I lifted my face and looked at him, he smiled. "Are you crying or laughing?"

I gulped. "You didn't tell them at your work that you were leaving yet, did you?"

"Not yet, but—"

I laughed and wiped tears from my cheeks. "Because I was going to call you tonight and tell you that I decided Sherri and I needed to come to the city and be with you and Jason. God has been working with me on trusting Him with my fears."

Alex stood quiet, looking into my face, then squeezed me harder. He laid his face against my hair. "We're going to be okay, honey," he whispered. "We're going to be okay."

THE KIDS HAD a hard time getting to sleep that night. We could hear them in Sherri's room, talking and giggling. Alex and I were up late talking too.

"I'll call Ron and ask him about coming back to work here." Alex sat beside me on the couch and picked up my hand.

"No." I shook my head. "The new job is the right place for you."

"Are you sure?" His voice cracked. "I should never have accepted the job without talking to you."

"I should never have let us all be separated." My lips trembled, and I pushed past a lump in my throat. "We need to start this whole thing over. The right way."

Alex caught a tear before it reached my cheek. "We'll start everything new," he whispered and pressed his cheek against mine. "God promises us new mercies every morning."

WHEN IT WAS time to go to bed, I looked in on the kids. From the light in the hall, I could see Jason's eyes, wide open where he lay on a blanket on the floor.

I knelt beside him and hesitated, then rested my hand on his shoulder. "Honey?"

His shoulder tensed under my hand.

Pushing forward, I took a breath. "I, I love you so much. And, and I'm so sorry for how I hurt you." My throat choked. "I know you're mad at me, and I don't blame you."

He turned away from me, but I heard the sob catch in his throat. I lay down beside him and wrapped him in my arms, fighting to swallow my own tears so I could talk to him.

"Jason, it's going to be okay. We're going to be together as a family. And I'm going to be the mom you can trust again." I gasped and coughed. "It's just going to take some time, but I'm going to be here for you."

He shook with quiet sobs, and I held him close. After a while, his breaths slowed, and finally he slept.

Sherri heard none of it. She curled up in her bed, one foot dangling over the side, grinning in her sleep.

Later, I lay in bed beside Alex and heard his quiet, even breathing. In spite of all the unknown that stretched ahead of us, peace wrapped around me.

"I know I'll still be afraid, God." I kept my voice soft. "Alex and I have to learn how to love each other better, how to be a team. I have to rebuild my relationship with Jason, to win his forgiveness." I swallowed. "But You are the God who will protect us, and help us." My eyes squeezed, but now they were tears of happiness. "Lord, I know You'll be beside us every step of the way."

Romans 15:13: "May the God of hope fill you with all joy and peace as you trust in him, so that you may overflow with hope by the power of the Holy Spirit."

THE END

FORGIVEN

CHAPTER 1

I knew I was running late when I finally got to the airport, but I thought I would still make it. Getting through security was not a problem, but I missed the plane by three minutes.

The next plane wasn't for four hours.

This would be a good time to pray. If only I could still pray.

When I'd called my mother a couple days earlier to ask if I could come home, I'd been scared. Would she even want to talk to me? I hadn't called the entire time I was gone.

Mom cried, she was so relieved to hear from me. "Please come home, Annie. As soon as you can."

Now I called to let her know I'd be arriving late.

"That's okay, honey. I'll be there. Just be safe. Be careful. Come home."

Come home. Would I ever feel at home again?

Holding a cup of coffee to my face, I breathed in the heat and comfort. Airport sounds and smells moved around me, and I closed my eyes and remembered.

NINE MONTHS EARLIER, I was wife and mom for a busy young family. Tony and I had been married for nine years.

Tony was a manager at a large department store and had a crazy schedule. I was a stay-at-home mom with two healthy, active kids, and I loved my job.

Then we found out I was pregnant.

We hadn't been planning on another baby, but we were glad. I was particularly excited.

"Jessica, I feel like this baby is a special gift from God for me," I told my best friend. "It makes me feel more important as a woman." I shrugged. "That doesn't make any sense, does it?"

She laughed and tapped me on the head. "No, but, you're pregnant. You're entitled to say dumb stuff."

When I lost the baby, I was so depressed I couldn't get out of bed for days.

Tony held me and cried with me, but he still had to go to work. My mother took the kids to stay with her for a week.

Alone in the house, I yelled at God. "Why did You let my baby die? Why did You give me this precious gift, then take it away?"

But screaming at God only exhausted me more. I stayed in bed. And cried.

Tony was gentle, but he started encouraging me to get up and keep moving. "I'm so sorry, sweetheart. I wanted this baby too. But we have two other kids, and they need you."

I got up, but my thoughts and movements were mechanical as I did the things that needed to be done around the house. It was as though I was walking in my sleep, and Tony still had to take care of the kids too often when he should have been at work.

"Mommy, don't cry."

Seated on the step outside the back door, my head in my hands, I was startled when little arms wrapped around my neck. "Please, Mommy. I'll still be your baby."

I looked up. Jake stood beside me, hugging me. Lizzy stood

behind him, holding a baby doll tight against her chest, tears streaming down her face.

Oh, God, how can I take care of these children?

One Saturday, Tony sat on the bed beside me. "Ann, I have to go in to work today. The kids have a birthday party to go to, at Alex's. I need you to take them."

I stared at him then blinked. "What?"

"Honey. The birthday party. We have a gift, wrapped and all ready to go. They need to be at the party at two o'clock. Ann?"

"Alex's house." Sitting up, I rubbed my face with my hands. "Two o'clock. Okay."

We made it to the party, but then I didn't know what to do. I left my car parked in the street and started walking, with no idea where I was headed.

"Ann? Ann, are you okay?" Someone stopped me with a hand on my shoulder.

I was crying. Again.

When I looked up, Doug stood in front of me. Doug was another parent we often saw at birthday parties and school activities. His son Jeff was in the same grade as Lizzie.

"Ann, can I help you with something?"

My mind fuzzy, I stared at him, my lips parted.

"Come on." We were at the park. He led me to a bench and helped me sit down. Drawing in a breath, I tried to stop crying. But my body shook with sobs. Doug wrapped his arms around me and held me.

When my breathing became more normal, I sat up. "I'm so sorry, Doug."

He shook his head. "You okay?"

Not hardly. Such an idiot.

But Doug looked kind and relaxed, like he was telling me, "This is no big deal."

"I'm okay." I took a deep breath. "Thank you. Do you know what time it is? I'm not even sure when we need to pick up the kids from the party."

"We've still got half an hour. Take your time. Would you like to talk about it?"

"No." I shook my head. "Give me a few minutes. I'll be okay."

He did. He leaned back against the bench and didn't say anything, while I found tissues in my purse and tried to get myself ready to go back to the party.

When it was time, we walked back together, and he didn't ask any more if I was okay or if I wanted to talk about it. He talked about the school year coming up and the new teacher Lizzie and Jeff would have. "We're running late on getting school supplies. How about you guys?"

"School supplies." I managed to smile. "Thanks for reminding me."

CHAPTER 2

*S*tanding at the front door, I watched Lizzie and Jake as they got on the bus. It was Jake's first day of kindergarten, but Lizzie was in first grade. She took Jake's hand and laughed with him as she helped him climb on to the bus. This was no big deal, she seemed to be saying to her little brother, who looked nervous.

I watched the bus until it turned the corner then closed the door. Now what was I going to do? It was my first day with no kids at home.

Making my way into the kitchen, I washed the breakfast dishes. In the kids' rooms, I made their beds and checked laundry baskets. Not enough to make it worth washing a load, even if I added mine and Tony's.

I walked around the house, picking up toys, straightening things on tables and shelves.

According to the clock, the kids had been gone twenty minutes.

I flopped onto the couch. "What in the world do I do now?"

The doorbell rang.

With a grateful sigh, I jumped up and ran to open the door.

Doug stood outside.

"Hey, Ann." He smiled, but he shuffled his feet and kept his eyes from meeting mine.

"Doug, hi. Come in."

"No, I mean—" He took a step backward and ran his hand through his hair. "What I mean is, would you like to go get some coffee?"

"Coffee?" I stared at him, not quite sure what to say.

He laughed. "I wondered if you might be feeling kind of lonely too, you know, first day of school. I thought we could keep each other company for a little while."

Then I remembered. Doug was a stay-at-home dad. His wife worked at the local hospital, and he did—I couldn't remember what —something from home. "Oh, coffee. Sure. That would be nice."

Seated at the coffee shop, with a warm cinnamon roll, I relaxed.

"So." Doug held up his mug. "What should we talk about? Not the kids."

I laughed and choked on a bite, then set my cinnamon roll back on the plate. "Is there anything else to talk about?"

He smiled and handed me a napkin.

After wiping my mouth, I fixed my gaze straight on him. "You first. What else happens in your life besides Jeff?"

He shrugged one shoulder. "You're right. Not much."

"What is your wife's job? I'm sorry, I can't remember her name."

"Jill. She works in the administration department at the hospital." He turned his head to look out the window. "Fortunately, she doesn't have to work late much and can spend a lot of time with Jeff."

"And you?" I searched my memory. "Didn't you used to work for one of the newspapers?"

"Yes." He turned back to me. "I quit to write freelance. I even get published sometimes." He made a mocking smile at himself. "I also work construction with Jill's brother part time. To help pay the bills, you know."

Sore subject. What else could I talk about? "Tony is under so much pressure at work. He has to work so many extra hours. Maybe

I should get a job." Puffing out a breath, I looked down at my empty cup. "It's going to be weird, now that I don't have kids at home anymore." I stopped and sucked in a breath. "I was going to have another baby at home with me soon." A lump caught in my throat. "I lost the baby."

I couldn't believe I was crying in public and again in front of Doug who, if he was a friend, was just a casual friend.

He reached over and rested his hand on mine. "I'm so sorry."

He had such a kind face.

We sat without talking for a few minutes, Doug's hand on mine.

Why can't I stop crying?

"Would you like to go home?" he asked, his voice soft.

"That sounds . . ." My shoulders jerked. "That sounds like a good idea."

When we got to the house Doug asked, "You still need some company?"

"No, I think I better just be by myself for a while."

He reached into the glove box and took out a pen and piece of paper. "This is my cell phone number." He wrote on the paper then handed it to me. "Please don't be afraid to call if you need somebody to talk to."

"Thanks." Climbing from the car, I hurried to the front door. I wanted to get out of his sight before I collapsed into a blubbering puddle.

CHAPTER 3

*F*or the next few weeks, I pushed myself to do what I had to do. Take care of the kids, the house. I tried to cry only when I was alone, but I wasn't always successful.

Doug started showing up almost every weekday. Once in a while we went out for coffee, but more often he stayed for a while and kept me company.

A few days after our first coffee outing, he knocked on the back door. They lived a couple blocks behind our house, so he walked over. He held a paper bag and grinned at me. "I brought bagels. You got any coffee?"

"Bagels? Coffee?" I was babbling. "Sure. Of course, I have coffee."

"Well." He tipped his head. "Are you going to let me in?"

"Oh. Sorry. Come in." I stepped back.

"I didn't know if you'd prefer bagels or doughnuts, so I thought I'd start with the safest."

"Good thought." Drawing in a long breath, I smiled at him. "You never know when a woman is trying to lose weight."

"Exactly." He poured coffee while I got plates for the bagels. "Now tell me, what do you think of Mrs. Bluffton?"

Mrs. Bluffton was our kids' first grade teacher. She was older, and according to Lizzie, a little forgetful. I relaxed. We spent quite a while laughing and talking about our kids' stories of their first few days of school. Doug was easy to talk to, easy to laugh with.

"Do you write humorous stories?" I wiped a crumb from my cheek.

"As a matter of fact, I do. And you can be sure Mrs. Bluffton will be finding her way into some of my stories this year."

"I'd like to read something you've written."

"Would you?" He looked away. "I'll bring you some stuff that's already been published someday." He stood and cleared the table before I could protest. "I'd better get home. I've got some things I need to finish before Jeff gets home."

"Oh. Right. Me too."

Little waited for me to attend to, but had we truly been talking for over two hours?

Pushing back my chair, I hurried to stand. "Thanks for the treat, Doug."

He stopped, his hand on the doorknob. "You're welcome." His face turned serious. As I watched him, neither of us saying anything else, I wished I could tell what he was thinking.

THE NEXT TIME Doug arrived at the back door, I was crying. I moved to turn away, but he caught my arm. "Hey, Ann, you don't have to hide anything from me. We're friends, aren't we?"

My throat was stuck, and I couldn't speak. He led me to the couch and sat holding me for a long time. We were friends. This felt good.

After that, when Doug was around and I started crying, I didn't turn away any more. I let him hold me. He didn't try to make me talk about what was going on. He sat with me, quiet, as long as I wanted. His company, and his arms, were a comfort to me.

Doug brought me a few of the stories he'd had published in family magazines. He wrote about his childhood, school happenings, college fiascos. "Doug, these are really funny."

"Yeah. Not all of them were very funny when they happened."

He had some sweeter stories about his little boy, as a baby and growing older.

"Don't you have any stories about your wife?" I winced as I saw his smile leave.

"Doug, I'm sorry. I didn't mean to—"

"It's okay." He reached over and covered my hand with his. "You've told me about things that are hurtful to you. We're friends." He sat quiet for a minute and then looked at me with a steady gaze. "Things haven't been good for me and Jill for several years." He took his hand away and clenched both fists against his knees.

No, Doug, don't tell me anymore.

He went on. "When I told Jill I wanted to quit working for the newspaper and try freelance writing full time, she was very support-ive. She had a good job, and I could find enough part time work to help us keep going." His jaw twitched. "But it wasn't too long until I started to notice a difference in how Jill looked at me. I don't know if it was dissatisfaction, or a loss of respect, or, or what. I'm not sure. But she was doing very well in her job, and I was getting only an occasional story published, and . . ." He rubbed his face with his hands. "I don't know. She just didn't seem so happy with me anymore. Is happy the right word? I'm not sure."

He got up and paced. "I asked her if she'd like me to go back to work full time. She said no, everything was fine. But it wasn't. It hasn't been since then."

What could I say? Saying I was sorry sounded empty. He'd always been such a help to me, and I couldn't think of anything to do to help him now.

He walked over and stood in front of me. He was smiling, but it was forced, not his usual grin. "It's okay, Ann. I'm okay. We just do the best that we can with our lives, right?"

I raised my eyes to his. No. I hadn't been doing the best with my life, and he had been helping me. He touched my shoulder and didn't speak for a minute. "I'm going to go now," he finally said. His voice rasped.

CHAPTER 4

September 24 was Lizzie's seventh birthday. Just the thought of trying to put together a celebration made me weep.

"What are we going to do for Lizzie's birthday?" Tony asked a couple of days before.

My head drooped. "I, I don't know."

He sighed. "Come on, Ann. We always do something fun for birthdays."

I swallowed. Was Tony starting to get impatient with me? "I'll try."

Sitting on my bed, I tried to make a list. Invitations for Lizzie's friends. Balloons and decorations. Games and prizes. Something special for dinner. Birthday cake.

My pen fell to the floor, and I wrapped my arms around my stomach. "Too much. It's too much."

"I'll take care of everything," Mom said when I was able to call her. "Let's just have a family party this year. We don't need to invite anyone else. Don't worry, honey, it will be okay."

Mom took me shopping and picked out a bunch of gifts: toys, books, two fancy dresses, and some pretty shoes. She knew better than me at this moment what Lizzie would like. In my mind, I thought this should hurt, but I was too numb.

Lizzie and I both pretended we were happy for the party.

Lizzie hugged everybody. "Thank you for the gifts." She smiled, but I saw a tear run down her cheek.

After Mom left and the kids were asleep, I collapsed in bed in tears. Tony was doing some work at his desk in the next room. With my pillow pressed against my face, I did my best to keep my sobs quiet.

What had happened to me? What kind of a mother was I? I used to be able to give the kids a fun birthday party with no trouble. Everything seemed to be too hard for me now.

"Maybe You were right, God, to take the third baby away from me."

The next morning, I couldn't make myself get out of bed.

"Honey, I have to get to work early for a meeting." Tony sat on the bed next to me. "I need you to get up and get the kids ready for school."

With my face turned toward the wall, I didn't say anything.

After a minute, Tony got up and left. In the kitchen, I heard him on the phone. "I'm going to be late. I'm sorry."

He hurried the kids through breakfast and made sure they had everything they needed in their backpacks.

After the bus came, Tony walked into our bedroom. "Ann, sit up. I need to talk to you."

He's mad.

Sitting up, I turned to face him. I was still crying.

Tony didn't come close to me. He stood by the door, his hands in his pockets. "Ann, you have to get over this. We need you around here. I need you. I've tried to do more with the kids, to let you have some time, but I'm falling behind at work. I need your help."

What could I say? My chest squeezed, and my eyes ached.

His voice rose. "You have to stop crying all the time."

"I don't know how." I wheezed with sobs. "Don't you care that we lost a baby?"

"I care." His fist slammed into the door. "But we have two other kids already here with us. Don't you care about them?"

He's yelling at me.

I couldn't remember the last time Tony yelled at me. Retching, I jumped up and ran to the bathroom.

After a minute, Tony spoke from the bedroom. "I have to get to work. I'll call you later."

When Doug came that morning, he found me still sobbing.

"Tony yelled at me." Was I screaming? I collapsed on the couch. "I can't take care of my kids anymore."

Doug sat on the couch with me, holding my hands, not talking while I sucked in breaths and tried to calm myself. After a few minutes, he put his hand on my chin and raised my face to look at him. "I was coming to tell you goodbye today." His voice was hoarse. "I can't stand it at home anymore. And I don't think they need me. Jill can take care of Jeff on her own. I need to get away. I feel like I don't belong in my own house."

He rubbed at my tears with his hand. "Come with me, Ann. I love you. I think I have been falling in love with you for a long time, even before that day on the street. Come with me. I'll help you. We can help each other."

I stared at him. Leave Tony and the kids?

Suddenly the idea of facing them all again that night felt like someone hit me with a truck.

I can't do it. I have nothing in me for my family anymore.

"Ann, please."

Doug needed me. He . . . he loved me.

In a fog, I packed a couple of suitcases. In my mind, it wasn't me doing this. I stood apart and watched someone else lock the door and leave her family.

My brain shut off any thought of Tony or Lizzie or Jake. I needed to get far away.

CHAPTER 5

*D*oug must have wanted to get far away too. We drove for two days before stopping at a cheap hotel where we could rent by the week. Over the next six months, we moved five times to different states. We always found a cheap place to stay: a hotel, a dumpy furnished apartment, a trailer.

I didn't call my mother or Tony. After the first couple of days, I wasn't in a fog anymore. I knew it was me doing this, and I was sick in my heart and soul.

No longer was the only thought in my head the sorrow for the lost baby.

Did I actually abandon my husband and kids?

Yes, Ann, you did.

And I couldn't see how there was any going back.

The physical relationship that began to happen between Doug and me was not what I wanted, but Doug said he loved me. He needed me. I was sure that was true, and I needed him: his kindness, his sympathy, and the feeling I was still someone worth loving. I was afraid of losing that comfort.

I had been a Christian since I was ten years old. Prayer had always been easy for me. Now, I couldn't pray, not even to yell for God to help me. I was sure I'd closed the door to His love too.

No going back. A wall grew up around my heart to keep out thoughts of all I'd lost.

WHEREVER WE LIVED, Doug and I would both get a job. He found work in stores, stocking shelves, bagging groceries, loading cars. I was usually able to find an opening waiting tables. Most of the time, I asked for double shifts. Doug spent his off hours writing, but I didn't have anything to do.

Doug worked on writing a book. "I've always wanted to try to write a novel, but I guess, maybe I've been afraid. Afraid I couldn't really do it." He set his jaw. "Now's the time. I've risked everything, so now's the time."

He wouldn't let me read what he was writing, even though I asked him often.

"I'm worried you wouldn't like it." He looked away from me. "And I don't know if I could stand that."

"Hey." I reached out and touched his hand. "I've liked everything of yours that I've read."

"But this is different. This is . . . my dream." He rubbed his hand over his face. "Please. Give me some time."

CHAPTER 6

*T*ime was of no use to either of us, though. More and more, I knew I was no help to Doug. He was never satisfied with what he was writing.

Often I'd get up in the middle of the night and find him at the computer. "Can't you sleep?"

"No. I'm sorry. Did I wake you?"

"No but—"

He slapped his hands on the table. "I can't stop my mind racing. I have to start this story over."

Doug was always good to me, caring and sweet. He'd stop whatever he was doing when I got home from work to spend time with me, to talk to me.

But he was restless. He kept wanting to move again, try a new start. But moving didn't help. Nothing did. This wasn't working for him, and my heart was a dead weight. Staying busy with work was the only thing I knew to do to keep my mind shut down.

But Christmas brought pain I couldn't turn off.

What have I done to my children?

I knew I'd caused sorrow for their Christmas. I was sure Doug was thinking about Jill and Jeff, too, but he didn't say anything. He worked to make it a special occasion for me.

I worked Christmas Day, but when I got home, Doug was waiting, the house was warm, and I could smell good food cooking. He put his arms around me. "Merry Christmas. Thank you for being here with me."

You need to make this a happy day for Doug.

I looked around the living room area. "You found a tree." It was a small tree, pretty smashed looking.

Did he find this after someone else threw it out?

But it was a fully loaded Christmas tree. "I love all this tinsel. And did you make all these chains and popcorn strings? And there are so many presents."

Walking into the kitchen, I stared at all the food. "Turkey, and stuffing. Cranberry salad. Oooohh, even pumpkin pie." I turned to face Doug and reached for his hand. "When did you do all this?"

He smiled. "You have been gone for twelve hours today, you know."

We both tried to make this a good day for each other, opening the gifts, singing along with the radio. But we were just pretending. This wasn't where either of us should be.

hen Jake's birthday came on February 23, I was a mess. I had to call in sick to work.

Curled up in bed, I tried to muffle my crying, so I wouldn't bother Doug. But he came in and held me, not talking. There was nothing to say.

"When is Jeff's birthday?" I finally asked him.

"January 16. He was seven."

"Doug?" I pushed myself up in bed. "Why didn't you tell me?"

His smile was sad. "Why? To give you something else to hurt about?"

After that, the wall I'd set up crashed down. I thought about my kids all the time. Missing them was a hard rock of pain in my stomach. I still didn't allow myself to think about Tony.

What was happening with the kids? Was school working out okay for Jake? Was he making friends? How was Lizzie doing with Mrs. Bluffton?

How much have they grown?

I knew Tony still read the Bible and prayed with them at bedtime. As far away from God as I'd moved, I still missed this time together.

One day as I came home from work, I stopped before entering the apartment building. "I have to go back."

The horrible thing I had done to my children could never be changed. Could they forgive me? I didn't know, but I had to try. They needed a mother, and I was their mother. I wanted to fill that need in their lives.

If they would let me. If Tony would let me.

I called my mother and asked if I could come home to her.

It was the morning I was packed and ready to leave before I told Doug. A cab waited for me downstairs.

Standing by his desk, I clenched my hands. My lips trembled. "I have to go back. I'm not able to help you. I know that now."

He stood up. "What . . . No."

"Please. You know I'm right." I stepped back and swallowed the lump in my throat. "And, I have to try to have some kind of relationship with my kids."

He stood still for a minute then took a deep breath, his face twisting. "You're very brave. I wish I had your courage. To try again with Jeff."

I wanted to say I would pray for him, but I knew I'd lost the right to talk to him like that. Before the tears behind my eyes could come, I took another step backwards. "Take care of yourself, Doug."

He reached out his hand toward me then drew it back. "You too," he whispered.

CHAPTER 8

$\mathcal{I}$t was late before I met my mother at the airport at home. My stomach twisted with shame and fear throughout the entire flight. How would my mother greet me?

She ran to me and hugged me, her face fighting tears and smiles. "Annie, thank God you're back. I've been so worried about you."

We stood for a long minute, holding each other, both of us crying. Then she whispered, "Let's go home."

For the next few days, I hid myself at my mother's house. She didn't ask me any questions about where I'd been or what I'd been doing.

Mom was gone most of the day. She worked half a day, then went to meet my kids when they got off the school bus. She fixed dinner for them and stayed with them until Tony came home. Alone in Mom's house, I had nothing to do but think.

Several evenings after I'd arrived, I walked into my mother's bedroom. "Mom, I want to see the kids." I licked my lips. "If I can."

Mom closed the Bible she'd been reading and patted the bed beside her. I walked to her and sat down.

She turned to face me. "Of course, you want to see them, honey. You should see them."

Leaning down, I picked up a piece of paper that fell from Mom's Bible. "I'm scared to talk to Tony. I, I don't know if I can. Can you ask him for me?"

She laid her hands on mine to keep me from crumpling the paper. "That's a prayer list from church I need."

"Oh." I let loose of the page, and it fell on the floor again. "I'm sorry. I'll get it."

Mom pressed her hand on my shoulder to stop me from bending over again. "It's okay. Sit still a second." She squeezed my hand. "I'll do anything for you, honey. You're going to have to talk to Tony eventually, but I'll ask him for you now."

Laying my head on her shoulder, I cried. She held me tight, and I felt like a little girl again. "Mom, I don't know how this will ever work out. I've messed up so bad."

She rubbed my hair and whispered, "Shh. I'll be here with you, and I'll pray."

Pray? I sat up and wiped my eyes. It was too late for prayer to help me. God didn't want anything to do with me anymore.

I knew I'd gone past God's forgiveness.

But I couldn't say that to my mom. Why should I hurt her more?

TWO DAYS later my mother planned to bring the kids to her house after school. When I tried to cook something for dinner, I only managed to spill things and break dishes. Finally, I sat down on the couch and just waited.

Jake came in first and ran toward me, stopping just a couple of feet away. Lizzie stood right inside the front door and stared at me.

"Hi, guys." My voice came out in a croak. I cleared my throat and tried again. "Hi."

Everybody was silent for a minute, then Jake jumped onto my lap and buried his head against my shoulder. "Mommy, you're really back. You really are. I didn't believe it."

I hugged him close. He was crying, and so was I, but I didn't try to stop.

After a minute I looked back up at Lizzie. "Hey, sweetie."

She kept her head down. "Hey."

"How's Mrs. Bluffton?"

She looked up and managed a small smile. "She's okay."

"Will you come and sit by me?"

She hesitated, then walked over to the couch and sat down, not touching me.

"You look very pretty today, sweetie."

"Daddy got me these bows for my hair." She still didn't want to look straight at me, but that was okay. I couldn't believe I was sitting in the same room as my children. My heart swelled.

CHAPTER 9

For the next couple of weeks, Mom brought the kids over almost every day after school to spend a couple hours with me. Jake was still teary, but if I asked him enough questions about the other kids and what went on at school, he usually started laughing.

Lizzie remained distant from me, but she always showed me her backpack, pictures and projects she'd worked on at school. I treasured this time together with them.

One afternoon when the kids arrived, I heard another voice.

Tony.

As I stood still in the kitchen, my breath stopped. My hand reached for the counter so I wouldn't fall.

Tony and Mom talked for a minute, then Mom and the kids left again.

Tony walked into the room and stopped, just looking at me. I looked back at him, trying to read what was in his eyes.

He walked over to the table. "Ann? Will you sit down with me?" His voice shook.

Is he as scared as I am?

My mouth grew dry. With my legs shaking, I took the chair across from him.

We sat in silence for a few minutes. Looking down, I twisted my hands together on the table, digging my fingernails into my palms.

Tony reached over and covered my hands with his. "Look at me. Please."

My entire body shaking, I brought my eyes up to his face. A tear rolled down his cheek. "Honey, please come home with me. We need you."

I don't know how long I sat with my head on my folded arms, crying. Tony came around the table and sat beside me, laying his hand on my shoulder, not pushing me in any way.

Finally I sat up, and he handed me some napkins. He went to the sink and brought me a glass of water.

When I felt like I could talk, I looked at him. "Tony, do you have any idea what I've done?"

"One of the neighbors said she saw you leave with Doug. I knew he'd been coming to visit you. I've got a pretty good idea of what's been happening."

My face tingled as the blood drain, but I tightened my jaw and managed to keep my eyes focused on his. "How can you want me to come back home?"

Tony paced for a minute, then came and sat down again. He didn't touch me, but he looked straight at me. "I love you. You're my wife."

Drawing in a long breath, I fought the tears that tried to come back. I remembered how much I'd cried last fall, and I didn't want that to be constant again. "How can you . . . Can you forgive me?"

"God has taught me a lot about forgiveness." His voice was hoarse. "He's forgiven me for all that I did wrong to you."

"Oh no." I clenched my hands. "Don't do that to yourself. You weren't bad to me. You were gentle. You tried to help me."

He reached over and held my hands in both of his. "No, honey. It's not that simple. You were hurting bad, and I didn't really try to understand that. I kept working like a crazy person and expected you to just get up and get going again. I didn't pay attention to the pain you were going through. Not like I should have. Not like you needed me to."

Looking down, I shook my head, not knowing what else to say.

"Honey, look at me please."

I swallowed and lifted my head.

He looked straight into my eyes. "Do you love me?"

"Ooohh." I gasped. "I always loved you. I never loved Doug. I—"

"No." Tony got up and paced again. "Listen. You don't ever need to tell me anything about what happened between you and Doug. I love you. I forgive you. If you still love me, if you forgive me, please come home to me. To us."

I wrapped my arms tight against my stomach, still trying not to cry. "I don't understand any of this."

Tony sat down by me. "We can't do this. But we can let God help us."

I was sure God wanted nothing to do with me, but I didn't say that then. "What about the kids? Are you sure they want me home?"

He smiled. "I'm sure. I'm not saying that they aren't hurt, or that it won't be hard. But you're their mama, honey. They want you back."

CHAPTER 10

*T*he memory is still clear in my mind of how everybody reacted that evening when Tony and I walked into our house with my suitcases. Jake ran to me and threw himself into my arms. Lizzie stood at a distance, her head down. Mom hugged me and cried. I must have gotten that from her.

Mom had dinner ready, but I don't think anyone ate much. Nobody talked. Jake asked if he could sit on my lap during dinner and said he wasn't hungry. Wrapping my arms around him, I buried my face in his hair, not looking at anyone else.

Mom left right after we finished the dishes. "You're going to be okay," she whispered, squeezing my shoulders. "Just take a lot of deep breaths, and don't forget to call me."

We always read the Bible and prayed with the kids before they went to bed. I felt strange sitting in on this, especially when Jake thanked Jesus for bringing Mommy home.

Before I left Lizzie's room, I asked if I could give her a hug. "Okay," she said, but she turned her head away from me.

"I love you, baby," I whispered. She didn't say anything.

I walked around the house, looking at all the familiar things, trying to feel at home. Was this my home?

Tony stood in the doorway to our bedroom. "Ann, come here."

I stood still, staring at him. My stomach grew sick. What did he want from me tonight? Walking toward him, I waded through mud.

Tony put his hands on my shoulders. "Why don't you go to bed? You look tired."

What should I say?

He moved us back into the room, turning me toward our bed. "Go to bed," he whispered. "For now, I'm going to sleep on the couch."

"No, Tony . . ."

He put his finger on my lips. "Yes. You know I can sleep anywhere. This just makes the most sense for right now. When you're ready for me to be back in our bed, you can let me know."

"But—"

"Shh." He wrapped his arms around me and laid his cheek on my hair. "I want to do anything I can for you to be comfortable."

"I, I don't know . . ." My eyes filled with tears.

Tony stepped back and held my hands in both of his. "We'll take things one day at a time. We don't need to rush anything." He wiped his hand on my face. "We're going to be okay, you, me, the kids. I'm sure of it. But let's just take it slow. One day at a time."

CHAPTER 11

One day at a time. That's what we had to do. The second night I was home I woke up in the middle of the night, because Jake was screaming. By the time I got to his room, Tony was already there, standing with Jake in his arms.

"Where's Mommy?" Jake's face was drenched with tears, and he gasped as he tried to talk. "I had a dream she was gone."

"Oh, baby." I put my face next to his on Tony's shoulder.

Tony put Jake in my arms, and he clutched at me. "Mommy, don't go away again."

Sitting on Jake's bed, I squeezed him tight and rocked. We both cried. He took more than an hour to fall back to sleep.

This dream reoccurred many nights.

The second week I was home, I heard Jake yelling for me when the bus dropped the kids off after school.

"Mommy? Mommy. Are you home?"

"Jake, I'm right here!" I ran and bent down to grab him in a hug, backpack and all.

There were tears on his cheeks, and his nose ran. "I got scared you wouldn't be home again."

It hit me that one night, I hadn't been there when they got home from school. Had anyone been there? Had Tony found out in time that I was gone?

My stomach flipped, and I wanted to throw up. But I stayed on the floor and held Jake. "I'm here, sweetie. I'm here."

I looked over at Lizzie. She stood quiet, unpacking her backpack at the couch. "Lizzie, is it okay if I give you a hug?"

"Okay." She walked over and let herself be wrapped in my arms with Jake. I looked back at him. His eyes were dry now.

How long will it be before he's not scared when he comes home on the bus? When he wakes in the middle of the night?

Lizzie was never rude. She didn't refuse to talk to me, but she kept herself at a distance. She was only a year and a half older than Jake, but she seemed even older. Although she didn't cry or wake with bad dreams the way he did, her pain showed deeper. I ached that I had done this to her.

Although I still couldn't believe God would listen to me, I started to plead with Him. "Dear Lord, please help my little girl."

CHAPTER 12

One night after the kids were in bed, I went out to sit on the back steps. Toward the end of May, it was a lovely night, warm, and the sun had not yet set. A few minutes later, Tony stood beside me. "Mind if I join you?"

"Of course not."

We sat together, quiet, and I bit my lip, wondering what he had to say.

"I wish you would come with us to church tomorrow."

I jerked. That was far from anything I might have expected.

I'd been back in our home for three weeks, and I hadn't left the house once. The idea of facing people terrified me. The neighbors who'd told Tony they'd seen me with Doug. People at church. Anyone.

"Honey." Tony went on, his voice soft. "I never bad-mouthed you to anyone at church."

"Oh. I, I know. But they still knew." Pulling my knees up to my chin, I wrapped my arms around them, feeling a sudden chill. "I'm afraid to see people," I whispered.

"I know." He put his arm around my shoulders. "But you have to give them a chance to accept you back. We'll never know how it will go unless we try." He squeezed me. "You had a lot of guts, to come back here to town, to the house. You can do this. I'll help you."

"I don't feel like I have guts." My mouth trembled. "And I don't feel like I belong in church." I choked. "I don't see how God can forgive me."

Tony stayed quiet for a long time. He was hoarse when he spoke. "Of course God forgives you. Otherwise I couldn't forgive you. I am not a good man."

"You are a good man." I grabbed at his hand. "You were good to me last year. You did try to help me, to do more with the kids, to take more time off work."

"Not as much as I should have." His body jerked as he gulped. "I didn't give you nearly what you needed. I never have. Work has always been first for me."

"Tony, no." I hugged his hand with both of mine.

"Think about it. It's eight-thirty on a Saturday night. Where would I have been last year at this time?"

"Last year? You . . ." I stopped.

"You know where I would have been. And most nights at eight-thirty. Look at how many fewer hours I'm spending at work now. But I still have a job. I still get a paycheck. We're still paying the bills."

His hand trembled inside mine. "But before, I had to work the long hours, I had to push myself, I wanted to climb the ladder." He took a deep breath. "I'm not a good man, Ann. I left you and the kids alone too much. Do you forgive me?"

I shook my head. "You're not . . . It's not the same."

He wrapped both arms around me and pulled me close. "It is the same. We just need to take care of each other. And God forgives us. He does."

I pressed my head against his chest. "I'm scared I can't believe that anymore." My voice shook. "Will you please pray for me?"

He lifted my face and rubbed away a tear on my cheek. "Yes, sweetheart. I'll pray for you. Of course, I will. I already have been."

CHAPTER 13

*O*ne morning as I wandered around the house trying to find things to do, the doorbell rang. I didn't want to answer it, but remembering Tony said I had guts, I did.

"Jessica?"

Jessica, my best friend since grade school, stood with her arms full of packages: flowers, food, I wasn't sure what all.

We stood staring at each other for a minute. Finally, she set all the packages down on the porch and hugged me. She was crying. We both were.

"Ann, I wanted to come see you sooner. I should have come to see you. I didn't know if you'd want to see me, but I should have come anyway."

She hugged me for a long time then said, "Come on. Let me in. I brought some stuff."

"I see that." I sniffed and wiped my eyes.

She handed me some of the packages, and we carried them all in and set them on the kitchen table.

"You brought me daisies. Thank you so much. You know I love daisies."

"I do know you love daisies." She managed a smile and gave me another squeeze.

"And look at all these groceries. We won't have to go to the store for a week. Well." I drew in a breath and laughed. "Tony won't have to go. I haven't quite made it to the grocery store yet. What's this casserole?"

"That's your dinner for tonight." Jessica laughed too. "From my mother. You know my mother."

Next I found a bag of books. "Oh, look, coloring books for the kids. How sweet you are." I lifted a book with "FORGIVENESS" in large letters on the front. "What's this?" My breath caught.

"That's a book that I thought you and I might read together, if you'd like." Jessica's voice was soft as she moved close to me and took hold of my arm.

My legs shook, and I hurried to sit down. "How did you know?" I asked in a whisper. I was crying again. No surprise.

Jessica knelt in front of me and took my hands in hers. Her hands were warm. Mine had turned cold and clammy.

"Because I know you. I knew you would struggle with forgiveness. Because I have struggled with it. The Bible has a lot to say about forgiveness." She got a napkin from the table and wiped my face. "Please let me help you, Ann, if I can. I love you." She wiped tears from her face, too, and squeezed my shoulders. "Let's try to stop crying and put these groceries away."

When we sat down to look at the little book, I clutched my hands on the sides of my chair. "Could you read it out loud to me? I don't think I can stop crying."

She smiled. "I can do that."

As Jessica read verses, I turned pages in my Bible to follow along. But I'd been right. I couldn't see the print through the tears. Jessica's voice spoke soft and steady.

"Okay. This is from Romans chapter 5. 'God demonstrates his own love for us in this: While we were still sinners, Christ died for us.'" Jessica stopped reading for a minute and pressed her hand on mine. "Listen to this, Ann." She went on. "'Since we have now been justified by his blood, how much more shall we be saved from God's wrath through him? For if, while we were God's enemies, we were reconciled to him through the death of his Son, how much more, having been reconciled, shall we be saved through his life? Not only is this so, but we also boast in God through our Lord Jesus Christ, through whom we have now received reconciliation.'"

Jessica stopped again, the kindness in her eyes reaching deep inside me.

My throat was tight, and I couldn't say anything.

She returned her attention to the book. "And this is from 1 John chapter 2. 'My dear children, I write this to you so that you will not sin. But if anyone does sin, we have an advocate with the Father—Jesus Christ the Righteous One. He is the atoning sacrifice for our sins.'"

Jessica laid the book on the table and took hold of my hands. "Father God." Her voice quivered as she cried with me. "Sometimes when we've been Christians for a long time, we get scared that You can't still forgive us if we sin. I know I get scared about that. Ann is afraid, Father." She drew in a breath. "But, Lord, in these verses, it seems like You're saying You know we'll sin even when we're Christians. And Jesus is still making sure that we are forgiven. It sounds like He's even working harder for us who are already Your children."

After she left, I sat with my face in my hands.

"Forgiveness," I whispered. A beautiful part of the faith I'd known for years.

"Dear God. Can I even ask? I don't deserve it." Pressing my hands against my chest, I stiffened my shoulders. "Please. Please, forgive me."

Had God sent me these people with their forgiveness? Tony? My mother? Jessica? Could it be that He was telling me that He forgave me too? That He still loved me? I was so scared to believe it.

CHAPTER 14

*T*he next Sunday, I decided to go with Tony and the kids to church. Maybe the only way to have the guts to do it was just to kick myself into taking the first step and go.

We picked up Mom on the way. When we got out of the car and walked toward the church building, she was on one side of me, Tony on the other, and the kids in front. We hadn't walked far when Jessica met us with her husband Dan, her parents, her brother and sister, and their families. They walked in with us and filled in the seats around us, to the sides, in front, and behind.

Should I cry or laugh?

My heart pounded hard, and my mind struggled to believe I had made it to this place. I didn't hear much of the Bible lesson that day or of the music or prayers.

But a sensation was forcing its way to the front of my awareness. A desire? A wish? A hope? Something that I was reaching for? Something I'd missed?

Yes, definitely something I'd missed. And I desperately wanted it back.

JESSICA CAME to see me the next morning. "So, how was church?" she asked, grinning.

"Good." I smiled back at her. "So nice to see your family. I don't know if I've ever had so many hugs before in one day."

"They were happy to see you. And, you can never have too many hugs." She sat down at the kitchen table. "I just wanted it to go easy for you the first time."

I hugged her. "I know. I appreciate it. We'll see how it is next week. I don't know if anyone else even spoke to me. Not that it would have been possible."

Jessica laughed. "They did. I noticed. Just wait. I think you'll find that people at church will be pretty happy to welcome you back."

Sitting beside her, I clasped my Bible between my hands. I wanted her to be right, but I didn't know if she could be.

She picked up the forgiveness book. "There was a verse I wanted to talk to you about. It's from Psalm 23. 'He restores my soul.'"

She leaned close to me. "Listen to me. I read about this verse in another book too. Psalm 23 is about God being our Shepherd, right? For believers? But why would He have to restore a believer's soul? Because . . ." She tapped my hand with the book. "Sometimes even Christians get lost, just like sheep do."

Biting my lip, I shook my head. "I don't know. I know God forgives people. Anything. I believe that. But I'd been a believer for so long. I don't mean perfect, but . . ."

She scooted her chair back and went to get coffee for both of us. "Okay, then what about Peter? Who'd been a believer for longer than he had? And after he denied Jesus, he went out and wept bitterly. It says that, remember? Who could have felt more like he had failed Jesus?"

She thumbed through the book. "Look at Mark chapter 16. Jesus sent a message to his disciples 'and Peter' after his resurrection, to tell them where to meet him."

She laid the book down again and grasped my hands. "Think

about it, Ann. Peter must have been feeling so bad. And Jesus knew that. So He singled him out. He said to tell the disciples, and specifically Peter. Don't you see? He wanted to make sure Peter knew He still included him."

I sat still, not speaking, my eyes on my lap.

"Ann, look at me."

I lifted my face to meet her gaze.

Jessica leaned back in her chair. "You've been a go-to person for more people than I can count, for advice. You're the one who led me to Christ."

My hands clenched into fists, but before I could say anything, she went on.

"I'd like you to take a minute and imagine it was me in your place right now. I'd left Dan for another man."

My mouth popped open. "Jessica—"

"Hear me out." Jessica interrupted me, raising her voice. "I'm coming to you now for guidance. I want to make it right with Dan, but I'm sure God can't forgive me."

"No. Please." My eyes filled with tears.

She bent closer, her face almost touching mine, her eyes demanding. "What would you say to me, Ann? Tell me. Would you say I'd gone too far for God's forgiveness?"

My head spun, and I dropped my eyes again. My shoulders shook.

Jessica stood and hugged me, not talking until I'd calmed. Then she knelt in front of me. "Honey, I just want you to remember that even if you don't feel forgiven, that's why Jesus came. It doesn't matter if you don't feel it. It's still true."

She picked up the book again. "I'm going to read you one more verse, then I'll leave. From 1 John 3: 'This is how we know that we belong to the truth and how we set our hearts at rest in his presence: If our hearts condemn us, we know that God is greater than our hearts, and he knows everything.'" She grasped my hands again. "Try to hold on to this. Even if you can't believe it right now, you know Jesus came to forgive, and He knows the truth of that, even if you don't."

After Jessica left, I picked up my Bible and turned pages until I found a passage I had underlined in Romans chapter 7. "So I find this law at work: Although I want to do good, evil is right there with me. For in my inner being I delight in God's law; but I see another law at work in me, waging war against the law of my mind and making me a prisoner of the law of sin at work within me. What a wretched man I am! Who will rescue me from this body that is subject to death? Thanks be to God, who delivers me through Jesus Christ our Lord!"

This passage had often struck home to me, and it did again today.

I covered my face with my hands and prayed. "Dear God, I am wretched. I need . . . help."

*W*ednesday, there was a family night at school for the last day of the year. I'd gone to church, so I figured I would have guts and go to school too.

It never occurred to me that I'd come face to face with Doug's wife Jill.

With my arms full of artwork, I almost collided with her as I came out of Lizzie's classroom. "Oh."

"Whoa. Excuse me," Jill said, stepping back.

She didn't recognize me. She looked distracted, glancing around, maybe trying to find someone?

I sped away from her as fast as I could, dropping most of Lizzie's artwork on the floor, banging heads with a couple other parents as they bent to help me pick it up.

And I absolutely hadn't expected to see Doug there. He did recognize me.

Our gaze met across the gym and held for a few seconds. Then he turned and walked out of the door.

When we were leaving for home, I saw Doug in the parking lot, in his car by himself. Jill and their son Jeff were in a separate car, and they drove away in different directions. He must be back but not living at home. My stomach went sick.

Later, as I lay in bed staring up at the ceiling, I kept seeing Jill's face, then Doug's, running through my mind. Why hadn't I thought about ever seeing them again?

The room was so hot, I thought I might suffocate. Then fever-like chills swept over me. Rolling from side to side on the bed, I tried to find a comfortable position. And turn off my thoughts.

Finally, I sat up then stood. I couldn't stay still.

Hurrying into the living room, I knelt down on the floor by the couch. Tony was asleep.

I hesitated, then bit my lip and put my hand on his arm. "Tony."

"Hmmm?" He moved then reached to turn on the lamp at the end of the couch. He leaned up on his elbow. "Ann?" His voice was groggy. "You okay?"

I swallowed. "No. I, I think I'm going crazy."

He lay there for a minute and blinked, then sat up. He reached his hands down and pulled me up beside him. Wrapping his arms around me, he pressed my head against his shoulder and held me without speaking for a long time.

I was out of breath, as if I'd been running. After sitting there for a while, my breathing settled, and my thoughts slowed down.

Lifting my head, I licked my lips. "I'm so scared."

"What are you scared of, honey?"

"What if, what if—" I choked, and my words came out in bursts. "I saw Doug tonight at school. Not that it's Doug. I never loved Doug. It could be anybody. I mean . . . Oh, sweetheart." Tears poured down my cheeks. "What if I fail you again?" Pushing my face into his shoulder, I clung to him and sobbed.

Tony didn't say anything for a long time. Then he moved me a little way back from him, lifting my chin so I could look into his eyes. "Honey." He laid his hand against my cheek. "I don't know if you can promise me that you won't mess up again. And there's nothing I can do to help you, no matter how much I want to. And it doesn't have anything to do with Doug. Believe me, there's nothing easy in my heart about forgiving him." He swallowed. "We can't do this ourselves. We have to depend on God to do it. One day at a time, we have to ask Him to help us to fight and to push on, and we have to trust that He's going to hold us together."

As I saw a tear trickle out of Tony's eye, I reached to wipe it away. "How, how can you love me? How can you forgive me?"

"Oh, honey." He choked. He pressed me against his chest and took a couple of deep breaths. "I'm not saying it was easy. I was mad at you. For a long time. But, like I told you, God helped me." He squeezed me tighter. "He taught me about what I needed forgiveness for. I'm so glad you're home. And not just for the kids. For you and me. We're supposed to be together. That's, that's just how it's supposed to be."

We sat without speaking for long minutes. When I lifted my head, I sucked in a deep breath and took a chance. "Please." My lips trembled. "Please come back to our room with me tonight. I need you with me. I, I love you."

Tony had held me many times since I came home, but this was the first time he kissed me. With my cheek pressed hard against his, I whispered, "I've missed you so."

As I lay on the bed, Tony stood next to me. "I don't want you to be afraid."

My eyes stung. "I'm not afraid of you."

He lowered himself into the bed. Wrapping his arms around me, he rested his face against mine. "I love you," he whispered. "So much."

*O*nce school was out, I became even more worried about Lizzie. Jake spent most of the day outside and at other kids' houses. But Lizzie stayed in her room almost all the time.

"Do you feel okay, sweetie? Are you sick?"

"No."

"Is there something you want to talk to me about?"

"No."

"Wouldn't you like to go outside and play with Jake?"

"Maybe later."

One morning, I heard something crash against the wall in Lizzie's room, then she yelled and started to cry.

I raced to her room. She was lying on her stomach on the bed, her face buried in her arms, shaking with sobs. Kneeling on the floor beside her, I rested my hand on her shoulder.

"Oh, sweetheart." I wanted to pick her up in my arms and sit down with her on my lap, but I knew I wouldn't be welcome. "Lizzie? What happened?"

She raised her head and put her hands on her face. "My doll made me mad. I beat her on the wall."

When I looked on the floor beside the bed, I found her doll lying broken, its head knocked loose.

My throat tightened. What could I say?

"Baby, why did you break your doll?" I finally managed to whisper.

"Because I was mad at her." She choked and scratched her fingers into her pillow.

"Why?"

She kept her face turned from me. "I'm just mad."

Reaching to pick up the doll, I examined it. I could probably fix it, but the head would still be wobbly. My stomach clenched.

Like I am.

I sucked in a deep breath.

"Lizzie?" I laid my head down on the bed next to hers. "I think I understand why you're mad. I think you're mad at me."

She didn't answer.

"I did a terrible thing to you, baby. I left you." I choked but pushed on. "There's no way I can ever make that go away. I can tell you how sorry I am. I am, so sorry."

Lizzie cried silently now, but my words came out in weeping gasps.

"I can try for the rest of my life to be the best Mommy I can ever be. I will. But I can never take away the terrible thing I did to you. And it's okay for you to be mad at me, honey. It's okay."

How could such a small child cry so loud or shake so hard? Picking her up in my arms, I cradled her close to me like a tiny baby. I don't know how long she cried. Or when she stopped, how long we sat in silence.

Finally she lifted her face to look at me. "Mommy, why did you leave? Was it because you were sad about the baby dying?"

I gasped then took a deep breath. "Yes."

"I wish you'd stayed, to take care of me. I was sad about the baby, too."

Pulling her close to me, I buried my face in her hair. "Dear God," I pleaded. "Thank You for giving me this wonderful little girl. Please help me be a better mother to her. She needs me, and I need Your help. Please help me."

CHAPTER 17

*T*he back step had become my place for sitting and thinking once the kids were in bed. With my elbow on my knee, I placed my chin in my hand. "Things are going pretty well."

With Mom's help, I'd managed to go to the grocery store again. She stood by me while I carried on brief conversations with people we met. I'd even said hello to several of my neighbors, including the woman I was sure told Tony I left with Doug. Going to church didn't scare me so much anymore.

Almost two weeks had passed since Jake woke up screaming in the middle of the night, and Lizzie was helping me make dinner again.

Last year, Lizzie and I talked about me showing her how to do cross stitch. A few days ago, I showed her a book with patterns and asked if she'd like to pick one for us to work on together.

"Not right now," she told me. Later that afternoon, though, I saw her looking through the book.

Now, I pressed my fingers against my forehead. "I know we have a long walk ahead of us, Lizzie," I whispered. "But I think we've made a start."

What I still couldn't shake was the fear that God would never forgive me. Even when I read the verses Jessica gave me, I could not push past the wall I'd put up in my mind. "How can You love me, God?"

Tony came out and sat beside me. Neither of us spoke for several minutes.

"I was thinking about something," he said after a bit, not turning to face me, his hands clasped tight on his knees.

I stayed quiet.

He cleared his throat. "How would you feel if we tried to have another baby?"

A fist pounded against my chest.

Tony went on. He kept his gaze straight ahead. "You know, the doctor last fall said that we should be able to, that there shouldn't be any problem. And I don't think we're too old." He turned to face me and picked up my hand. "What do you think?"

I took a breath, tried to speak, then took another breath. "I think I don't deserve you." My voice croaked.

"No, you don't." He tucked a strand of hair behind my ear. "I'm sorry about that."

"Oh, Tony, you know what I mean." Tears slid down my cheeks, and I swiped at them with my hand. "I'm sorry for crying so much."

He wrapped his arms around me and held me close against him. "It's okay. It's okay." After a minute he asked, "Do you want a boy or a girl?"

"Both," I finally managed to sputter, my face against his chest. "I want twins."

CHAPTER 18

*A*nother night after the kids were in bed, I walked through the kitchen and noticed the forgiveness book lying on the counter. Picking it up, I flipped through the pages. When I found a page circled heavily by highlighter, with a liberal dotting of smiley faces and exclamation marks, I smiled and flopped onto the floor. "I guess I'm supposed to look at this chapter."

Oh sure, I know this one, the prodigal son.

Drawing my lip between my teeth, I started reading the story in Luke 15.

The son who had as good as told his father, "I wish you were dead."

He took everything and ran away, wasting his father's money in sinful living.

As I read, my hands began to shake.

The son found himself wishing he could eat the slop he fed to pigs. He decided he'd go home, admit to his father how horrible he'd acted, and beg to be his father's slave.

When my vision blurred with tears, I bit down on my lip and tried to swipe them away.

This was a part of the Bible I'd read and heard many times. But when I came to the place where the father was watching for the son, was filled with compassion for him and welcomed him back as his own child, I let the book drop out of my hands.

A wave of cold fell over me, and I wrapped my arms around my knees.

"This scripture was written for me at this time."

The son showed such ugliness, even hatred, toward his father. But the father watched for him, saw him coming from a long way off, and ran to him and gave him back his full place in the family before the young man could barely begin to spit out his planned speech.

This was my story.

"Lord God, I've treated You with such ugliness, such hatred."

Could this mean that the whole time I was gone, He still loved me? He was watching for me?

"You surely ran to meet me as soon as I started to limp home."

God gave me a mother with such a huge heart to welcome me back with all the help she could think of. He gave me the chance to work at making things right with my kids.

I swallowed. "You've given me a husband who has accepted me back with unbelievable love. With tenderness."

My lips trembled as I was able to smile. He'd given me a friend who led me with such gentleness to parts of His Word that spoke straight to me.

"What more do I want from You?"

My chest ached as I rocked back and forth.

"I'm so sorry, Lord. You've been trying to show me You forgive me, and I, I put up a wall against You. I said this wasn't something You were able to do. I'm so sorry."

I picked up the book and opened it again to the passage from Luke 15. "But while he was still a long way off, his father saw him and was filled with compassion for him; he ran to his son, threw his arms around him and kissed him."

The book fell from my hands again.

353

KATHY MCKINSEY

"Oh, dear Lord, I believe You still love me. I want to be Your daughter." My voice cracked. "I love You, Father."

Quiet now, I rested my face against my knees and let cleansing tears fall.

I hadn't heard Tony come into the room, but he was there then, wrapping his arms around me and resting his face against mine.

Gulping, I pushed back from him. "No, no, it's okay. I'm happy."

He tipped up my face so he could look at me. His smile was a little crooked. "I'd like to see you happy more often, I think." He rubbed my face with his hand to dry the tears.

"No. It's really okay." I pointed to the Bible verses. "I think I can finally see that God has forgiven me."

Tony looked down at the book, then looked back up and pulled me closer. His eyes were wet too. "Yes, honey. Oh yes."

I rested my head on his shoulder for a minute, then I raised my face to lay it against his. I was sure we still had work to do to get through this tough time. But for the first time in months, I knew what it was like to have hope.

ABOUT THE AUTHOR

Kathy McKinsey grew up on a pig farm in Missouri, and although she's lived in cities for nearly 40 years, she still considers herself a farm girl.

She's been married to Murray for 31 years, and they have five adult children.

She's had two careers before writing—being a stay-at-home-Mom and working as a rehabilitation teacher of the blind.

Now she lives in Lakewood, Ohio with her husband and two of her children. Besides writing, she enjoys activities with her church, editing for other writers, braille transcribing, crocheting, knitting, and playing with the cat and dogs.

Contact Kathy at:

Kathy.mckinsey@gmail.com

Visit her at: http://kathymckinseyauthor.blogspot.com/

Books Afloat

Columbia River Undercurrents

Book One

Blaming herself for her childhood role in the Oklahoma farm truck accident that cost her grandfather's life, Anne Mettles is determined to make her life count. She wants to do it all–captain her library boat and resist Japanese attacks to keep America safe. But failing her pilot's exam requires her to bring others onboard.

Will she go it alone? Or will she team with the unlikely but (mostly) lovable characters? One is a saboteur, one an unlikely hero, and one, she discovers, is the man of her dreams.

~

Ring of Death

Cozy Mystery

Dorey Cameron just wants to do her job. But that's nearly impossible when her dental patients don't show up for appointments. The bizarre accidents causing them not to appear can't be a coincidence. Someone is sabotaging her. But why?

Things take a terrible turn when vandalism, mugging and murder have the police pointing the finger at Dorey. Something in her possession must be worth killing for. If Dorey can't figure out the mystery in time, will she be the next victim?

September Shadows

Book One - Justice, Montana Series

A mystery

After the sudden death of their parents, Jess Thomas and her sisters, Sly and Maggie, start creating a new life for themselves. But when Sly is accused of a crime she didn't commit, the young sisters are threatened with separation through foster care. Jess is determined to prove Sly's innocence, even at the cost of her own life.

Cole McBride has been Jess's best friend since they were children. Now his feelings are deepening, just as Jess takes risks to protect her family. Can Cole convince Jess to trust him—and God—to help her?

Scrivenings
PRESS
Quench your thirst for story.
www.ScriveningsPress.com

Stay up-to-date on your favorite books and authors with our free e-newsletters.

ScriveningsPress.com

www.ingramcontent.com/pod-product-compliance
Lightning Source LLC
Chambersburg PA
CBHW060619100726
47907CB00006B/1684